Heart

A novel in two parts

Hearts and Minds

A novel in two parts

Speak the truth when you can.
Lie when you have to.

Guy Harston

This is a work of fiction. Names, characters, places, and incidents either are the product of the author's imagination or are used fictitiously. Any resemblance to actual persons, living or dead, events, or locales is entirely coincidental.

FIRST EDITION

Paperback ISBN: 978-1-80541-095-9
eBook ISBN: 978-1-80227-698-5

We see the world refracted through
the twin prisms of intellect and emotion

—Vittorio Barlini, 1704-1779

Guy Harston was born in London.
And has never married.

Contents

Part Two: From the Heart

Part One: From the Head

The Good Europeans

Prologue

Today the European Commission is pleased to announce the creation of a new state, the European Federal Republic. The greatest the world has ever seen.

Based in Lausanne, covering an area of 5 million km^2. It is committed to the freedom, diversity, welfare and prosperity of its 470 million citizens.

Its flag will be the familiar gold stars on a blue background. Now circling a large single central star.

At midday tomorrow, identical statues of its founding father Jean Monnet will be unveiled in the capital cities of each of the member states that comprise the EFR.

We salute one man, one vision, one people.

From this day forth the 12th May will be called Founding Fathers' Day. And celebrated every year as a national holiday, with parades through the great cities of the EFR.

Chapter One

Anderson MacKinnon

"Welcome to Anderson MacKinnon." The Senior Partner shook her hand. "We're delighted you've decided to join us, Louise. And you've picked a good day for it. It's Andrew's Annual Staff Briefing this afternoon. It will be a great opportunity to see everyone."

A couple of hours later, in the huge conference room overlooking London's Docklands, Andrew MacKinnon stood to speak in front of a packed house.

Through the full-height windows behind him, beyond the distant arc of the river, the silhouette of The Shard stood tall and jagged against the sky.

Every seat was taken. With many more standing at the back.

"Welcome friends and colleagues," he said. "Thank you for coming this afternoon.

And as is customary at these events, we are joined by a number of distinguished guests today."

He read out a dozen names or so. A mix of cabinet ministers, chief executives and senior partners of major City institutions.

Then he said, "this is a very special year for us. It is exactly forty years since my late father started the firm. From a single room, above a parade of shops in Sheffield. And we have come a long way since then. But despite offices in London, New York and Dubai, we are still the same family law firm we've always been. And I know that's the reason many of you chose to make your career with us."

The sound of polite applause echoed around the room. He waited a moment for the noise to subside. Then he continued. In a quieter, more personal tone.

"I made a promise to my father when I succeeded him, that I would always maintain the same ethical and professional standards he demanded of himself. Every day of his life." He walked to the edge of the raised platform. His head bowed as if in contemplation. Then he looked up.

"And it is a promise I will never break."

He walked slowly about the stage as he spoke. "Many of our thirty-seven partners are non-executive directors of major multi-national companies. We mix professionally and socially with the international political, business and media elite. Which gives our practice an influence far beyond just the legal world." He slowly looked around the room. "Compared to us, other major City law firms seem lazy and complacent. And that's why we're taking clients off them. And beating them to new ones. And why, year on year our earnings per partner exceed theirs."

The sound of loud applause filled the room.

"And that," he said raising his voice. "Is why they say if you're not good enough for Anderson MacKinnon, try the Magic Circle."

The applause grew louder. "So, what is the key to our success?"

He paused a moment. The room fell quiet.

"Is it our generous salaries? Or exceptional benefits package?"

His eyes scanned the faces of the audience before him. The room was silent now.

"No," he said. "It's much simpler than that."

He let his words hang in the air a moment.

And when he spoke again, there was a passion in his voice. "Because the best attracts the best. And we *are* the best. Many apply. But few are chosen. And if you are invited to join our family, then you have proved yourself to be exceptional.

The fact you are here today, listening to me is proof you are the best of the best. I salute you. And I admire you. Each and every one of you."

Thunderous applause echoed around the room.

Then he said, his words barely heard above the noise, "now I would like to invite Sir William Rees-Watson, President of the Law Society to speak to us".

He returned to his seat in the front row to more loud applause. While his guest took his place on the podium.

"Thank you for inviting me Andrew," he said. "It's a privilege to be here today. And an honour to have the opportunity to say a few words to you.

I know you are all very busy people. And I don't want to keep you from your work. So I'll be brief.

I have been fortunate to know this firm for many years. And it attracts a certain type of person. A certain type of person who behaves in a certain kind of way. I like to think of it as the Anderson MacKinnon way."

His words were met by the sound of enthusiastic applause.

"And you should be very proud of yourselves," he continued. "You deserve your success. It has been earned through hard work, dedication and a commitment to the highest ethical standards. So I congratulate you on behalf of the Law Society of England."

He returned to his seat to loud applause. When he sat down Andrew leant across to shake his hand.

After that various Partners and Associates reported on the company's activities for the next hour or so.

Finally Andrew MacKinnon stood up to speak again. "Thank you all for coming. Please help yourself to the food and drink laid out behind you. Enjoy yourselves tonight, because the hard work starts again tomorrow morning."

The crowd clapped enthusiastically and made their way to the bar at the back of the room.

The guide held up a torch to draw everyone around her.

"Welcome to our newest, and possibly most fascinating London tour," she said.

"The Palace of Westminster has been shut for nearly five years now. As you can see the condition of the building has deteriorated considerably in that period. So please be careful where you tread."

Then she said, "sadly this is unlikely to be one of our longer running tours. The Cultural Commission is expected to approve its conversion to luxury apartments in the autumn.

So enjoy this fine old building while you can. And its extraordinary history. Dating back to a time when Britain was a separate autonomous self-governing state.

Now if you follow me, we will make our way deeper into the building. Please keep close because some parts are unsafe."

The group followed as she walked across a patterned stone floor, towards a pair of large and ornately carved solid oak doors. With a push they opened to reveal a bare and empty space beyond. It was hard to make out its size in the dull glow of temporary lights, high in the roof above.

"This was the lower chamber, called the House of Commons. You will have to imagine the tiers of wooden benches that used to line the hall, rising up on either side. Elected members would be seated according to their party membership. As we stand here the government benches were to the left. And the opposition benches to the right. At the far end stood the Speaker's chair.

It's hard to believe now, but at one time nearly a third of the world's population was ruled from this very room.

And even as recently as five years ago, a small staff of about twenty still worked here under delegated powers from Lausanne.

But before that, for more than five hundred years Members of Parliament would debate the issues of the day.

And unlike our modern European Parliament today, individual delegates were permitted to question the President. Or as he was called then, the Prime Minister. And equally surprising to our modern concept of democracy, legislation could only become law if it obtained a majority in a vote put to the whole House. There was also a second chamber it had to pass through to be ratified. As you can imagine it was a very slow and cumbersome process. With draft bills being scrutinised and debated for months. Today's procedure of drafting and enacting legislation by private committee without debate is much more efficient. Enabling far more laws and statutes to be created with minimum delay.

And incredibly, and chillingly, decisions were taken on several occasions in this very chamber, to go to war with our European partners. Indeed, less than a hundred years ago approval was given to invade mainland Europe. And to lay waste to our great cities. And kill millions of our fellow citizens. Hard to believe I know. But it happened right here. In this very chamber, where we're standing now. That is surely the most shameful aspect of this building's often rather grim history."

The following morning one of the Associates introduced Louise to her new colleagues.

"And finally," she said. Tapping lightly on a glass door. "And most importantly, Robert Waters. The Partner in charge of your section."

She opened the door. And stood aside to let Louise enter the room.

"I'll leave you two to get acquainted," she said. And closed the door quietly behind her.

He was sitting on the corner of his desk. Studying his phone. He didn't look up.

Louise went to shake his hand.

Instead he walked to a Nespresso machine by the window.

"What we need here Louise," he said, inserting a cartridge. "Isn't something you learn."

He closed the lid.

"Or something that can be taught."

And swiped his finger across the touch screen.

"Either you have it. Or you don't."

He studied his phone as coffee slowly drained into the cup.

"If you can rise to the challenge here," he said. "The next few years could be very good for you."

He put the phone down. And took the cup from the machine.

"But if you can't."

Finally, he looked up. His eyes met hers.

"Your time here will be brief. And not very pleasant."

Then he said, "we work hard here. And we play hard. I expect to see you in *The Witness Box* on Friday."

In the rubble and social dislocation of the war they seized their opportunity. The destruction of the old order gave rise to a new elite, the anonymous unelected bureaucrat. They took control of life on the home front during the conflict. And were not about to give it up in peacetime.

In post war Europe especially, they learnt the lesson of invasion without destruction. To take possession of a country, its people and infrastructure whole and intact. And to overlay the existing government with a higher level of authority. Before dismantling democracy and erasing national borders.

And like all new elites, they demonstrated their power by destroying the monuments to the old Gods.

Hundreds of historic buildings were demolished, to make way for the London County Council Architect's concept of a modern post war city. A brutalist vision that crushed the human spirit. And whose grey and joyless character reflected their own.

Henry closed the book. And put it back on his shelf.

"That was published almost twenty years ago," he said. "There's still a few unsold copies around. I saw half a dozen in Judd Books last summer. They didn't ask me to write another."

By four o'clock on a Friday afternoon *The Witness Box* was very hot, noisy and packed with Anderson MacKinnon staff. Dozens of tall glasses lined the length of the bar.

Robert Waters, eyes glazed, shirt and jacket creased and stained with sweat, put his arm around Louise's shoulder. He leaned in close. The smell of alcohol and stale cigarettes on his breath. "Welcome to *The Witness Box*," he shouted above the noise. His words were beginning to slur.

The unmistakable scent of cannabis hung in the air. Huge brandy glasses on each corner of the bar and on every table were filled with different coloured pills, red, blue and yellow. "Just help yourself," he said, taking a handful.

"Of course they can be charming when they want to be," said Henry.

"I remember when I was first elected to the House many years ago. A former Foreign Secretary who had always been a hero of mine, long before I became an MP, came and spoke to me.

He even knew my name. He asked me to support a motion he was proposing. And with a delightful twinkle in his eye, he said if you don't I will never speak to you again. I was thrilled. So I did. And he never spoke to me again."

She recognised the distinctive voice of her old tutor on the phone

"Hello Louise," he said. "I was just wondering how you were getting on at MacKinnons?"

"Not very well I'm afraid, Bruce."

"I'm sorry to hear that. But I can't say I'm very surprised. It takes a certain type."

Then he said, "if you want a bit of time out to look for another practice, the bursar here does some fund raising for the government. They're always looking for people to help in central office. I'm sure she'd be happy to make an introduction for you."

"I don't know, Bruce," she said. "I'm not sure what to do."

"Just for a month or two. While you find somewhere else."

The Kalatou Development Agency is proud to announce the construction of the world's finest luxury resort. Located on the shores of one of West Africa's most beautiful lakes, two hundred miles north of the capital Kalatou City.

It will include a new multi-million euro international airport with direct transport links from Europe, Asia and North America.

The new city, conceived by the country's visionary leader President Henri Maboteau, is intended to become the holiday destination of choice for the super-rich.

It will feature the finest 6 star hotels, designed by the world's most celebrated architects. The most prestigious and expensive shops from Europe and America will line the boulevards. Along with 24 hour super-casinos and restaurants, run by internationally renowned Michelin starred chefs.

"It's very good to meet you Louise." The Party Chairman shook her hand.

"But are you sure you really want to be a fund raiser? I'm certain we could find something more appropriate for an Anderson MacKinnon lawyer."

Then he said, "Alan Wells, the MP for Bradford South is looking for a Special Political Advisor. He's a junior minister and a rising star of the Party. We could go and have a chat with him if you're interested?"

They made the short taxi ride from the Party HQ to the Minister's private office in Portcullis House.

"Good morning, Alan."

The Minister looked up from the document he was reading.

"I'd like to introduce you to Louise Hemmings."

Alan took off his glasses and shook her hand.

"Louise is a lawyer at Anderson MacKinnon. But we're hoping to persuade her to come and join us instead. Perhaps for your Political Advisor's job?"

"Anderson McKindle?"

"The top international law firm."

"Yes I know," said Alan. He turned to Louise. "So you're thinking of giving up a lucrative career for a life of public service. I like that. I did something similar myself."

A smartly dressed little man stepped forward. And shook her hand.

"Pleased to meet you Louise," he said. "I'm Jez Evans, the Minister's agent."

He looked at Alan. "You never know when we might want a little legal advice."

The minister put down his papers. "I'm speaking in my constituency in a couple of days. Why don't you come along."

"No Henry, there's no way." She shook her head.

"But with a convoy of mobile operating theatres and refrigerated storage containers could it be done?"

"It's monstrous and barbaric."

"Yes, but is it possible?"

"In theory. But no medical practitioner would ever get involved in such a thing."

"No, of course not."

"I can assure you there's no black market for human blood or organs. For goodness sake Henry, we're talking about hugely respected international institutions. Operating to the highest moral and ethical standards."

"Yes of course," said Henry. "You don't need to say anymore."

Against the low evening sun, two and a half hours out of Kings Cross, she saw the distinctive chimneys of Shipley railway station. Outside a taxi waited to take her to the venue where Alan was speaking.

There was already a large crowd inside the hall when

she arrived. A security guard directed her to a small office at the back of the building.

Jez looked up as she closed the door.

"Hi Louise," he said. "Good to see you again. We're expecting a full house tonight."

A few yards away, Alan was pacing back and forth. Oblivious to everything and everyone around him. Mouthing silent words to himself, making gestures and movements with his hands. They left him and took a couple of seats near the back of the hall.

Moments later, the house lights dimmed. A single spotlight shone towards the back of the hall. Everyone turned to look.

"Here he comes," she heard someone say.

The audience stood and clapped. He emerged into the light in a dark suit and white shirt.

A single spotlight followed him as he walked towards the front of the hall. Past countless mobile phones held high above the heads of the crowd.

And maybe it was just the cut of his clothes, but he looked a little taller and more heroic than she remembered. But his progress was slowed by the countless hands extended to him as he passed. He shook them all, smiled and thanked them for coming. Stopping every few yards to say a word or two to someone in the crowd.

Finally he arrived at the stage and bounded athletically up the three steps. A single circle of light illuminated him in the darkness.

At the lectern he stood a moment. A lone figure bathed in light. The hall completely silent now. He bowed his head. Perhaps to collect his thoughts. Or maybe momentarily overcome with emotion. It was hard to tell. Then he slowly looked up.

"Thank you," he said humbly.

The crowd clapped and cheered.

"It's always a privilege to come home," he said above the noise.

The sound of cheering grew louder.

He raised his voice to be heard. "To come home. And be amongst my own people.

I know so many of you here tonight. I've been a guest in your homes. I've shared in your achievements. And I've been there for you in your troubles. Some may call it a constituency. But to me it's a family. My family."

He scanned the darkened hall before him. Shielding his eyes from the glare of the spotlight, his gaze shifted across the faces in the crowd before him.

A smile lit up his face. He raised his hand towards a distant part of the room. "Emily," he said. "And David. A pleasure to see you again. Mark and Carol too. And the Robertson family," he said. "Who I know are here with us tonight."

Then he moved away from the lectern, and walked slowly towards the front of the stage.

He stood there a moment. Now quiet and introspective. And this time, when he spoke his voice was grave and measured.

"As a government Minister, I mix with many very powerful people," he said. "Men and women whose decisions affect the lives of millions around the world. Including every one of us here in this room tonight. Yet these people know little of you. And I regret to say, they care even less."

Standing at the very front of the stage now. Barely a couple of feet from the first row of the audience.

"But when I speak." He paused a moment. "They listen."

His eyes directed now to the furthest depths of the hall.

"And do you know why?" His voice suddenly louder.

"Because they can see it in my eyes. They can see the steel in my soul."

And with a pointing gesture to the audience. "The same steel that's in all of you. Because we've had to fight. To fight for everything we've got. No one has ever given us anything.

And it's made us tough." His hands moving now in short sharp thrusts in rhythm with his words. "And it's made us strong! And it's made us proud!"

Then suddenly calmer. His voice quieter. His movements slower and less animated.

"It's what gives someone like me. The son of a farm labourer and a factory worker, the confidence to talk to them as equals. Because they know." He paused a moment. His words hung in the air. He repeated them again, only louder. "Because they know." His eyes icy cold now. "I won't let them take advantage of honest hardworking people. People like you. People like my parents. People like me. And what strength I have, I draw from you. Each and every one of you."

Almost unnoticed the lights in the hall grew brighter. "And for that I thank you from the bottom of my heart. For without you I am nothing."

Even as he spoke several people stood to applaud. Then the entire hall was on its feet, giving him a standing ovation. He tried to speak on. But unable to make himself heard he fell silent. And bowed his head. When he looked up, there were tears in his eyes.

Then the house lights dimmed. And a single spotlight fell upon him again. The noise in the room stilled to silence. He stood impassive and introspective under the intense gaze of every person in the hall.

And when finally he spoke, it was in a quiet voice. And with great humility.

"I don't like to talk about myself," he said. Slowly looking around the hall. "But I know I have been an inspiration to many of you here tonight."

Jez tapped Louise on the arm and whispered they had things to do. They quietly left their seats. And returned to the room at the back of the hall. Leaving Alan speaking to the crowd.

Closing the door behind him Jez took her aside.

"I've been meaning to talk to you," he said in a hushed tone. "About a delicate matter."

"Yes?" said Louise.

"Someone's making allegations against Alan."

"What sort of allegations?"

He waved his hand dismissively. "It's nothing," he said. "Just a misunderstanding. But if the media get hold of it. You know how they twist things." Then he said, "or Heaven help us, Henry bloody Douglas".

"Of course I'll do whatever I can," said Louise.

He looked at her. "Maybe you could go and see someone?"

"If you think it would help."

"Yes," he replied. "I do." Then he said, "and like a good Anderson McKenzie lawyer frighten the shit out of them".

Louise looked startled.

"That really isn't what I do," she said.

"For fuck's sake!" He raised his voice.

Tears welled up in her eyes.

He opened his briefcase and took out a thick plain brown envelope.

"Then give her this." He thrust the envelope towards her. "You can at least do that can't you?" he said angrily.

"I'm very sorry Jez, but I don't think I'm the right person for you and Alan."

He was silent for a moment. Then in a warmer, more conciliatory tone, "come on Louise," he said. "We're doing great work here."

He put his arm around her shoulder. "You saw the people out there. They need us. We can't let them down."

He put the envelope back in his briefcase.

"We can talk about this another time," he said.

Shortly after Alan re-joined them. The applause of the crowd still echoing behind him. Jez handed him a glass of red wine. The shirt under his jacket was soaked with sweat. And the heavy stage make up caked on his face was starting to melt.

Dark eyeliner ran down his deathly white face like a trail of black tears. Down almost to his bright red lips.

That night she typed the name *Henry Douglas* into her laptop.

In a warehouse in the old industrial quarter of Kalatou City, lie several hundred wooden crates of rusting steel plate. Writes our West African correspondent Paul Reynolds.

Each crate bears the mark of the Kalatou Atomic Agency. An EFR funded government organisation. Tasked with delivering President Maboteau's pledge of a carbon nett zero economy within ten years.

The centre of the country's nuclear industry is located a day and a half's drive north of the capital city. Where for the past three years Chinese engineers have been re-building an East German reactor from the 1960s. Originally de-commissioned forty years ago, after German re-unification.

Various key components were missing. A Swiss company has been employed to scour scrap yards in eastern Europe and Russia. And to re-manufacture obsolete parts from old drawings. And from what we could see, mostly using local backstreet workshops. Some barely better equipped than a blacksmith.

An accurate measure of progress is hard to come by. Access to that part of the country is restricted due to reports of anti-government militia operating in the area.

From time to time the Director of the Nuclear Energy programme, President Maboteau's oldest son Jean-Paul, announces the imminent start of a commissioning programme.

And Heaven help us if they do try to fire it up. But there seems little likelihood of that. Many industry experts doubt it will ever work. And some suspect the government has no intention of completing it. Not so long as generous EFR funding continues to be available.

"Hello Ms Hemmings," said the voice on the phone. It was after 9pm. "This is Paul Hay, Chairman of the New Democracy Party. I hope you don't mind me calling you at home this time of night."

"No, not at all," she replied politely.

"We're forming a new parliamentary party. And we would like to talk to you about an exciting opportunity. Perhaps you could spare the time to meet me in our office in St James's. And we could see if our aspirations match your own."

A couple of days later she made the short walk from Westminster, across College Green to an office in Carlton House Terrace.

Inside it was light and airy. Sparsely, but expensively furnished.

Paul Hay introduced himself. A tall, smartly dressed man with an easy smile.

"I'm delighted you could come and see us Ms Hemmings," he said. "Please take a seat."

He motioned to a richly upholstered leather Chesterfield. And poured a glass of water from a crystal jug.

"Before we start, I need to ask that you treat our conversation today in the strictest confidence. And not to repeat anything we discuss. Especially to your colleagues and the media. Are you comfortable with that?"

"Yes of course."

Then he said, "I'm sure an ambitious young woman like yourself must look around the Palace of Westminster and despair. I mean compared to the Executive in Lausanne it's a disgrace isn't it. Covered in scaffolding to stop it falling down. Just like the British political system itself," he smiled.

"And that's why we are creating a new political party to deliver a pro-EFR agenda. And we need talented and ambitious young people like you Louise, to represent us at the next General Election. With the complete backing of Lausanne, we will be the most exciting and dynamic party this country has ever known. And we will transform the British political landscape. It will be glamorous, aspirational politics. The like of which has never been seen before in Britain. Young voters will be a vital element in our success. And we will ensure our appeal to them is irresistible.

Our launch night will be a huge multi-media event. The biggest and the brightest in British political history. With a celebrity audience of reality TV stars, social media influencers and other famous people.

But we only want the best, Louise. And we are prepared to pay for them. As a prospective candidate you would become an employee of the Party. With a very generous salary, expense allowance, pension and benefits package. Which I am very confident will be comfortably in excess of what you're earning now.

We think it demonstrates just how serious we are. About the project. And about you."

He sat back in his chair.

"So Louise, what do you think? Is joining the New Democracy Party something that interests you?"

"Yes, indeed."

"I thought it might," he smiled.

"Let me tell you a bit about our election strategy.

We will not contest every seat. We have no interest in becoming the largest party. We'll leave that to others.

Our route to government is through coalition. Holding the balance of power is all we're interested in. We want the influence without the infrastructure. It will be our shortcut to government.

And we will get it through targeting key marginal seats to achieve a disproportionate return on our investment.

We will position ourselves as the natural coalition partner of choice. And we can hold the balance of power with as few as fifteen seats.

That's enough to control the country. While our majority partner provides the hundreds of MP's required to carry out the administrative and regulatory functions of government.

And that's how we will leverage a small percentage of the vote into huge political power and influence. Way out of proportion to our size and number of MP's.

All of which means many of our candidates will become ministers in the next government.

So there you have it Louise. That's our route to power and influence. And should you choose to join us, it will be yours too. What other Party could offer you that?"

Then he added, "there's a reception next Thursday at the French Commissioner's official residence near Paris.

Why don't you come along? I think you'd find it very interesting.

And it would be a good opportunity to meet some senior officials of the Federation. We'll take care of all your travel arrangements."

"Someone wants to pass me some classified information this evening in Hyde Park."

"Are you going?"

"I made my mind up a long time ago about this sort of thing. I always go."

"But it seems so suspicious."

"How else would it seem if someone was passing classified information? All sorts of people contact me. Sometimes it's worthwhile. And sometimes it's not. You can never tell. But I've learnt one thing over the years, you find friends in the unlikeliest places. But I won't hang around. I'll do a circuit of the lake, and once it starts getting dark I'll leave."

"I don't think you should go."

"I shall be very careful."

"Don't get into any cars, and keep out in the open."

"I have done this before you know, young lady," said Henry. "One day you may have to do something similar yourself."

Chapter Two

A Change of Career

A few days later a limousine with darkened windows pulled up outside her house. Ready to make the short journey across town to London City Airport.

Approaching Connaught Bridge it turned onto an unmarked road. A row of tall steel bollards sank into the tarmac to let it pass. The road came out on the far side of the airport. Well away from the main terminal building.

The limousine stopped next to an executive jet. A uniformed flight attendant welcomed her aboard. There were several other passengers. All young men and women like herself. Smartly dressed, in their early to mid-twenties.

Forty-five minutes later the jet touched down at a private airfield. More limousines were waiting. A short drive down a deserted expressway brought them to the gates of a huge chateau. Just visible through the trees.

In a grand tapestry-hung reception hall, white gloved attendants handed out name badges.

She saw Paul Hay.

"Hello Louise," he said. "How nice to see you again. I hope you had a good trip."

"Yes, thank you."

"There's lots of people I'd like you to meet." He touched the arm of someone walking past.

"Jean-Pierre, can I introduce Louise Hemmings. One of our prospective candidates for the British parliament next year."

"Hello Louise," he said. "Welcome to Rambouillet."

"Thank you," she replied.

"I think it is very wise for a young person like you to join us. The UK is finished. What is the point of the House of Commons? Lausanne is the centre of Europe. London is nothing. Your country is an embarrassment, no?"

Paul Hay smiled and laughed politely. "So many people to meet," he said. "I hardly know where to start."

Shortly after a discreet bell sounded.

"Time for the opening speech," said Paul. "The guest of honour tonight is Henri Maboteau, President of the Democratic Republic of Kalatou. He's a great friend of the EFR."

She followed Paul into the grand hall. And took a seat next to him under the vast chandeliers. A tiny earpiece sealed in plastic hung on the back of the seat in front.

"You might find that useful," he said. "If your French is a bit rusty."

The host for the evening stepped up onto a raised platform at the front of the hall.

"Welcome ladies and gentlemen," the English translation echoed in her ear.

"It is my great pleasure to introduce our special guest.

Someone who has kindly taken time out of his visit to Lausanne to say a few words to us tonight.

He is a leading member of the bold new generation of progressive African leaders. Ladies and gentlemen, le President de la Republique Democratique du Kalatou, Monsieur Henri Maboteau."

A tall, slim man in an expensively cut German suit walked to the lectern. He looked to be in his early fifties. But might have been older.

"Thank you Monsieur Commissionaire," he said. " It is an honour to be invited here to speak to you tonight. And for the opportunity to tell you about the great work the EFR is doing in my country."

The sound of applause echoed around the room.

The President smiled and waited a moment for the noise to subside.

"Thanks to the generous support of our friends in the European Federal Republic, we are undertaking the largest infrastructure investment programme ever seen in Africa.

And to oversee the construction of these works we have created an organisation called the Agence Kalatouse de Developpement. This company will be responsible for spending a budget in excess of e50 billion over the next eight years."

The President spoke on for several minutes. When he finished Paul leant across and pointed out a small man in the crowd, clapping enthusiastically. "That's the EFR Overseas Aid Commissioner. It shows the importance the EFR attaches to the graduate programme that he's taken the trouble to be with us tonight."

Then he asked, "were you familiar with President Maboteau before?".

"No, I must admit I'd never heard of him."

"He is a great statesman and democrat. You'd never get the opportunity in Westminster to be involved in the building of a new nation, would you?"

"No, I suppose not."

"But here in the Federation we do. There is a much larger pool of talent to draw on here than in the UK. Which is why there are so many fine politicians on the continent. And almost none in Britain."

The host returned to the stage. "Now ladies and gentlemen for our closing address tonight I would like to welcome Roger Vallecourt, the Commissioner for Training & Personal Development."

The Commissioner walked up to the lectern to polite applause.

"Good evening everyone" he smiled. "It's very good to see you all here tonight. I hope you are enjoying our event. And learning a bit more about us."

Then he paused a moment.

"But I have to tell you something."

The warmth seemed to drain from his face.

"Mistakes have been made."

He studied the faces of the delegates seated before him.

"And we have been too accommodating."

He paused again. Then he said, "it was in the mud, the blood and the wire of northern France and Belgium where the origins of the EFR are to be found.

Fortunately, history has not called upon recent generations to make such a terrible sacrifice. But perhaps because of that we have lost the courage of our convictions.

The people of Europe deserve bold and decisive leadership. The sort that only the EFR can give. And yet despite that. Even now, after all these years Jean Monnet's dream of European Unity has still not been achieved."

He looked around the room.

"Was it because his great plan was flawed?"

He paused a moment.

"No it was not!" He slammed his hand down on the lectern startling the audience.

"It was because we let others hold us back. But no longer. The time has come for everyone to contribute their fair share. And there can be no exceptions.

Our place in the world will be our legacy to future generations. And believe me my friends, they will not thank us if we fail.

Instead, they will ask why did they not act when they could? Because now it is too late. And we must live with the consequences of their weakness."

There was a fury in his voice. "Is that how we want to be remembered?"

He gripped the sides of the lectern. "Is it? Because we will be. If we do nothing."

Then he smiled. And the warmth returned to his face. "But that is for tomorrow," he said.

"Today our work is done. And tonight we eat and drink. Our food has been prepared for us by some of Europe's finest chefs. Complimented by the best wines from the cellars here at le Chateau de Rambouillet."

"Is that it?"

"Does that surprise you?"

The Construction Director looked at the half dozen sheets of paper, roughly stapled together.

"To win a contract of that scale and complexity, against some of the finest civil engineering contractors in the world." He shook his head. "With a tender like that is frankly beyond belief. The New Mabotoville International Airport was one of the most challenging projects I have ever been involved in.

A tender for a job like that should be hundreds of pages long. We had a team of twelve people working on it for six months. It cost over half a million pounds to produce."

"Would it also surprise you then," asked the journalist. "To hear the company that won the contract was formed less than twelve months ago."

"It would astonish me."

"It's true."

"No," he said in disbelief. "That's not possible. There was a very strict pre-qualification process. We had to submit a 5 m euro on-demand performance bond. Provide six years of company accounts and evidence of similar projects completed. Some of the biggest contractors in the world failed to make the short list."

"So would you say, in your opinion this project was awarded in a fair and transparent way?" he asked. Before adding, "or would you say it was a fix?"

"That's not something I want to get into. The Client's Project Manager is a highly respected international practice. And we need to work with them in the future."

"Will you pursue any more EFR Development funded work after this?"

He considered his response for a moment.

Then he said, "they are a very important client."

The next morning after a breakfast of coffee and croissants, many of the delegates congregated outside in the courtyard. Talking in small groups and enjoying the sunshine. Louise and Paul Hay among them.

A small crowd of curious onlookers had gathered on the other side of the railings. One of them, an unshaven man in an old combat jacket caught Louise's eye. He pointed at two of the Kalatou delegation. Then he shouted, "genocidiares! Ils sont genocidiares!".

Several gendarmes pushed their way through the crowd towards him. He was quickly bundled away.

"Did you see that?" she said to Paul.

He shrugged his shoulders.

"You don't want to be late for your induction this morning," he replied. "I'll show you the way."

The training suite was in a modern annexe, away from the main building. About a dozen young men and women were already there. She recognised most of them from the flight the day before.

A few moments later the trainer arrived. He shut the door. And locked it.

"Good morning ladies and gentlemen," he said. "Please take your seats and we'll begin."

He took off his jacket and hung it on the back of his chair.

"You have been invited here because you are the brightest and most talented of your generation. Drawn from the world of media, law, PR and advertising."

He walked slowly around the room as he spoke.

"And we want you to join us in a special project. One that will change the face of modern Britain. And put you at the very forefront of its return to the heart of Europe.

Paul Hay has met each of you individually in London. And now that you've had a chance to meet some of our senior delegates." He paused a moment. "It's time to decide if you want to join us on this exciting journey."

The room was silent.

"Ask yourselves this, do you want to change your life? And the lives of millions of others? Do you want to fulfil your own personal potential? And enjoy all the benefits that will bring? Because that's the unique opportunity we're offering you today.

Right here. Right now. In this room."

He stopped walking, and stood before them.

"But if any of you feel this is not what you want. Or you're not up to the challenge. Then walk away now."

He held up the key to the door. "Does anyone want this?"

He studied their faces.

"Well? Do you? Anyone?"

There was silence. No one moved.

Finally, he spoke again. "I want you to put your hand on the shoulder of the person next to you. Look them in the eye. And say, "*we are the future. Together we will change the world.*"

They murmured the words.

"No, no!" he raised his voice. "That's not good enough."

They said it again. A little louder this time.

"You can do better than that," he said angrily. "Do it again."

He made them repeat the words over and over. Louder and louder. Ten, twelve, twenty times and more. Until the noise in the room was almost deafening.

Then he held up his hands for quiet. A hush descended.

"Now I want you to close your eyes. And be still."

A minute passed. Maybe longer, before he spoke again. "OK," he said.

"Going forward you will undertake a course of instruction in public speaking and interview techniques. You will be assessed by an image consultant. And we may require some minor cosmetic procedures to be carried out.

You will be enrolled on a six month fully-sponsored post graduate course, at the College of Europe in Bruges. Where you will enjoy the latest state of the art learning and leisure facilities. And meet fellow like-minded successful and ambitious young professionals from all across Europe.

Our Alumni Association in Lausanne offers unique and privileged access to a network of the most important and powerful people in Europe.

And our range of influence spreads far beyond the political sphere. Into commerce, industry and all forms of the media, including cinema, TV and music. The opportunities are almost limitless. Our on-line Alumni Directory will enable you to identify exactly the right person to contact. Whatever your needs. And they will do everything they can to help you."

Then he said, "OK everyone, let's take a break."

He unlocked the door.

"We'll reconvene in ten minutes."

Louise returned to the courtyard for some fresh air. And to collect her thoughts. The crowd at the fence had thinned since the morning. But the old soldier had returned. He gestured her over.

"Ou sont vos amis, les genocidieres?" he said with contempt.

"I'm sorry, I don't understand," Louise replied politely.

"Vous etes anglais? English?"

"Yes I'm English."

"Que faites vous ici?"

Louise shook her head. "I'm sorry."

"Why are you 'ere, English?"

Before she could reply the old man took a piece of paper from his pocket. And wrote an address on it. He pushed it through the railings to her.

"Rencontrez moi ici a midi. Meet me 'ere." He snatched it back and drew a circle, like a clock face. With the hands at midday. "If you want to know the truth about your friends."

"A fair and inclusive democratic capitalist system," said Henry. Addressing a disappointingly small crowd at a London Chamber of Commerce meeting in Saddlers' Hall. "Is far from an inevitable development of society. Indeed like life itself, its evolution is as random and tenuous as its biological

counter-part. What takes root and flourishes in one society, may never occur in another.

And it can take many decades, centuries even, for a sufficient distribution of wealth to occur to sustain a just and equitable system.

Even once established, such a system may prosper for a while, then wither. And ultimately fail. Because it needs time and space to grow. Not choked by excessive political interference and over-regulation.

And I fear here in Europe just such a process is occurring now. Something which has often brought me into conflict with my fellow MP's in Westminster. And the EFR in Lausanne."

When they reconvened the trainer left the door unlocked this time.

"In this session we'll talk briefly about the philosophy of the EFR."

He sat on the corner of the desk. The atmosphere a little less intense now.

"It is a fundamental truth that modern political and economic issues are too complex for ordinary citizens to understand. The disastrous Brexit referendum a decade ago is a tragic case in point.

And that is why the EFR has moved beyond the simplistic democratic system of the 20th century, to a much more sophisticated 21st century post-democratic model.

Only unelected professional career politicians can plan for a future twenty or thirty years ahead. Unlike elected short term here-today-gone-tomorrow politicians, we can take unpopular decisions without consideration of public opinion.

We deal with major strategic planning and policy making. And leave the day to day administration and politics to local and nationally elected officials. They ride the ebb and flow of ignorant and fickle popularism, while we exercise the real power at federal level.

And we maintain that power by targeting key demographics. Young people especially are drawn to our message. And we will channel their as-yet unshaken certainty and self-belief, by making you the political influencers of your generation. Yours will be the voice of trust they listen to.

And as statesmen and women of the future, you will be required to exercise a level of wisdom and insight far above that of the ordinary person. And to understand the concept that it is *Our Truth* that is important. Not the literal one. Because neither truth nor untruth has any inherent moral value in itself.

An untruth that sustains or promotes the greater good is of a higher moral value than a truth that doesn't. And that's a judgement only we can make.

And should we ever choose to explain our actions to the people, it has to be in language they can understand. And if in that inevitable process of simplification, the facts become distorted. So be it. You must learn that it's OK to lie to them. We speak the truth when we can. Lie when we have to.

And it's inevitable at times some member states need to make sacrifices. But to us the concept of being a Good

European is second nature. It is absolutely normal to put the needs of the EFR first. Even when it goes against our own national interest.

And it's not a burden. It's a privilege. One we are happy to embrace and share equally.

And it's your great good fortune to be the golden generation. The one that will reap the benefits of the hard work done by those who went before you.

For all the measures are now in place. Tax and language harmonisation, a common legal and judicial system. We have a European parliament and a European Army. And EFR embassies or consular representation in every country of the world."

Then he paused a moment.

"But a key piece is missing. A single thick black line still stains the map of Europe.

And this, and only this stands in the way of the European Federal Republic becoming the greatest political and economic super-power the world has ever seen.

And it is our job, every one of us here in this room, to make sure that national border is erased. Because we must speak to the rest of the world with one voice. There can be no deviation from EFR policy. No European state can be allowed to take unilateral action. Or to hold any position contrary to the EFR.

All states must commit their resources to the common good. And the EFR, and the EFR alone, will determine how best to use those resources. Without recourse to consultation, consent or approval.

This great organisation is too important to have one country hold it back. Britain is part of Europe. Whether it likes it or not. The philosophy of the EFR is a complete one. It cannot be partially implemented. It has to be swallowed whole. And it has to be swallowed now. And each of you in this room will play a major role in ensuring that process is executed."

Soon after they broke for lunch. Louise slipped away into town.

The address on the scrap of paper led her to a shabby internet café, in a run-down district. There was no sign of the old soldier. She took a seat at a tired outdated machine. And typed the words *President Maboteau.*

French language websites filled the screen. She scrolled down until she saw one in English. And then another.

President's Son Appointed to Run Family Firm

"For a position of such huge responsibility, only the very best candidate can be chosen for the role of Chief Executive of the Kalatou Development Agency.

The selection process must be rigorous and exhaustive to make sure we have the right person. Someone who combines the necessary skills, training, integrity and experience to deliver this hugely complex multi-billion euro programme of works.

And to ensure complete impartiality, I entrusted the entire selection and appointment process to an independent panel of experts. Over whom I had no influence.

And so it gives me particular pleasure to tell you they have chosen my son for this prestigious and demanding position. And I commend the selection committee on their excellent choice."

Kalatou Joins the Technological Elite in Formula One

"Welcome Mr President, are you enjoying your first visit to a Grand Prix?"

"Yes, very much, thank you."

"Rumour has it this won't be your last."

"No, indeed. Next year you will be speaking to me on the grid of my own Grand Prix. The streets of our new capital city Mabatoville will be laid out to form the track. And I have a personal invite from the President of the world governing body of motorsport in Paris.

They are very keen to meet me, and to sign the contract. And no doubt you have noticed Le Societe Mineraux de Kalatou logos on several drivers' helmets?"

"Yes, of course Mr President. And could you comment on the rumours we may soon see the SMK name among the ranks of Grand Prix teams."

"Yes, we are in the market to buy a Formula One franchise. My advisors are in discussions with several team owners. We are a young, confident and wealthy nation. And Formula 1 is a natural environment for us."

The old soldier took a seat opposite her. Faint purple bruising around his eyes, and three fresh stitches at the corner of his mouth. Despite his grey hair and the lines on his face, she saw he was not an old man. Probably only in his forties.

"This is the most safe internet café in town," he said. "The machines are slow. But too old to be traced."

"That man this morning?" asked Louise. "The man you were shouting at?"

"Il est *Colonel Manches Courtes*. A Minister in Maboteau's government. In English you say Colonel…". He hesitated, searching for the right word.

Then he made a chopping motion with his hand against his arm. Just above the elbow.

"The shirt with the short sleeve."

He saw she didn't understand.

"His soldiers," he said. "They cut all the arms."

Then he added, "the Minister of Justice, *Colonel Manches Longues*. He only cut the hands."

He continued, "I was part of the EFR's peace keeping mission, Operation Ghibli. When we arrived in Kalatou City it was like the liberation of Paris in the war. Crowds cheering and the EFR flags everywhere. They thought we had come to protect them."

His gaze shifted from Louise's eyes, to somewhere in the distance over her shoulder. His mind returning to earlier, darker times.

"We were on patrol with Maboteau's militia. They stopped a school bus. My men raised their weapons to defend the women and children. But I had to give the order to stand down. And do nothing. We could not fight Maboteau's men. The EFR forbid it."

He shook his head at the memory of it. "And they killed them all. Toutes mortes, toutes les mamas et les enfants."

There were tears in his eyes.

He fell silent for a moment.

Then he reached into his pocket. He pulled out a small newspaper cutting with a faded photograph.

"Here," he said. "Look at this. Maboteau's coronation as President ten years ago."

Louise studied the photograph.

"Look at the crowd. Can't you see?" The piece of paper shook in his unsteady hand. "Where are the adults and the old people?" he said animatedly.

C'est un pays des orphans! Everyone of more than 15 years was killed. And the memory of the genocide and the genocidiares died with them. Those who lived were too young, and know only Maboteau as President."

"Does the EFR know this?"

"Bien sur, of course they know. But they choose to forget. And that's why I am here. And why…" He touched the fresh stitches at the corner of his mouth.

Then he said, "and Maboteau's L'Armee des Vampyrs? You know of that?"

Louise shook her head.

"Bodies without blood, without hearts. You don't believe me? It's true. I've seen it with my own eyes."

The Speaker of the House called on Alan Wells to address the chamber.

As he got to his feet several colleagues moved to fill the empty seats around him, in a show of solidarity and support.

"Thank you Mr Speaker," he said. "As I explained when I was called before the Select Committee, pricing a company for floatation is not an exact science. Especially one held in public ownership for so long. It takes a combination of skill, experience and fine judgement.

So let me tell you, my Honourable and Right Honourable friends, I am very proud of the return my team and I delivered for the taxpayer. We called the value of the company correctly. It was the market that got it wrong. And I am confident the share price will drop back down to our IPO level in due course."

Murmurings of agreement echoed around the chamber.

"As for any criticism of me personally." He shook his head. "That is something I cannot accept.

And I say that as someone who has worked tirelessly throughout his career to support the working people of this great country.

My purchase of those shares was merely a gesture of solidarity with the employees. A loyal and dedicated workforce, for whom I have the highest regard and admiration."

His words were drowned out by the enthusiastic calls of "hear, hear" from those seated around him.

He raised his voice. "And as a purely symbolic act, let me assure the House my stake holding was never acquired with any thought of profit or long term ownership."

He sat down to more cries of "hear, hear" from his colleagues.

The Speaker invited the Prime Minister to reply.

"Thank you Mr Speaker. And thank you to the Honourable member for his heartfelt words. He has always served

the government and the people of this country selflessly. And my cabinet colleagues and I look forward to him continuing to do so for many years to come.

And despite the claims of the National Audit Office and the Business Innovation and Skills committee, he has satisfied the House he behaved honourably and correctly. And the matter is now closed. And I'm sure I speak for all in this chamber when I say too much valuable parliamentary time has been wasted on this already. And that we should turn our attention to issues that the electorate actually cares about."

The Clerk pointed to a small unlit stairway she had never noticed before.

"Up there," he said. "To the top." Then he added, "it's a long way".

She climbed a hundred steps and more until she reached a corridor high in the roof of the old building. Up at that level there was no expensive wallpaper or luxurious carpet. Just plain white walls and bare wooden floorboards.

And but for a door with the faded words *Henry Douglas MP*, no sign anyone ever went up there.

She knocked on the door. A moment later an elderly man opened it.

"Come in," he said. "You found it OK then?"

It was a tiny office with a sloping roof. So low Louise could barely stand up in half of it. The only daylight through a small skylight, And the only warmth from an old cast iron radiator. The smell of damp hung in the air.

"Thank you for agreeing to see me," she said.

"You're welcome," he smiled. " I don't get many visitors. I'm one of the last MP's left in the old building. And not by choice, I can tell you." Then he asked, "would you like a cup of tea?"

He seemed a kindly fellow, in his late sixties or early seventies.

"Please, take a seat," he said, and switched on the kettle. "So, Louise Hemmings, who are you? And how can I help you?"

"I work as a Special Political Assistant."

The old man put a tea bag in a cup.

"Oh yes?" he said. "May I ask who for?"

"Alan Wells."

He looked up.

"And how long have you worked for him?"

"Only a couple of months."

"And before that?"

"I was a lawyer."

He was silent for a moment. Then he said, "with whom?"

"Anderson MacKinnon."

The old man shook his head.

"I'm very sorry, young woman," he said. "But I have to tell you I loathe Alan Wells. And I despise lawyers. Especially Anderson MacKinnon ones. Me and several thousand Yorkshire miners cheated out of their redundancy pay. To name but a few.

I don't wish to appear rude. But I don't think we could possibly have anything to discuss."

"I was just hoping for some advice," said Louise.

He was silent for a moment. Then he said, "you have just walked up one hundred and eight steps. I suppose I ought to give you a couple of minutes. Speak."

"I was invited to an EFR reception near Paris last week."

The kettle boiled. The old man ignored it. "Go on," he said.

"You have to admire the principles of the EFR don't you? A brotherhood of nations, working together for the greater good, tolerance, peace and understanding. But when I went to see them…" Her voice trailed off. Then she said, "but nobody said the EFR was perfect did they?".

"No," said Henry. "No one's ever said that."

"And maybe that's the best reason to join them. You can't improve something unless you're part of it. And perhaps my generation can be the one to turn the great idea into reality."

The old man was silent for a moment. Then he said, "you asked my advice". He looked at her sternly. "Find yourself another career. And as far away from Westminster as you can. Politics is a filthy business."

He got up and walked towards the door.

"But if you are determined to make a career here or in Lausanne, coming to see me is a very bad way to go about it. I am not popular amongst my colleagues. Either here or in Europe."

He opened the door.

"But fortunately, I have the most inaccessible office in Westminster. So no one will ever know you were here. And I suggest you don't tell anyone we met. Good day."

"Campaigning starts tomorrow in the South Cambridgeshire by-election, following the Prime Minister's recent resignation on health grounds.

Deposits have been received from candidates representing all the major parties. Including the recently launched pro-EFR New Democracy Party. Along with the inevitable handful of independents and protest groups. Of which, surely the most interesting is Henry Douglas's New Independent Party. Although whether he will find it worth the value of the deposit he's bound to lose remains to be seen. Because his candidate, an unknown former Anderson MacKinnon lawyer and political advisor will surely sink without trace."

A couple of days later Henry called.

"Our meeting the other day," he said. "It's been troubling me.

You have a very gruesome CV. And you've fallen in with the worst elements in Westminster and Lausanne. But despite that, you seem an honest and genuine young woman. And it would be a great shame to let them ruin that.

So, if it's of any interest there is a position available as my political advisor. Although I must warn you, working for me is not generally considered a good career move. Which is why the position is available. And has been for some time.

But if that doesn't put you off, I'd be happy to talk to you about it."

"When the chairman of the Law Society asked you three months ago, in this very room Mr MacKinnon, you assured the committee that all SRA regulations had been adhered to. And yet we subsequently learnt the information you provided was not correct. Which is why we have called you back here today to explain yourself."

"Mr Chairman, I answered all your questions in good faith. And to the best of my knowledge, based on the information provided to me at the time.

Please let me assure you, no one feels more let down than me by the actions of a small number of junior employees. Who, despite the best endeavours and outstanding example of the Partner in charge of their section, chose to disregard the company's strict code of conduct."

He paused a moment.

"But I can assure the committee, we have taken the necessary steps to ensure these young men and women never work in the profession again."

They took their places in the five hundred seat circular Roosevelt lecture theatre, just off Tottenham Court Road. Louise waited patiently, Henry wrote in a little pocket book.

The lights came up on the stage.

"Good evening ladies and gentlemen," announced the host to a packed house. "It's my great pleasure to welcome you tonight to the launch of a bold and exciting new initiative, *A New Dawn for Africa*. Created to reach out and forge new partnerships with the young and emerging nations of that great continent.

And to tell us all about it, I'm delighted to introduce our guest speaker. The highly respected international businessman and tireless charity campaigner, Mr David Arnoud."

Henry turned to Louise. "And son of the EFR President," he said quietly.

To the sound of loud and enthusiastic applause, he walked briskly up to the podium in an expensively tailored suit. Gold cufflinks glinting under the lights.

"Good evening everyone," he said. "I'm very pleased to have the opportunity tonight to talk to you about a subject I feel very passionate about.

I have always been fascinated by the history and politics of Africa. And through my extensive charitable works, I have been lucky enough to visit that great continent many times. And get to know the extraordinary and inspiring people who live there.

So when I was invited to lend my support to this new initiative. I knew in my heart it was the right thing to do. Because things are changing in Africa. And changing fast.

With your help we can drive that pace of change. And release the vast economic potential embedded in this exciting and dynamic region. Believe me, the financial opportunities are immense. And that is why we have formed the *New Dawn for Africa Corporation*.

Over the last decade, stronger and more stable governance has all but eliminated risk in the region. A new generation of enlightened leaders, like President Maboteau are leading their countries into a golden age of democracy, freedom and opportunity.

So trust me, when I say this is somewhere you can do business. And very profitable business at that.

But let me tell you a secret. Some of the big global institutions are beginning to notice. So I urge you to get ahead of the market, and sign up to our new business initiative without delay. And take advantage of our unparalleled network of the region's most powerful and influential decision makers. But don't think about it too long. Time is short. And this opportunity won't last.

So join me today in this commitment to the people of Africa. And together we can achieve results unseen in modern times. Your journey to almost unimaginable financial success starts here. And it starts tonight. Sign up to our initiative. And make your pledge.

A minimum investment of just £100,000 will get you on board. There's no upper limit. And we will ensure your money is wisely and ethically invested for the best possible return.

And believe me when I tell you, the level of those returns will be exceptional. I guarantee it. Forget what you're used to in European, US or Far Eastern markets. Because once enrolled in the New Dawn Business Initiative, you will have to completely re-calibrate your expectations. What you might consider outstanding now, will soon seem quite ordinary.

So, ladies and gentlemen, it's time to open your eyes. And see the possibilities. And to turn those possibilities into reality. You won't regret it. Thank you," he said, concluding his speech.

He left the stage to loud applause.

The host returned.

"And now I would like to call on Monsieur Roland Nkweta, Business Development Director at the Kalatou Ministry of Finance."

He stepped up onto the stage. "Good evening ladies and gentlemen. Thank you for the opportunity to speak to you tonight. And to emphasise my country's commitment to this new and exciting venture.

La Republique Democratique du Kalatou provides one of the world's most progressive and risk free economic environments in which to conduct business.

We place no restrictions on the repatriation of the proceeds of investment or capital return. And whilst of course our legal and financial regulatory systems comply with all international standards, we understand the many and varied requirements of the overseas investor. And our financial institutions can provide the necessary flexibility and diversity to suit every type of business interest.

I can say with complete confidence, that the RDK offers the most dynamic and secure low tax investment platform anywhere in the world. And a perfect political and economic environment in which to create, manage and develop your business."

As he spoke Henry continued to make notes. And when he finished speaking, David Arnoud returned to the stage.

"Ladies and gentlemen," he said. "The pledge desks are now open. We accept all forms of cash or money transfer. And have representatives from all the major commercial, private, on-line, high street banks and cryptocurrency dealers with us tonight. There are no upper limits. Whatever the figure, we can invest it for you. And the greater your investment, the greater your return."

He raised his arms aloft. Like the Pope on the balcony of the Vatican drawing the faithful.

"So come join us," he said. "Add your name to the list of internationally recognised and respected figures from the world of politics, business and sport, who have already done so. It was the right choice for them. And it's the right choice for you."

Afterwards on the pavement outside, Henry called for a taxi on his phone. He looked at the screen. "There's no service in this area."

"We're in the middle of the west end," said Louise.

She got a signal on her phone immediately.

"When did you last update your phone?"

He shrugged his shoulders. "I don't." Then he said, "I think we ought to find out a bit more about the Democratic Republic of Kalatou".

It was the first time Henry had accompanied the Prime Minister in the back of his official car. They sat in silence. Each alone with his thoughts.

Then the Prime Minister said, "a week ago I was at the United Nations in New York. Speaking to some of the most powerful people in the world. But in a year or so the Great British public will probably put me out of a job." He shook his head. "What do they know? They don't have a clue. I mean look at him." He pointed at someone standing on the pavement as they passed. "My future rests in his hands, and people like him. It's a bloody joke isn't it. Would you rely on someone like that. Or that," he said pointing at someone else standing by the side of the road. "Or him… or her." He jabbed his finger against the inside of the glass as the car moved slowly down the street.

At first Henry thought he was joking. But then he slammed the palm of his hand against the window. He'd never seen him like this.

"Look at those bastards out there" he shouted. "Gormless half-witted fuckers."

His face contorted in a sudden fury. Great gobs of saliva collected at the corner of his mouth. Spots of spit sprayed onto the glass window in front of his face. Making obscene gestures and shaking his fist at passers-by. Oblivious, all of them to his silent and invisible rage behind the smoked glass windows of his soundproofed car.

"What sort of stupid fucking system is it where they get to decide if I keep my job.

It's a fucking disgrace."

He pounded his fist into the soft upholstery of the door next to him. The car momentarily stopped in traffic, began to rock on its suspension.

CHAPTER THREE

Friends in High Places

"I've asked Paul Reynolds, the West African correspondent of the Times to come and talk to us," said Henry. "He's written several articles about Maboteau. And he's bringing a member of the exiled Kalatou opposition party with him."

Henry set out his traditional welcome of tea and chocolate biscuits.

Then he said, "a word of caution about journalists, Louise".

He carefully arranged the biscuits on the plate.

"Don't ever think of them as friends. They'd never think of you as one. They're only interested when they believe there's a story in it. Or a valuable new contact. So if they're nice to you don't take it personally. Or indeed, if they're not."

Then he added, "but I find it pays to let them think you could be useful."

A few minutes later his guests arrived.

"Thank you very much for coming, gentlemen," he said.

"Thank you for inviting us Henry," replied Paul Reynolds. "Let me introduce Patrice Kabala, London representative of the Kalatou Democratic Party."

He shook Henry's hand.

"I'm very pleased to meet you Mr Douglas," he said. "And thank you for your interest in my country."

He handed Henry a business card.

"You're very welcome," said Henry. "And this is my colleague, Louise Hemmings.

Previously Louise was a lawyer at Anderson MacKinnon."

Patrice Kabala leant across the table to shake her hand. "Very pleased to meet you Ms Hemmings," he said. And handed her a business card.

"Hi," said Paul, studying the biscuit selection.

"And," said Henry. "She had the dubious pleasure of meeting President Maboteau recently at an EFR event in Paris."

The journalist looked up.

"That's very interesting, Louise," he said. " I'd like to hear more about that. Perhaps I could buy you lunch," he smiled. "I'll give you a call."

Then he turned to Henry. "So why the interest in Maboteau? I didn't think African politics was your area."

"His name keeps coming up," said Henry. "In all sorts of places."

"It wasn't always like that," replied the journalist. "Not until he got control of the state mining company, *Le Societe Mineraux de Kalatou*. It's a *very* profitable business. Mining for copper, coltan and other key elements in the manufacture of computers and mobile phones. And it's made Maboteau one of the richest men in Africa."

Then Patrice Kabala spoke. "Our country's mineral reserves should be our most precious asset. But in Maboteau's hands they have been a curse upon us. None of my countrymen have benefitted. But millions have died. He has made himself and his family rich beyond imagination. And condemned his compatriots to live in poverty.

Yet in Europe you support him. And this is something we do not understand. You say you support democracy. And yet you support Maboteau. It makes no sense. He is a criminal. A very bad man. There is a saying in my country, *Maboteau is President, but corruption is King.*

Even the son of your EFR President is a friend and business associate of Maboteau and his family. How can the EFR say he is the legitimate President, when he has murdered or imprisoned all who oppose him.

I would like to invite you and Ms Hemmings to visit my country, to see for yourself. But I cannot. While Maboteau is in power I can never return.

But here in London, in Europe there is very little interest in the ordinary people of my country. And that is why I am honoured to come and speak to you today.

But even here, on the streets of this great city I fear for my family. Not for myself. But for them, should anything happen to me. But it is a risk I have to take.

He must not be allowed to steal another election. And if there is anything you, Mr Douglas as a member of the British Parliament can do to bring attention to this, the people of my country would thank you from the bottom of their hearts. We need the support of the international community to bring Maboteau to justice for the crimes he has committed. And for what he has done to our country."

Paul shook his head.

"Maboteau has a lot of friends in high places," he said. "All of whom are extremely keen to see him stay right where he is. Educational establishments, charities, business organisations, you name it. They've all done extremely well out of him. And intend to do so for a long time to come. And that includes several of your Party's most generous donors, Henry."

"Why don't you report this in your paper?"

"Come on Henry," he replied. "You know it's not that simple. London's not called the libel capital of the world for nothing. And the Royal Charter put press freedoms back to the dark ages. These are very powerful people and institutions. Who can afford the sort of legal protection money can't buy."

Then he said, "as it happens Maboteau's coming to London next month. To open a new state of the art lecture theatre he's funded at the Maddox Business School in Islington. His son's a student there, loosely speaking. When he's not wasted in exclusive West End clubs."

The journalist took another biscuit.

"I'm afraid the politics are very complicated out there, Henry. You have to remember the European concept of a nation state is pretty irrelevant in much of that part of Africa. Many of the national borders are old colonial relics. Just lines on a map that mean very little on the ground. And Kalatou is typical of that. A French creation that rode roughshod over existing tribal and ethnic boundaries. An example of shameful colonialism at its worst. The northern province has sought independence ever since they left in the 1950s.

And there's been an undeclared civil war in the country for decades. Large parts of it are no go areas for aid-workers, NGO's and journalists. No one really knows what's going on in there."

Then Louise spoke for the first time. "I understand French paratroopers were sent in a few years ago?"

"Yes," said Patrice. "That is correct."

"Operation Ghibli," said Louise.

"You are a well-informed young woman," said Patrice. "The EFR sent a peace keeping force. But they did nothing, while Maboteau's army murdered thousands of civilians."

"And Maboteau's Vampire Army?" said Louise.

"You are a *very* well-informed young woman," said Patrice.

"Vampire Army?" asked Henry. "What's that?"

"Superstitious nonsense," said Paul.

"It is not superstition!" said Patrice angrily. "L'Armee des Vampyrs exists. I have seen their filthy work with my own eyes. Bodies drained of blood. Hearts, kidneys and livers removed.

But it is not a contract with the devil Maboteau has made. It is a Chinese healthcare company. To sell human blood and organs to medical institutions in Europe, Asia and America. Maboteau's L'Armee des Vampyrs is a business. A business that murders for profit. It is true, I assure you."

Over the past year Lausanne based broadcasting company EuroSat have been producing a weekly political satire. It's syndicated across the EFR and has built up a huge following. Writes our media correspondent Roger Perry.

Channel 4 have bought the rights to air it in the UK. And it's scheduled to start its British transmission next month.

Earlier this week I was invited to join a group of journalists to watch a preview tape at their offices in London.

In the main it pokes gentle fun at EFR and other European political leaders. It's hardly satire at its most biting. But it is quite amusing.

There are certain themes that run through it. Every time you see a British politician they're shown in black and white, like an old Movietone news. With jerky out of sync movements and speech. Simulated marks on the film and hairs flickering across the screen. And they're always shown wearing old fashioned crumpled clothes, driving around in dull 1950's British cars, belching exhaust smoke. Whereas the EFR politicians are all young and attractive, driving the latest top of the range electric Audi's, Mercedes and BMW's.

Our favourite among the cast of minor unnamed characters, and surely a caricature of Henry Douglas, is an aging buffoon who's always tripping up and dropping his papers on the floor.

It has particularly large viewing figures among the 18 to 30 demographic on the continent, so the advertisers love it.

The Speaker called on Henry to address the House.

Murmurs of disapproval echoed around the chamber.

"Order," cried the Speaker.

Henry got to his feet. And waited a moment for quiet. But in vain.

He started to speak. "I wish to draw the attention of the House to the forthcoming visit…"

But still the noise persisted.

"Order! Order!" repeated the Speaker.

Henry raised his voice. "… Of the President of Kalatou to open a new lecture hall at the Maddox Business School in central London."

Finally the noise began to subside.

"And let me ask the Prime Minister this."

At last the chamber fell quiet.

"Is it right for a prestigious British educational establishment to accept gifts from a man with such an appalling human rights record?

Indeed, should such a man even be allowed to set foot in this country? Let alone welcomed here to distribute handouts and donations to all sorts of organisations.

He is personally responsible for the death of thousands of his countrymen, through civil war and genocide. He has ransacked the natural wealth of the country. And left his people starving and destitute.

So I hereby call on the government to freeze all President Maboteau's assets held in the UK, while an audit is carried out to determine their legitimacy.

The British government and the EFR must decide what is more important to them. Lucrative trade deals and generous gifts. Or human rights and the rule of law. Because with President Maboteau you cannot have both. Which is it to be, Mr Speaker?"

The Prime Minister rose irritably to his feet to respond.

"There will be no investigation. Or freezing of any assets. I must ask the Honourable member not to waste the House's valuable time with such silly requests. The President is a democratically elected head of state. Whose financial affairs and human rights record satisfies all international standards.

And the Honourable Member would do well to remember that the President is a good friend to this country. And should be treated with respect.

Not used in a crude attempt to embarrass the government, or highly regarded educational establishments in this country."

Then raising his voice, he said, "when in fact the only embarrassment."

He paused a moment.

"Is the Honourable Gentleman himself."

The chamber erupted into loud and mocking laughter. With much finger-pointing in Henry's direction, and shouts of "you're an embarrassment!".

"We were deeply sorry to learn of the passing of Mr Douglas. He was a good friend to our country. We were very thankful for his support in our struggle for freedom and justice. And for the kindness he showed our colleague Patrice Kabala. Who, he himself also sadly fell in the struggle. And I speak on behalf of the New Democratic government of Kalatou,

when I say we always hoped one day to show our gratitude to him personally. But sadly now we cannot.

And I fear it will take many years to rebuild our country. We are finally rid of Maboteau. But his legacy is a terrible civil war, that is tearing our country apart. And massive international debts we cannot repay. It saddens me more than I can say, to tell you ours will remain a deeply divided and impoverished nation for many years to come. And it will be a very long time before we can even think about trying to bring the son of the EFR President to justice, for the crimes he has committed in our country. Much as we want to."

He took a memory stick from his pocket. And placed it carefully on the table in front of Louise.

"Especially now we have access to many incriminating documents we never had before."

"Those bloody yanks," said Henry. "Someone needs to sit down and really explain it to them."

"What's happened?" asked Louise.

"The US Secretary of State's in Lausanne." He lifted the screen of his laptop.

Images appeared of a press conference recorded earlier in the day.

"… Yes we do believe it would be in the best interests of the British government to seek closer integration with the EFR…"

The image froze.

"Give it a moment," said Henry irritably.

"… and as a close ally to both parties we would welcome any opportunity to…".

The image froze again for a few seconds. "*... do whatever we can to encourage that. We believe this will benefit both the UK and the EFR. And also the wider global community, including ourselves...* ".

It froze again. He switched it off in frustration.

"They don't get it," he said. "And I don't know why.

The US would never be part of an organisation like the EFR. It's completely at odds with the whole concept of the US constitution.

Taxation without representation was too much for them, for God's sake. And the EFR is government without representation."

Then he said, "of course I understand they deal with Lausanne because they have to. But don't stir the bloody pot for us. The stakes are much higher over here. There are powerful factions in Westminster looking for any opportunity to engineer our integration into the EFR. The Foreign Secretary and his gang for a start."

He leant back in his chair for a moment. Seemingly lost in thought. Then he said, "you know the Founding Fathers of the United States were quite remarkable men. Eighteenth century American political philosophy may not have been democracy as we think of it today. But it was very bold and enlightened for its time."

He sat up in his chair. "To have been in Philadelphia in that glorious summer of 1787." He shook his head in wonder. "And to see Franklin, Washington, Madison and the other Framers at work in the State House. Following the arguments back and forth, as the great charter takes shape before your eyes."

In his mind it seemed the events were as vivid as the day they happened.

"Can you imagine it?" he said. "To be present at one of the greatest moments in political history." He was becoming very animated now. This was a side of Henry she had never seen before. "And to witness the birth of a nation," he continued. "And not just any nation. But the most powerful and progressive the world has ever known. And to see how a group of ordinary people could produce such an extraordinary document. And in doing so become great themselves."

Then his mood darkened.

"But who are the successors to those remarkable men?" he asked. "Not Jean Monnet, that's for sure. Even now, nearly three hundred years later we're still waiting for the next great advance in political thinking. And believe me," he said. The shadow of the modern world closing in around him again. "The EFR isn't it. Instead they've taken us back to the dark ages."

"Why the fuck would I want to go back to London? Why do you think I left in the first place for Christ's sake? I despise my fellow countrymen. And I have a very good life here in Lausanne. When I left British politics eight years ago, I had no intention of ever going back. And nothing's changed."

"We'll arrange a peerage for you Sir Stephen. How do you like the sound of Lord Fowkes of… wherever. And you'd have Chequers and the flat above Number 10."

"Big fucking deal," he replied.

"There would be a very generous salary, bonus and benefits package. And of course you'd continue to draw your full EFR entitlements as well."

"And they've agreed to this?"

"They will. When we tell them to."

"I want to keep my fully staffed office and apartment here in Lausanne. I'm only prepared to work in London three days a week. "

"Yes, yes, all that can be accommodated."

"You really think they would accept that?"

"They don't have a choice. They signed it all away at Augsburg."

"I must warn you, if you insist I take this job there's going to be some almighty rows. Because I won't take any shit from those fuckers."

"That's fine. It doesn't matter if you upset them. In fact, we like the idea."

"The Honourable member for Brentwood & Ongar," called The Speaker.

Henry rose from his place on the back benches, to the usual murmurs of irritation from all sides of the chamber.

"I wish to draw the attention of the House to the continuing civil unrest on the streets of Kalatou City. The shooting of protestors and mass arrest of political dissidents."

His words were met with indifference from all sides of the House.

"The legacy of years of corrupt and oppressive rule," he said. "By a President this government gives millions of pounds of aid money to every year."

The opposition benches stirred. A few half-hearted cries of "shame, shame" echoed around the chamber.

"Money that has been mis-spent," continued Henry. "On military hardware and personnel to maintain his grip on power.

So will the Prime Minster confirm to the House the suspension of all financial aid to this discredited regime, with immediate effect. Until President Maboteau steps down and calls an election."

The Prime Minister rose to the Despatch Box. "President Maboteau is one of Africa's most respected and longest serving elected leaders. He has proved himself a committed advocate of democracy and social reform. His track record is beyond reproach.

Which is why we have supported him and his government in the past. And why we will continue to do so through these difficult times.

We respect and endorse whatever action the President takes to prevent rogue elements destabilising the country and its economy, and to maintain the rule of law."

Henry got to his feet, to exercise his parliamentary right of reply.

"The rogue element destabilising the country and its economy is the President himself."

The Prime Minister shook his head wearily, and said something to the Foreign Secretary on his left.

"And will the Prime Minister state for the record, that this continued support owes nothing to protecting the interests of wealthy Party donors. Many with lucrative and quite possibly criminal business links to…"

Cries of "shame! shame!" rang out from the opposition benches. Much louder and more vigorously this time.

"… with links to this government of murderers and gangsters."

On his own benches his colleagues sat in silence. Staring straight ahead or slowly shaking their heads.

"Order! Order!" called the Speaker.

Raising his voice, Henry continued. "And who have used this blood money to help sustain a party, which at this moment in time I am ashamed to be associated with."

He sat down to enthusiastic cheers from the opposition benches, and cries of "hear! hear!".

The Prime Minister returned to the Despatch Box.

"I will not be drawn into this silly argument. Or respond to these ill-considered and offensive remarks."

Then he raised his voice sharply. "But I will say this." He looked around the chamber. "If the Honourable member is so ashamed of his Party." He paused a moment. Then he said, "I suggest he does us all a favour. And resigns."

Loud cheering and laughter rang out from both sides of the House. And a ragged chorus of "do us all a favour," echoed around the chamber.

The Returning Officer spoke up above the deafening noise in the hall. "Ladies and gentlemen" he called out. "If you please. Ladies and gentlemen, please." But his appeals for quiet went unheeded. "I hereby declare…," he tried again. But it was impossible to make himself heard. He waited a moment for calm.

Finally, he gave up waiting. "I hereby declare Louise Ann Hemmings duly elected member of Parliament for South Cambridgeshire."

Several candidates shook her hand. The government candidate turned away. The New Democratic Party candidate looked at the floor, and shook her head.

Louise walked to the front of the stage as dawn was breaking outside. She stood to address the crowd. Her hands behind her back, so no one could see them shaking.

A few yards away on the other side of the stage, a BBC Newsnight Reporter spoke to the defeated government candidate. He leaned in to catch her words above the noise.

"You must be very disappointed with tonight's result," she said.

"Of course I am," he replied curtly. "Not for myself. But for the people of this constituency. Because they have made a big mistake."

"Do you think the dirty tricks campaign against her influenced the outcome?"

"What dirty tricks?"

"And actually worked in her favour?"

He pushed his way past the reporter. And disappeared into the crowd on the floor of the counting hall. The New Democratic Party candidate had already left the stage.

Henry tore open the hand written envelope. Two e-tickets fell out onto his desk.

"The EFR Tour of European universities rolls into London this week," he said. "They're at the Maddox Business School tomorrow night. It's a closed event. Students and invited guests only." He smiled, "no riff-raff".

He handed one of the tickets to Louise.

"You really do have friends in unlikely places," she said.

"Of course the QR codes won't match our ID," he said. "But if it's busy enough no one will notice. You'd be surprised the places I've got into like that."

Inside the auditorium there was space for three or four hundred people in steeply tiered rows of luxurious seats. The stage was lit by a huge and complicated lighting system.

"You can see why these universities suck up to people like Maboteau," he said.

A few minutes later, the EFR Commissioner for Training & Personal Development walked to the lectern to address the audience. Louise recalled his face from Rambouillet.

He spoke for about forty minutes, describing the benefits of a career with the EFR. Henry scribbled notes in a shorthand note pad.

Then he said, "and for the last half hour I would be delighted to take questions from the audience. Zonal microphones are located around the hall."

He looked up at the audience before him. "The first question please."

Henry raised his arm. One of about a dozen delegates around the auditorium to do so.

After responding to a couple of other questions, the Commissioner motioned his hand towards Henry.

"The gentleman, here to my right," he said. "Your question please."

"Good evening, Monsieur Commissionaire," said Henry.

"And good evening to you sir," he replied affably.

"Could you please explain the EFR's policy on the payment of bonuses."

"Yes of course," said the Commissioner. "As an organisation we are committed to continually driving up standards year on year. And the payment of bonuses recognises dedicated and outstanding staff who have excelled against rigorous performance criteria."

He looked elsewhere for another question.

But Henry spoke again. His voice loud and clear across the chamber.

"Last year the EFR paid out over 100m euros in bonuses. And they were paid to almost three quarters of all staff. So they are not incentives at all, are they? Merely a device to conceal the massive salaries paid to EFR staff from public scrutiny."

Everyone turned to see who was asking the question.

"Your figures are not correct," replied the Commissioner brusquely. Then in a more measured tone he said, "but I do acknowledge the quality of our staff is exceptional. Justifying an appropriate level of pay to match. And we make no apology for that.

Every bonus paid generates efficiency savings. And if a significant proportion of our staff receive the maximum bonus, then it just demonstrates how much money has been saved. The day we pay 100% staff bonuses will be a tremendous validation of our pay policy. And a great day for the EFR, and the people of Europe it serves."

Then he turned sharply away, and looked for another question from the other side of the hall.

Henry spoke again. This time the microphone failed to pick up his voice.

Under his breath he said to Louise, "I suggest we leave separately. I'll see you in the morning."

After one more question the host drew the session to a close.

"I think they're trying to get rid of me, Henry."

"Why do you say that, Prime Minister?"

"It's just a feeling."

Before Henry could say any more, the Prime Minister held up his hand. Indicating him to be silent.

He took his phone from his pocket. And studied it for a moment.

Then he opened his desk drawer, and removed a roll of aluminium kitchen foil. He tore off a length. And wrapped it tightly around the phone. Then he put it back in his drawer. And locked it.

He gave Henry a knowing look.

Then got up from his chair. And walked to the window. He parted the net curtain an inch or two and looked out. He stood there for several minutes.

"Is everything alright Prime Minister?" asked Henry.

Making their way through the crowd to the ticket barriers at Westminster underground station, Louise heard a loud noise behind her. She turned to see Henry fall to the ground. The contents of his briefcase spilled out over the floor and under the feet of passers-by.

She helped him up off the ground. People nearby gathered up his papers and other items.

"That was a bloody policeman," he said.

Someone handed him back his briefcase, which had slid several yards across the polished tile floor.

Louise thanked them as Henry put his papers back into it.

"I really don't think it was a policeman Henry," she said. "He didn't look like one."

"Precisely," replied Henry. "Plain clothes."

Before a large gathering of international press and TV, the President of the EFR and a delegation of senior officials waited on the tarmac at Geneva International Airport.

A Dassault Falcon executive jet taxied slowly towards them. Red and green lights on its wing tips pierced the gathering dusk of evening. It rolled silently to a halt.

Moments later, the President's son emerged from the plane. Wearing a Gucci leather jacket, faded jeans and cowboy boots. His eyes concealed behind expensive sunglasses. Gold jewellery glinted in the lights of the TV cameras.

The President embraced him. Then spoke into a microphone to address the media.

"I am delighted to welcome home our precious and beloved son."

The emotion clear in his voice.

"And I would like to thank President Maboteau, without whom he would not be with us tonight."

He looked across at his son.

"And thanks also," he added. "To the Special Forces personnel, who rescued him from anti-government militia earlier today in Kalatou City."

Then David Arnoud stepped forward to the microphone.

"I am not someone who seeks publicity," he said. "Either for myself, or for the many charitable causes I support. But I want to stress my enthusiasm and affection for the people of Africa remains as strong as ever. And I plan to return as soon as I can. To continue my work there improving the lives of ordinary people. My own personal safety will always be secondary to that. And now I would like to go home and get some rest."

"In the summer of 1945, the people of Europe looked out across a wasteland where great cities once stood. They saw the infrastructure and industry of an entire continent destroyed. Whole populations displaced and homeless. The tragic result of American economic & military imperialism. And the centuries old territorial ambitions of European nation states.

And the people were determined it would never happen again. And spoke with one voice to demand change. And Europe's greatest political thinkers, led by Jean Monnet and Robert Schumann answered the call. And so began the process that brought forth the creation of today's European Federal Republic."

Henry closed the book.

"That," he said. "Is pure propaganda. The EFR is re-writing history to portray itself as a great populist movement driven by the grateful people of Europe."

Then he held up the book to show the words printed on the front cover: Approved EFR History Text for 10 to 14 Year olds.

"And they are doing it by targeting the youngest and most impressionable in our society. And it is as cynical as it is shameless. But they can't help themselves. It's in their nature. Bureaucrats and politicians can never have enough power. Why be a national politician when you can be an international statesman? Why regulate a country when you can regulate a continent? The draw of power and control is irresistible to them. And which is why I have such a deep distrust of all political elites and institutions. And the EFR embodies everything that is wrong with those sorts of organisations."

"Henry's off again," said the Minister sitting to his left, sarcastically.

"No, Henry is not off again," he snapped. "You try to mock me because you're one of them."

"From anyone else Henry, that would be deeply offensive. But you are such a ridiculous old man, nobody cares what you think. How you ever got elected to parliament is a mystery. And the sooner your constituency comes to their senses the better."

The TV presenter raised his hands for calm. " I think we'll have to leave it there," he said. "We're out of time."

The studio lights dimmed. But as the figures faded to silhouette their animated body language showed they hadn't finished.

Chapter Four

A Serious and Credible Candidate

President Maboteau stood in front of the packed assembly chamber in the parliament building in Kalatou City.

His eyes slowly scanned the faces of the delegates before him.

"If the gangsters and criminals who roam our streets, and abduct innocent foreigners want an election so badly." His voice echoed around the chamber. "Then I say to them, OK. Let's have one."

For a moment there was silence in the assembly hall. Then hushed murmurings of shock and anguish filled the air.

"But these thugs and troublemakers will be sorry," he continued.

"Because they will hear the voice of the people. And it will say you belong in jail."

Then he said. "And let me tell you. When I am re-elected, I will be very happy to oblige.

So I intend to submit my resignation. And sign the executive order for an election to be held. And I call on every man and woman of this great country, to exercise their sacred and democratic rights at the ballot box.

And to ensure this election is conducted without fear or intimidation, anyone with criminal connections, or links with extremist groups will be forbidden to stand. This sends a powerful message affirming our commitment to a free, fair and fully democratic process."

His words were heard in complete silence.

"And yet despite this." He looked around the chamber, in apparent disbelief.

"Where are the opposition party leaders?"

He raised his hands in amazement.

"They are finally getting the election they say they want so badly. And they are not even here."

The sound of loud and enthusiastic laughter filled the air.

"What does that tell you about their commitment to democracy?"

Again he looked around the chamber.

"I think we all know the answer to that," he laughed. "We have called their bluff."

The President sat down to loud and sustained applause, lasting several minutes.

Finally the noise in the chamber began to subside. Another delegate got to his feet to speak.

"Thank you for your words of wisdom, Mr President," he said.

"Of course we respect your wish to submit yourself for re-election. Demonstrating yet again the depth of your personal integrity. And absolute commitment to democracy. But I know I speak for all, when I say it distresses us to see you, our great President, subjected to such an indignity. You are the Father of the Nation. And you are too beloved, and too precious for that.

And besides, what is the point? Why go to the trouble and expense? When we already know the outcome the people want.

So instead, I would like to propose an amendment to our constitution. An amendment that would bestow upon you title of President for Life. And surely, honouring the will of the people in this way is a perfect example of democracy in its purest form."

The President rose to his feet to respond.

"Thank you for your kind and gracious words my friend," he said. "I have to tell you this is not something I would ever seek for myself. But if it is the will of the people, then how can I refuse? As a nation dedicated to the highest democratic principles, it is my duty and obligation to respect that.

And if in the future, it is the will of the people that my son be appointed my successor as President for Life. Then I would have to respect that too.

And certainly, no one could deny the logic of it. The son of the President is literally born to lead. It's in his genes, his very DNA. It is indeed our great good fortune that in my son the process of natural selection, and the will of the people have combined to create the perfect candidate."

Public Notice to all persons residing, working, visiting or otherwise affected within the postcodes listed in the attached appendix.

A major security exercise will take place in the City of London over the last weekend of February.

This exercise will test procedures for dealing with a major terrorist incident in London's financial district.

Under powers granted by the Prevention of Terrorism Act 2006, only authorised persons and vehicular access will be permitted within the designated area, from midday Friday until 5am Monday.

All commercial, residential, religious, leisure and other premises must be closed and vacated. And all unauthorised personnel and vehicles must leave the area for the duration of the exercise. Failure to do so may result in an unlimited fine and or imprisonment.

Any unauthorised vehicles will be removed by the Police and may be destroyed. All rail, road and air links into and out of the City, and all overflight clearance will be suspended during this time.

Even from fifty yards, Louise could see the dents and scratches.

"Are you sure you're safe to drive Henry?"

"Sorry about the car," he said. "It keeps getting vandalised."

"Have you reported it to the police?"

He shook his head. "There's no point."

"Why not?"

"They do it."

"Why on earth would you think that?"

"I don't think. I know."

"You've seen them?"

"I don't need to. I'm afraid I am an outlaw in the true historical sense of the word. Their duty to protect and defend every individual in this country, irrespective of race, creed or colour does not extend to me. And to make the point, they commit acts of petty criminal damage to my property. No doubt you think I'm crazy. But you're too polite to say it."

"Henry, I'm sure they have far more important things to do."

"If I didn't know better I'd think the same. And that's the point. If I speak out about it no one would believe me. They'd think I was mad."

"But what possible reason could they have to do it?"

"To intimidate me, to undermine my resolve, force my withdrawal from public life. In some countries political dissidents are imprisoned. But here they harass you just below the conscious level. At first you don't realise it's happening.

It took me years to work it out. But now I have, it's obvious. My internet connection is hopelessly slow and drops out all the time. And no doubt my phone is tapped and my email hacked."

Then he said, "If they are monitoring my movements on CCTV I don't make it easy for them. Tube stations are very useful. Especially ones with several exits. Tottenham Court Road has six. Piccadilly Circus seven. And Bank, best of all has nine. Department stores too are very good.

Before the new extension there were eleven exits from Selfridges. Now there's twelve. I know. I counted. And I have used every one."

"It is *very* hard to believe, Henry."

"Precisely," he said. "I doubt it myself sometimes. Which is exactly what they want."

We are delighted to announce the launch of our new Integrated Social Credit Programme. To be progressively rolled out across the Federation over the next five years. Developed with our international A.I. technology partners, to empower the citizens of the EFR to live safe, happy and fulfilled lives.

By rewarding a healthy, public-spirited and socially responsible life-style with enhanced social service and welfare access, borrowing potential and other entitlements. Whilst targeting wasteful, irresponsible and anti-social behaviour.

A single cloud-based portal will consolidate all public, private and personal data, social media networking and internet access into one convenient place.

The system's powerful facial recognition software will create a cashless, paperless society. Where your face will be the only password you need.

"I'd like to get Patrice Kabala's view on David Arnoud's business activities," said Henry.

He unlocked the bottom drawer of his desk. Louise saw it was full of SIM cards.

He slipped the back off his phone and switched cards.

"You might want to get some of these yourself," he said.

"They're unnumbered and untraceable. They sell them in the Members' Bar."

He made the call. But there was no answer. He removed the SIM card and put it back in the drawer. Then took a well-worn London A-to-Z off the shelf.

"Can't risk the internet," he said.

He leafed through it. Found the page and studied it for a moment.

"It's near Elephant & Castle," he said. "But we'll take a cab. There's too many cameras on the underground."

"Does it really matter?" asked Louise.

"I don't mind them knowing a little about my business," he said. "But not too much. With a bit of luck they might think I know more than I do."

They walked to the corner of Great College Street, where he hailed a cab.

"Could you take us via Queenstown Road please cabbie," he asked.

"But that's the opposite direction, Guv."

"I like that route," replied Henry with a charming smile.

The taxi driver shook his head as they drove off.

Finally south of the river, they turned onto Clapham Road and headed north east. Twenty minutes later the driver turned to them. "This is the street, Guv."

Henry studied the passing shopfronts. Reading the numbers out loud. Until he stopped, opposite a vacant shop. With a *To Let* sign in the window. He checked the business card again.

"Sorry, cabbie," he said quietly through the glass. "Could you take us back to the Commons." Then he added, "the most direct route".

He sat back in the seat with a haunted look on his face.

"Maybe he moved away," said Louise.

Henry shook his head. "Because I asked a question in the House," he said.

"He asked you to do what you could. And you did."

"And his wife and children? They didn't ask me. He said that was his greatest fear. And because of me it's happened."

He stared out the window.

The lift doors opened at street level. The commuters waiting for their trains surged forward. While she slipped away to the right, down the emergency stairs.

Slowing her pace, a stranger drew alongside in the narrow circular stairwell.

"Thank you for agreeing to meet me," he said. "I'm sure you understand I can't tell you who I am. Or how I came by this information."

He passed her a folded piece of paper. "But I assure you it's genuine."

She took it without looking at it. And slipped it into her coat pocket.

"I am taking a huge risk giving you that. But I'm deeply troubled by the current negotiations between the government and the EFR in Augsburg. And when you read that e-mail you'll understand." The sound of their footsteps on the steel stair treads masked. his hushed voice.

"And why I beg you to reveal its contents under Parliamentary Privilege. Just as Henry would have."

They timed their arrival at the bottom of the stairs to the noise of the lift doors opening. And blended back into the crowd of travellers. She joined the group making the short walk straight ahead to the northbound platform. While he took the steps down to the left with the others, southbound to Morden.

It was an hour before dawn. Events had moved quickly overnight. Henry waited to be interviewed inside the Sky News mobile studio. Outside the wind and rain swept across a deserted College Green.

On a small TV monitor he watched live pictures of the former Foreign Secretary arriving at Broadcasting House. His car surrounded by media reporters and TV crews. Flanked by several policemen, he made his way through the crowd towards the building.

The sound played in Henry's earpiece. Someone shouted out, "what's your reaction to the reshuffle Mr Ross?".

He ignored the question.

"Why were you sacked?" called out another.

He didn't react.

"Were you planning a leadership challenge?"

He stopped a moment, in front of the bronze art deco entrance doors. "I have always acted in the best interests of the Party. And done whatever the Party wanted me to do. I've nothing more to add, thank you."

An hour later former Foreign Secretary John Ross spoke on BBC Radio 4's *Today programme.*

"Of course the Prime Minister is entitled to reshuffle his Cabinet," he said.

"No one has an issue with that. Least of all me. But to replace it almost in its entirety with a group of totally inexperienced Ministers, less than a year away from an election." He shook his head. "Is madness. The A Team are in the dressing room, while the B Team are out on the pitch. The people of this country deserve better than this government of nobodies."

"I'd hardly call Henry Douglas a nobody," replied the host.

"And that's the final insult. Promoting that man to the cabinet is outrageous. He is totally unfit to hold any office of state. Let alone one of the highest in the land."

"But with your poll ratings, surely decisive action was needed. And the Prime Minister's taken it. You're just sore it's come at your expense."

"No, not at all. One bad opinion poll and the Prime Minister loses his nerve."

"It wasn't just one."

"Mid-term polls mean nothing. Until this ridiculous re-shuffle the Party was on course to maintain its majority at the next election. The Prime Minister is undoing all the good work this government has done over the past nine years."

"You would say that wouldn't you? You lost your job."

"My job is not important. What's important is the people of this country get the best possible government. That's all I'm interested in."

"And by that presumably, you mean one led by you. If the rumours arc to be believed."

"That's a decision for others to make. Not me."

"I call on The Foreign Secretary," said the Speaker.

Silence fell across the House.

Getting up from an unaccustomed place on the government front bench, Henry stood to make his maiden speech as a Minister. With the eyes of every MP, journalist and visitor in the packed Spectator's Gallery fixed upon him.

"My Honourable and Right Honourable friends," he said. Microphones and TV cameras recording his every word and gesture.

"Our friends and colleagues in Lausanne, and those who went before them have achieved many admirable things over the years."

His words prompted a few murmurs of agreement.

"For which," he continued. "We should all be grateful.

As the European Coal & Steel Community it played a vital role in rebuilding the shattered post-war economies of western Europe. And the EEC that followed laid the foundations for the prosperity we all enjoy today."

Cries of "hear, hear," rang out around the chamber from all sides.

Henry waited a moment for the noise to subside. Then he continued. And in a more sombre tone. "But it always had much bigger and more sinister ambitions than that."

An uneasy silence descended on the House.

"From the very start they planned the world's first post-democratic super-state." Murmurings of discontent reverberated around the chamber from all sides.

"Order, order," called the Speaker.

The House quietened again. And Henry continued. "Run by an unelected ruling elite who created themselves out of nothing. At vast expense. And at the request of no one."

The noise in the chamber began to increase.

Henry raised his voice above it.

"Hollowing out the institutions of national government like a grotesque parasite."

Shouts of "no! no!" rang out across the chamber from all sides.

Raising his voice still further he said, "until only the empty husk of its host remains."

"Order! Order!" called the Speaker. "I must ask the Minister to moderate his use of language in the House."

The noise subsided again. And Henry continued.

"But I ask the House not to mistake my anti-EFR sentiments for anti-Europeanism. The EFR have succeeded in creating a myth that to criticize it, is to attack Europe. And this is a falsehood. A falsehood they have inculcated into the minds of many people."

The Speaker interrupted him again. "I must remind the Honourable Member to observe the rules of the House. And refrain from the use of unparliamentary language."

Undeterred Henry spoke on.

"For despite the darker chapters in our shared history, we have all reaped the benefits of two thousand years and more of economic, social, cultural and scientific development. But in spite of those great advances, politically Europe has returned to the dark ages.

And that is the EFR's wretched contribution to the history of this great continent. And why I personally cannot support it."

There was silence in the House.

"But I say this." His voice loud and clear across the chamber. "If it is indeed the will of the people to join the EFR. Then so be it."

He was silent for a moment. Then in a quieter and more reflective tone, he said it again. "So be it."

Before raising his voice once more. "But for some of my colleagues to have tried to set this process in train by subterfuge, is a betrayal of everything this House stands for. Never, Mr Speaker, never have the words *my Honourable* and *Right Honourable friend* been less appropriate in connection with those of whom I speak."

The silence was broken by uproar in the House.

"Order! Order!" cried the Speaker.

Henry continued speaking above the noise. "Let the guilty members of this House, and those who went before them hang their heads in shame."

While those around him reacted furiously, the former Foreign Secretary sat stony faced and impassive on the back benches.

There were shouts of "shame! shame!" from government and opposition benches alike. The noise in the chamber was almost deafening. Members on both sides of the House were on their feet.

"Order! Order!" called the Speaker yet again. "I must demand that the Minister use more temperate language in the House. Or face the consequences."

Henry tried to continue. But his words could barely be heard above the noise.

"But I have a message for the Bureaucrats of Lausanne," he said.

The Speaker banged his staff on the floor. The clamour in the chamber quietened a little. And a sense of order returned to the packed House.

"I have already asked you to moderate your language. I will not ask you again."

He leant forward to the two wigged clerks in front of him.

"Strike that last passage from the record," he said.

Henry waited a moment. A sense of anticipation charged the air.

"But I have a message for the Bureaucrats of Lausanne," he repeated again. "Your agents have been banished from their positions of influence in this House."

The Speaker banged his staff on the floor a second time. "If you continue to disregard the rules of the House, I will suspend you from the chamber."

Henry continued. "Replaced instead by men and women of integrity. Who unlike them, respect the principles of democracy."

Members on both sides of the House were on their feet again. The noise in the chamber even louder than before. But Henry carried on. Raising his voice again, in a vain attempt to be heard. "Men and women who will not allow the creeping shadow of federalism to steal across this land unchecked."

Shouts of "shame! shame!" echoed from all corners of the House. The former Foreign Secretary leant across and said something to a colleague next to him.

The Speaker shouted, "Order! Order! Order in the House! The Minister's language is completely unacceptable. I have no alternative but to demand the Honourable Member withdraw from the House under Standing Order 43, for the remainder of the day's sitting."

And for the second time he ordered the Clerks to strike his words from the record.

Henry collected his papers. And left the Chamber to insults from all sides of the House.

Late afternoon in Mayfair, and the light was fading. At that time of year it would be dark in another twenty minutes.

She walked past the front of the shop. Turned down a narrow alleyway alongside. And entered by an unmarked entrance.

"If a conventional body-worn camera is too big, or too conspicuous for your purposes," said the salesman. "Then a wireless button camera is the ideal solution."

He placed a tiny round object in the palm of her hand. Barely the size of a small copper coin. And weighing about as much.

"This is one of our best-selling models," he said. "It's been used by law enforcement agencies around the world for many years. And I can assure you, whatever your intentions you will find it highly effective."

"Hello Henry, thank you for coming to see me."

"You're welcome, Prime Minister."

"How are you?"

"I'm fine thank you."

"Good, I'm pleased to hear it."

He gestured towards a small table with a selection of tea, coffee and biscuits.

"Please help yourself," he said. "And take a seat."

Henry poured a cup of tea from a china pot.

The Prime Minister waited for him to sit down before he spoke again.

"This is a very significant day," he said.

"Yes? Prime Minister."

"Today I became the tenth longest serving Prime Minister in British history."

"Congratulations," Henry replied. "That's a great achievement."

"Thank you. And although our majority is very slim. And our ratings at their lowest ebb." He looked at Henry intently. "I am certain to become the longest serving of all time."

He sat back in his chair. "And do you know why?"

Before Henry could think of something to say, the Prime Minister continued.

"It's His will."

He leant forward.

"The will of God."

Henry tried to read the expression on the Prime Minister's face, to see if he was joking.

"I've thought about this a great deal in the last few

months. And it's become clear to me. I have been placed on this earth to carry out His work. And I must have no fear or concern what others may think. Because when you know something is right in your heart. But others doubt you. And sometimes you doubt yourself, that's when He's testing you.

And when you're alone. And you hear the voice of your conscience. That's really His voice speaking to you. And then you *know* it's the right thing to do."

Henry was silent for a moment. Then he said, "have you spoken to anyone else about this?".

"I wanted you to be the first Henry. In the short time we have worked together I've come to regard you as my most trusted and faithful colleague."

"Thank you Prime Minister. I appreciate that. And I think perhaps we ought to keep this to ourselves. Just for the moment."

"But Henry, that's exactly what we can't do. The people must be told. Because nothing will be the same again. There will be no more elections. As God's own Party we will be in power forever. Never to appease an ignorant electorate again. And in years to come when he is old enough, my son will take my place. You do understand what I'm saying, don't you Henry?"

"Yes of course, Prime Minister. And that's why we need to think very carefully about how we communicate this to the electorate."

"You're absolutely right, Henry. I was thinking of doing a national TV or You Tube broadcast. We have to speak directly to the people."

"It's an interesting idea, Prime Minister. But before you do anything could you give me a little time to think about this. To come up with a strategy. It's vital we get this right."

"OK, Henry. But it's not something we can keep to ourselves for long. It's our duty to spread the message."

"Of course, Prime Minister. Let's talk about this in the morning. In the meantime may I ask you not to speak to anyone else about this."

"Alright, Henry. But only for a day or two. The people must be told."

"Yes of course, Prime Minister. And thank you for letting me know."

"You're not concerned about this are you Henry?"

"No, not at all."

He stood looking out the window. His office in deep shadow. Lit by the glow of a single desk lamp. Outside the evening traffic was still heavy on Victoria Embankment. And the lights of Westminster Bridge reflected on the still flat surface of the river.

He didn't look round when Louise came into the room.

"Is everything OK Henry?" she asked. "I got here as soon as I could."

A moment passed before he spoke.

"I always knew it would end, of course," he said. "But not like this. Not so soon."

It is now almost one hundred and twenty years, since Aristide Briand inspired Europe's greatest political thinkers to challenge the pernicious forces of nationalism.

And to conceive of a fairer, more tolerant and inclusive society, in the spirit of federal partnership and co-operation.

And as President of The EFR, let me assure you the great post war ideal of total and indivisible European unity is within our grasp.

Yet despite that, some national governments still continue to frustrate the hopes and aspirations of their people, under the false cloak of sovereignty.

And history has taught us nothing if not that this way lies only xenophobia, division and distrust. And a breeding ground for intolerance, hatred and prejudice.

But fear not citizens, redemption is close at hand. And when the time comes we will leave no one behind.

Because none are free until all are free. The EFR is Europe. And Europe is the EFR.

"I cannot remain silent much longer. You're not trying to stall me are you?"

"No, not at all," said Henry. "Just give me a few more days to finalise our strategy."

"He is getting impatient. And we must not displease Him."

"No, of course Prime Minister."

"And it's not fair on the people. They have a right to know. And to share in the glory of *The Great Revelation*."

"Yes of course, Prime Minister. But we need to make sure the timing is right."

"He is testing us. And we must show Him we are worthy of the task He has selected us for." The Prime Minister looked at Henry. "And we are, aren't we Henry?"

"Yes, Prime Minister."

Returning through the Members Lobby he saw the political correspondent of the Daily Telegraph.

"Hello Henry, good to see you."

"You too," said Henry, less enthusiastically.

"The PM seems to have found a new lease of life. There's a real sense of conviction about him these days."

"You could say that."

"Look, Henry, you know I've always helped you out in the past. We'd love to get an exclusive with him. If there's anything we can do for you just say. I'm sure we can make it worth your while."

"Matthew, this is not a good time. He's very busy. But I'll see what I can do."

"Thanks very much, Henry. You're not just saying that are you?"

"No, not at all."

On another day of rising violence on the streets of the capital Kalatou City, demonstrators protesting against government corruption clashed with riot police and troops. In response to the rapidly deteriorating situation President Maboteau has declared a state of emergency. Closing schools, banks, factories and offices. And imposing a strict curfew. Rioters and known dissidents have been rounded up and interned. The numbers detained are unknown.

And the President has called on international support to secure his position in power. The EFR and the British government are monitoring the situation closely.

At the centre of the long table in the Cabinet Office, Prime Minister John Ross took his place. For the first time.

"As you are all aware there will be an election in less than 12 months. And our priority is to retain our lead in the polls, following the regrettable resignation of my predecessor yesterday.

There will be no speaking to journalists, except in the presence of Press Officers. And no answering of any questions without clearance from Number 10 first. Anyone unable to follow these directives should leave now. I will announce a revised cabinet at 3pm today. Thank you."

And with that he dismissed them. Except Henry. He indicated for him to stay behind. He waited for the last person to leave.

"Of course none of that applies to you Henry. Because your career is over. Don't think our thin majority will save you. You will sign this letter of resignation."

He slid a typed piece of paper across the table towards him.

"You will retire as a Minister and an MP with immediate effect. You will not be heard from again. And live out the rest of your life in obscurity. Do you understand?"

"I will not resign," said Henry. "And after you've sacked me John. I shall continue my work more vigorously than ever."

"That would be deeply unwise. You have made some very important people extremely unhappy. So I suggest you think long and hard before you say or do anything you may come to regret."

"On the contrary, outside the Party I will be able to speak much more freely than I ever could before."

"Henry, there are very powerful forces at work against you. And I cannot protect you. Even if I wanted to. Which of course, I don't."

"So," said Henry. "The EFR got their man out just in time. Seeing him arrested and put on trial in Kalatou City was the last thing they wanted. Can you imagine what would have come out.

And now Maboteau's in Lausanne they're stuck with him. They made him out to be a great democrat and statesman, but now he's a huge liability. And a very expensive one too. It must cost a fortune for round the clock security. Can you imagine it if agents of the new democratic government kidnapped him off the street in Paris, and took him back." Then he smiled. "Here's hoping."

"What will you do now?" asked Louise.

"The only thing I can do," said Henry. "I will form my own political party.

I will resign after the summer recess, and stand for re-election. And hopefully retain enough of my majority to be returned to the House.

But first, I am determined my new Party will put up a candidate at next month's by-election for the former Prime Minister's seat. And not just any candidate. But a serious and credible one. One who could win it."

"But who?"

"With your permission Louise, I would like to submit your name."

He saw the look on her face.

"I know your distaste for politics. Which I think surpasses even my own. But that is yet another compelling reason why you are the right person.

And I can't say you won't regret it. Or one day you'll thank me for it. Because we both know that's not true.

But despite that, you must accept. This is not the time to walk away and find another career. Maybe later. But not now.

And of course you will have my complete support. And as the first appearance of our new Party, I am sure we will attract a lot of media attention."

The phone rang. It was London Times political correspondent Andy Smart.

"Hello Louise," he said. "Is Henry around?"

"He'll be back shortly. Can I take a message?"

"Actually it was you I wanted to speak to. I hear you're putting your name forward for the South Cambridgeshire by-election."

"Yes, that's right."

"Are you sure that's something you really want to do? It will be a very rough ride. Henry is the most hated man in Westminster and Lausanne. They may hate him for different reasons, but they all hate him just the same. And it will get very ugly.

And it's not just the politicians. It's also the media, the political lobby, pressure groups, everyone. They're all out to get him. And you too, if you stand. Your life will never be the same again. And I fear your career as a prospective parliamentary candidate will be very short. And extremely unpleasant.

So I suggest you think very carefully before you allow him to put your name forward."

Henry returned a couple of hours later.

"Andy Smart rang."

"Oh yes," he said. "What did he want?"

"He offered me some advice about standing in South Cambridgeshire."

"What did he say?"

"Nothing I didn't already know."

Chapter Five

A Night on The Town

Barely within a minute or two of its posting the BBC reported it. And within minutes of that, every news agency in the UK carried the story. Most reproducing the text of the statement in full. Exactly as it appeared on the New Independent Party website. Just before 8pm, all two hundred and nineteen words of it.

A Personal Message from Louise Hemmings:

Earlier today I checked myself into a private rehabilitation clinic for the treatment of drug and alcohol abuse.

To my deep shame and regret this is something I have concealed for many years from my family, friends and colleagues. But such is the level of my dependency now, I can no longer hide its very damaging effects. On both my personal and professional life.

I sincerely apologise for the hurt and distress my irresponsible actions and poor judgement have caused. And I ask for the forgiveness and patience of all those who have been affected.

It would of course be completely inappropriate for me to continue to seek public office at this time. So I am withdraw-

ing from the forthcoming South Cambridgeshire by-election and will cease all public appearances with immediate effect.

I would like to ask that my family and myself are given the time and the privacy for the healing process to begin.

And it is my hope one day perhaps, to resume a life of public service in some way. But as to when, and in what capacity I cannot say.

I trust everyone will understand I that do not wish to comment further, or answer any questions on what is now a private matter for myself and my family."

The Prime Minister took a few moments out from an engagement at the Guild Hall to speak to a crowd of reporters.

"Yes," he said. "I've heard the news. It's very sad. But you know running for public office is a very challenging experience. And I'm afraid, as we have tragically seen tonight, it quickly exposes any physical or mental weakness. I'm sure everyone in Westminster will join me in wishing her a complete recovery. And I echo her request to be given the privacy she needs. As I fear her recovery will be a long and difficult one."

Across London, Alan Hay, chairman of the pro-EFR New Democratic Party spoke to a group of journalists outside his home.

"It takes a brave person to publicly admit their failings. And I feel for her. I really do. She is clearly a very vulnerable and deeply troubled young woman. Clearly wholly unfit ever to have been a candidate. But let's be quite clear. It is Henry Douglas who bears the responsibility for this. He has sacrificed this poor unfortunate young woman on the altar of his own ambition. Shame on him. Not that he will care about her of course. He's only concerned how it affects him."

As the first foreign journalists to visit the site since work began, we were shocked and dismayed at what we saw. Writes our West African correspondent Paul Reynolds.

Six and a half thousand acres of the country's finest agricultural land is now just a dirt brown desert, as far as the eye can see.

Silent and deserted under a relentless and unforgiving sun, that bakes the ground as hard as concrete. Deep cracks and fissures snake out across the surface in all directions.

Excavators and dumper trucks lie abandoned. Slowly leaking diesel into the earth around them. Half a dozen tower cranes stand idle against the sky. The wind whistling through their rusting masts.

And the great runway, intended to be the longest in the world at more than three miles, is little more than a rough outline on the ground. We walked the length of it. Our boots kicking up clouds of fine dust that hung in the air behind us. We paced it out at no more than a mile at best.

And of the famous terminal building, whose startling post-modernist design had been selected from a shortlist of the world's leading architects, there were just a few steel columns sticking out of the ground.

And that was it. All there was to show for two years' work. And several hundred million euros borrowed from the EFR Central Development Agency in Lausanne.

Outside her house from the early hours, the noise of car doors slamming and loud voices. And inside, the incessant ringtone of her mobile phone and the sound of SMS alerts.

Closing her eyes and taking several long deep breaths, she steeled herself for a moment. Before opening the front door to a barrage of blinding camera flashes and TV lights. Instinctively, she stepped back and turned away. Emboldened by her retreat they pressed home their attack.

"What sort of organisation doesn't notice a rogue message posted on its website," one of them called out.

"Until it's been splashed across the media for six hours?" shouted another.

"Is this a serious political party you're representing? Or some kind of joke?"

"Good luck with your campaign," someone said sarcastically. "You're going to need it."

"Do you know who did this?" asked someone else.

She shook her head. "No," she said. Her voice barely heard above the noise. "I don't."

"The same people who vandalised your car?"

"Perhaps."

"… and broke into your house?"

A couple of hours later Henry sat at her kitchen table. His head in his hands.

"I'm so sorry," he said. "I got here as soon as I heard."

He looked up at her. "I should never have asked you to stand. What was I thinking?"

He shook his head. "I always said politics is a filthy business." Then he said, "they've beaten us. It's too much. I'm withdrawing our nomination."

"No," she replied. "We have to carry on. Now more than ever."

The new Prime Minister stood at the despatch box.

"I am pleased to inform the House, the Foreign Secretary and the Secretary of State for Trade will meet their European counterparts in Lausanne today. Where they will hold crucial talks aimed at enhancing our trading relationship with the EFR. These will be the most important and far-reaching discussions since the creation of the EFR, over a decade ago."

He sat down to loud cheers of approval from the government benches behind him. And many others around the chamber.

Then the Speaker called for the first question.

Henry rose from his place on the back benches. To the usual murmurs of derision from across the House.

"Will the Prime Minister come clean and admit the first act of his new government, and the real purpose of this trip, is to engineer our integration into the EFR through the back door. Something he has no mandate to do."

Shouts of "shut up!" from the government benches echoed around the chamber.

Henry raised his voice. "Fortunately," he said. Before pausing a moment for quiet.

"Order! Order!" cried the Speaker. But in vain. So Henry continued.

"Fortunately," he said above the noise. "With an election in a few months' time, the British people will soon have the opportunity to discard this unelected Prime Minister, and his wretched government."

Loud mocking laughter from the opposition benches filled the air.

The Prime Minister slowly shook his head. While other colleagues around him sat stony-faced.

Then he got to his feet to respond. The noise in the chamber subsided again.

"Time in the House is too valuable to waste responding to silly questions like that. So I will be brief. The Honourable member is talking nonsense," he said. Before adding, "as usual".

MP's on the benches behind him cheered and stamped their feet.

"I can assure the House, we are just tidying up and rationalising existing trade agreements. This is good for Britain. And good for Europe.

And whatever prosperity we have enjoyed since leaving the EU, will only be enhanced by even closer trading links with our friends in Europe. A collaborative working relationship between the UK and the EFR is in the interests of both parties. And long overdue.

And not helped I might add over the past few months, by the antagonistic attitude of the Honourable gentleman himself.

And as for his comments about this government, I think he would do well to reflect on his own recent fall from grace and expulsion from government." He sat down to the sound of laughter and cheers from both sides of the chamber.

After the session adjourned for the day, Henry walked across College Green to the Politics Channel studios. The Foreign Secretary was already there when he arrived.

"Thank you for joining us, both of you," said the host.

"You're welcome," replied Henry.

The Foreign Secretary nodded his head in acknowledgement.

"So, Mr Douglas what's wrong with negotiating trade deals with the EFR? We do it with everyone else. Why not them?"

"I'm afraid it's not as simple as that," said Henry. "Let me tell you the mood in Lausanne is not as our new Prime Minister would have us believe.

They are determined no myth should ever take hold, either here or anywhere else that Britain took on the EFR and got what it wanted.

These new trade terms will be so harsh and so punitive we could never survive outside the EFR again. They want to send out a clear message that no European state can question their authority."

The correspondent turned to the Foreign Secretary. Who shook his head and smiled.

"Henry's been talking rubbish like that for years. The EFR needs us as much as we need them. It is a negotiation of equals. And both sides will treat the other with the respect they deserve. It is simply not in the interests of either party to try to gain an advantage over the other. The ethos of the EFR is to establish a close and collaborative partnership among friends and allies. And to work together for the common good. What benefits the EFR benefits Britain, and vice versa. We must all do our bit to be Good Europeans.

And we are not joining the EFR. So for goodness sake Henry shut up. You are a complete irrelevance to modern political debate. And the sooner you and your ridiculous little Party disappear the better for everyone."

"Perhaps in twenty years' time a more balanced view of him will emerge.

Surely much of the disrespectful and emotive language associated with him will have been forgotten. And we may find history is kinder to him than we might imagine today.

And maybe on reflection, we should have treated him better. Too often it seemed the normal rules of politeness and respect did not apply to him. Both from his colleagues in Westminster and those of us in the media.

Some said the better you knew Henry, the more you liked him. And judging by the loyal support of his constituency over many years, perhaps that was true. But the rest of us never bothered to find out.

He went too far in what he said sometimes. Even he admitted that on occasion. But possibly if we'd listened, we might have found some merit in what he had to say. But now he's gone, it's too late.

And although rarely acknowledged in his lifetime, one of his greatest achievements was to have the Right of Reply protocol incorporated into PM's Question Time. Something a former Prime Minister once described as the most infuriating waste of parliamentary time since the Freedom of Infor-

mation Act. Something which must have given him great satisfaction.

But perhaps one day his contribution will be recognised as much more than that.

Only time will tell.

"I don't believe it's an anti-terrorist exercise."

"Why not?" asked Louise.

Henry took a small piece of blue cloth from his pocket.

"Because I never believe anything they say."

He took off his glasses. And wiped each lens with it.

"So, what do you think it is?"

"I don't know."

He held his glasses up to the light. "But something's going on. I'm sure of it."

He looked at her. "And I'm usually more right than wrong about these things."

"Well, whatever it is," she said. "You'd never get close enough to find out. There'll be hundreds of Police on the streets."

A few days later Henry invited her to his home.

"Come in Louise," he said. "There's someone here I'd like you to meet."

She followed him into the lounge. It was a sunny winter's afternoon, but the curtains were drawn. And the room in deep shadow. Henry's traditional greeting of tea and biscuits was laid out on the table.

"Let me introduce *John Smith*."

A tall man with closely cropped hair stepped forward to shake her hand.

"Pleased to meet you Louise," he said.

"He's a security advisor," continued Henry. "And he's very kindly agreed to lend us this rather fascinating piece of equipment."

He gestured towards a tiny device on the table. Similar in size and shape to an old fashioned fountain pen. But with a tiny propeller on the top. And another at one end.

"It's a surveillance drone," said Henry. "And," he added. "It's worth £20,000."

"So please try not to lose it," said his guest.

Louise looked at Henry. "And we need one of these?" she asked.

"Yes," said Henry enthusiastically. "We do."

He handed her a cup of tea.

"Now we'll be able to see what's really going on in the City over the weekend."

Henry's guest spoke again.

"It's heavily RF shielded, and virtually undetectable. Ideal for close range urban reconnaissance.

He held up what looked like a small TV remote control. "Using this device we can pre-programme it. So all you have to do on the night is enter the activation code.

Then he picked up his briefcase. Flicked open the catches. And took out a piece of heavily folded linen-backed paper.

"I'm afraid we'll have to do this the old fashioned way," he said.

He opened it out on the dining table. To reveal a large map of central London.

We don't want to broadcast our intentions," he said. "Any more than we have to."

Henry gave Louise a knowing look. She ignored him.

He over-laid a smaller clear acetate sheet on top of it. Marked with a number of concentric circles, radiating out from a central point. He positioned it over Bank underground station. "As good a place as any," he said.

He carefully slid the sheet across the surface of the map. Moving it an inch or two to the left and to the right. And up and down.

He leant back in his chair. "Unfortunately," he said. "And as I suspected. Due to the size of the exclusion zone, it will be necessary to enter it to release the device."

He looked at the map again. "That's a risk," he said. "But a manageable one. Provided you're careful.

It's such a large area, they can't secure it all. So they'll concentrate their resources close to the centre. And with your OTH visual capability you can remain comfortably outside that."

"What about the CCTV cameras?" asked Louise.

He reached into his briefcase again. And took out what appeared to be an old walkie talkie. With four short rubberised ariels.

"This is a military grade frequency jammer," he said. "Highly illegal, and not available in this country. If you're found in possession you'll be arrested under Section 25 of the Theft Act, *Going Equipped for Burglary*. And with good reason," he said.

"When you get within range it will freeze the video picture. But leave the timer running. Particularly effective in scenarios devoid of intrinsic movement. Such as a deserted night-time urban environment.

No doubt GCHQ will be monitoring all transmissions in the area. And they will pick it up. But it's highly advanced location-spoofing software will place you miles away. And by the time they've worked out what's going on, you'll be long gone."

He turned his attention back to the map. Slowly tracing the course of various streets and alleyways with his finger. Trying to visualise the reality on the ground from the complex ribbons of coloured ink on the paper.

Finally he pointed to a spot near the top of Fleet Street.

"There," he said. "That's where you should release the device."

He looked up from the map. "Much of the old medieval street pattern still remains in that part of town. And there's lots of little alleyways and courtyards to give you cover."

Then he asked, "are either of you familiar with that area?".

"I did a summer placement at the Inns of Court around there," said Louise.

"Good," he replied. "Because it's confusing enough in daylight. And naturally they'll cut the street lighting. Take a torch. But don't use it. Except in an emergency. Nothing less than a broken ankle. Because they'll see you a mile off.

And leave your phones at home. They'll triangulate your position in seconds."

Now they knew their destination, they had to reverse engineer their way into town and back out again.

Eventually, hours later, long after night had fallen they had their route. Every yard of it, every landmark and every timing point along the way. Written on small cards, a mix of words, numbers and symbols. All to be committed faultlessly to memory over the next five days.

The government press officer stepped up to the lectern.

"Welcome to this morning's media briefing," he said. "The Home Secretary would like to make a short statement."

"Good morning ladies and gentlemen," she said. "I am very pleased to announce the appointment of a Pre-Crime Commissioner. Who will lead a new and specialist division within the Metropolitan Police. Tasked with the early recognition and recording of activities or beliefs that could potentially lead to an unlawful act.

A similar pre-crime early warning system has been operational in the EFR for a number of years. And has proved highly effective in pre-empting the future causes of crime.

A Pre-Crime Caution (PCC) can be issued to an individual either as a result of direct police enquiries. Or on information provided by responsible and community-minded members of the public, via an easily accessed phone app. Penalties could include a fine or possible imprisonment.

And through this partnership of the police and private individuals exercising their civic duty, we can create a powerful force for freedom, tolerance and social justice. One in which the ordinary citizen will play a vital role in creating a compassionate and law abiding society. One that prioritises the well-being, safety and security of all, through the early identification and mitigation of potential future criminal intent. And reaches out to prevent the most vulnerable from being drawn into unlawful activity in the first place.

Supported by a robust policy of data share and close co-operation, this new appointment will facilitate a more harmonised and effective relationship with our law enforcement colleagues in the Federation."

Elsewhere in the city, it was a typical Friday night.

The pubs and bars packed with revellers, celebrating the end of the working week.

They arrived at Kings Cross soon after nightfall. And approached the City from the north on foot. Careful to activate the jammer only once they left the crowded Euston Road behind them.

Still a couple of miles from the exclusion zone, they followed a tortuous route towards Mecklenburgh Square. And along the tree lined Doughty Street.

Mindful of the need to swing east before they advanced too deep into town. They broke cover to cross the wide and well-lit Gray's Inn Road, for the shadows of Elm Street. And Leather Lane beyond.

Finally entering the exclusion zone, they left the lights of twenty-first century London. And returned to the blacked out streets of 1940. It was a moonless night. And no doubt not solely by chance so. A low cloud robbed them of even the faintest starlight to steer by.

"I can't see my hand in front of my face," whispered Henry.

They had studied the route for days. And knew its every step. And so far it had served them well. Their only obstacle a length of black and yellow tape tied across the road.

But now in the pitch dark, they found themselves adrift in another world. One without form or substance. Where time and distance held no meaning. And familiar landmarks ceased to exist.

But they were not alone. Noises unnoticed on any other night echoed around them in the darkness. The scampering of tiny feet close by. The screech of an owl circling distant rooftops.

As their eyes adjusted to the dark their progress quickened a little. Until at last, two hundred yards beyond Butler's bronze of John Wilkes, the smooth pavement beneath their feet gave way to the cobble stones of Gough Square.

But now, for the first time their progress faltered.

Unable to find the statue of Hodge, the final landmark before the tiny passageway of Bolt Court, they became disorientated. And fearful they had strayed too far ever to find the route again, risked consulting the map by torchlight. Casting giant shadows that danced around them like evil spirits. To discover they were only yards from where they needed to be.

A minute or two later they emerged onto Fleet Street. The dark outline of St Paul's just visible ahead of them, against an even blacker sky. And like a distant drum beat, the sound of helicopters carried on the still night air.

Safely out of range, they stood in silence. A moment at last to collect their thoughts.

Then, a sudden movement in the shadows. They froze.

A blinding light dazzled them. A dog growled menacingly.

Shielding their eyes they could make out the yellow jacket of a police officer standing in front of them.

He pointed the light away. And lowered his head to speak into his collar mounted microphone.

"Nothing to report here," he said. "Just a faulty security light."

He turned his attention back to them.

"Good evening Henry," he said. "And Ms Hemmings. May I suggest you stop waving that torch around. Or you'll have the whole Met down on top of you. And not all my colleagues are as understanding."

"Very sorry officer," replied Henry apologetically.

"It's not much of a night to be out on the town," said the policeman. "Or haven't you heard?"

"We were just wondering what was going on, officer."

"I don't know any more than you, Henry. It's a military operation. We're just here to close the roads. But I can tell you some massive trucks have come through here. And there's more on the way."

Then he said, "take my advice, go home. You're wasting your time. You'll never see anything. And the way you're carrying on, likely as not spend a night or two in the cells for your trouble."

Then he wished them good luck. And vanished back into the darkness as abruptly as he had appeared.

Working with a renewed sense of urgency, Louise entered the activation code into the hand controller. And released the drone into the night sky.

They quickly crossed Fleet Street and disappeared into the shadows of Pleydell Court.

Louise led the way, recalling past visits to the chambers there. Henry followed close behind. They penetrated deep into the labyrinth of tiny alleyways around Inner Temple. Heading west through the narrow twists and turns of the old medieval city, tracking broadly parallel to the Strand. Moving as quickly and quietly as they could over the ancient and uneven stone paving. On either side archways and passages led off blindly into the darkness. Through some they felt the occasional draught of chill damp air coming off the water close by.

Navigating a series of lefts and rights they made their way towards tiny Devereux Court. The ground rarely level, either rising up towards the Strand or falling away towards the river.

Finally they emerged onto the wider eighteenth century Essex Street. Where a hundred yards ahead, obscured still in the darkness stood the great red brick Gateway Arch. And beneath it their second way station of the night. A flight of steep and narrow steps. That led down and out of sight into Milford Lane, thirty feet below.

Where half way down, they took a step each for a seat to sit out the drone's return.

Concealed at last, not just by the archway overhead. But also from the street behind, the deserted Embankment in front and the water beyond.

Henry set his rucksack down on the step beside him. He took out a flask of tea and two cups. He poured one for Louise. And the other for himself.

"You really *do* find friends in the unlikeliest places," she said.

The hot tea warmed them a little against the bitter cold. No longer on the move they felt it keenly now. And for the first time that night. Henry rubbed his hands together. His breath clouded in front of his face. Louise pulled her coat tight around her.

They sensed it first. Not so much a sound, more a faint disturbance in the air. Low and barely audible. Felt, rather than heard. Then as a distant hum borne on the chill night breeze. That grew louder and louder. Echoing off the buildings all around them. Suddenly so loud it was impossible to think. And impossible to tell where it was coming from.

Seconds later, a helicopter passed at great speed over the open stretch of river in front of them. Barely sixty feet above the water. A flash of the blue and gold central and circling stars of the EFR on its flank. Then it was gone. As quickly as it came. Reduced to a fading hum again. And a single red light dwindling into the distance.

Sometime after that they heard a police siren. And a dog barking. They sounded close by, but on a night so still they could have been miles away.

It was barely midnight. But they had walked two miles already, and not easy ones at that. With the prospect of the same again before dawn. Louise closed her eyes.

She felt a vibration deep in her coat pocket. It seemed only a minute or two later. But it could have been an hour or more.

She looked at the remote control. Images were flickering across the tiny screen. She roused Henry. Dozing on the step below, or maybe deep in thought. Together they studied the screen.

Looking down from a height of a hundred feet or so above the ground, dark and empty streets passed silently beneath. Up ahead a distant glow lit the night sky.

In Throgmorton Street they saw a long convoy of trucks. Rubble and debris lay strewn across the road. And a huge flood lit mobile crane stood parked in the narrow confines of Lothbury.

Rising up now, high into the night sky. Soaring above green and patinaed domes and cupolas. Before swooping low past the gilded bronze of Ariel. Down at street level they saw the decapitated statue of Sir John Soane. Torn off its pedestal, shattered on the ground. Then the mouth of a giant gaping maw opened up below them. Exposing vaults deep underground. And the glint of precious metal.

They stared at the screen. Astonished and appalled.

"That's not an anti-terrorist exercise," gasped Louise.

"It's a bloody bank robbery!" cried Henry. "The biggest in history."

The Speaker called on the Home Secretary to address the chamber.

"It is wholly irresponsible for anyone," he said. "Least of all members of this House, to attempt to publish images of a classified anti-terrorist exercise. Which is why we have obtained an emergency injunction this morning.

Disabling the *New Independent Party's* website and social media outlets. And I have instructed the Director of Public Prosecution to urgently determine what further legal action can be taken against the individuals concerned."

Across town, the Chief Secretary of the Treasury's office issued a press release.

We are delighted to announce the start of a multi-million pound upgrade and modernisation of the Bank of England's infrastructure and security systems.

Once complete, these works will restore this magnificent and historic building to its rightful place as one of the world's most secure bullion storage facilities. These are the most significant works undertaken since Sir Herbert Baker's glorious and sympathetic re-modelling of the original building in the 1920s.

The extent of these works has necessitated the temporary re-location of the UK gold reserve.

"As usual, Henry's getting bent out of shape over nothing," said the Home Secretary speaking on the one o'clock news. "Does it really matter where our gold is stored? It's still our gold. I think the Great British public are a lot smarter than Henry gives them credit for.

And once the Bank has been upgraded we can have it back.

So we should be grateful to the EFR for their help. It's good to see international government's co-operating so effectively on security matters. And to know we have friends and neighbours we can rely on."

"In which case," asked the interviewer. "And to quote Henry Douglas, *why the cover story?*".

"That's just the sort of ridiculous nonsense you'd expect from that man. There is no cover story. There was an anti-terrorist exercise in the City. And to minimise disruption it made sense to carry out an element of the Bank refurbishment at the same time. That's all."

"So," said the host. "And to use Henry's words again, it wasn't a *smash and grab.*"

The Home Secretary shook his head. "That man should be ashamed of himself."

The Code for Crown Prosecutors, tenth edition, places a responsibility on the CPS to pursue only cases that have a realistic prospect of conviction.

Accordingly, the documentary evidence you submitted with regard to alleged criminal acts of Mr David Francois Arnoud has been assessed. And found to be of insufficient credibility and integrity to pass stage one of the Full Code Test.

The case is therefore judged inappropriate to present to a criminal court under Section 10 of the Prosecution of Offences Act, 1985.

The door of Number 10 opened. The Prime Minster walked to the lectern set up on the pavement outside.

He stood a moment, in respectful silence. Then he spoke. "It was with great sadness and regret I learned this morning of the death of Henry Douglas and his wife Margaret, in a car accident while holidaying in France yesterday.

He was a fine parliamentarian, who earned the respect and admiration of all who knew him. His loss will be deeply felt by everyone in Westminster."

A journalist called out. "Can you give us any more details of the accident?"

The Prime Minister continued. "And I wish to convey our thanks to the French authorities for their sensitive and professional handling of this tragic incident."

Then, ignoring the questions of hundreds of journalists, he turned away. The black door behind him opened. And he disappeared inside.

A couple of hours later Charlie Freeman's daily Westminster Blog devoted less than fifty words to the news.

Today we write the obituary not just of Henry Douglas, but also of his ill-conceived New Independent Party. Certain now to recede still further into irrelevance and obscurity. Its sole remaining MP destined to be nothing more than the tiniest of insignificant historical footnotes.

Chapter Six

A Treaty is Signed

"The Prime Minister," announced the Speaker.

He stood at the despatch box to address the chamber.

"Mr Speaker, Honourable and Right Honourable friends, I am pleased to inform the House that trade negotiations with the EFR are progressing well. And we are on track to achieve the prized status of *Principal Trading Partner* within the next few weeks. Which I am delighted to tell you will shortly be ratified by the signing of an historic agreement in the ancient city of Augsburg."

Cheers echoed around the chamber. Then the Speaker called for the first question of the session. "I call on the Honourable Member for Bedford."

From the benches behind the Prime Minister a young man got to his feet.

"I know I speak for the whole House," he said. "And indeed the whole country, when I express profound gratitude to the government's dedicated team of negotiators. And whose unstinting efforts on our behalf, I commend to the House."

His words were met with murmurs of "hear, hear" from across the chamber.

Then the speaker called, "The Honourable Member for South Cambridgeshire."

Louise stood to address the House. "Thank you, Mr Speaker."

The sound of her voice echoing around the chamber for the very first time.

"It is true Prime Minister, is it not, that these so called trade discussions in Lausanne are not in fact negotiations at all. On account of this government's policy to secure an agreement as quickly as possible. And at any price."

The Prime Minister rose to respond.

"My Honourable friend is wholly misinformed. That is not the case at all.

And whilst I am not able to advise the House of the exact terms of our agreement, as the final details have yet to be ratified. I can assure My Honourable colleague we have secured extremely fair and equitable terms. And that the future prosperity of this country has now been assured."

The Prime Minister returned to his place on the front bench to an enthusiastic chorus of "hear, hear" from around the chamber

Exercising her right to reply, Louise got to her feet again. A piece of paper in her right hand. She held it high above her head. Like an exhibit in a court of law.

"I have here," she said. "A copy of an e-mail from the head of the EFR Legal Commission."

The Prime Minister looked across at the Home Secretary.

She read aloud from the piece of paper: *"The commission will not consider the UK government's application to join the EFR, until it provides absolute and unconditional agreement to pre-accept, without negotiation, whatever terms and conditions are set out by the Federation. Then, and only then can the UK's process of entry begin."*

There was silence in the House.

She continued. "And written in pen. In the Prime Minister's own hand is this note:

"accept, but must never become public knowledge".

And Mr Speaker, let me tell you the word *"never"* is twice underlined."

Her words sparked uproar. MP's on all sides of the House leapt to their feet, shouting, "shame, shame!".

She spoke on, raising her voice. "I put it to the House." But few could hear her above the noise.

"Order! Order!" cried the Speaker trying to restore calm.

She carried on, struggling to be heard. "I put it to the House, this is one of the most shameful documents in our nation's history. And I demand on behalf of the people of this country…"

"Order! Order!" called the Speaker again.

"The immediate cessation of these negotiations. And the resignation…"

The Prime Minster jumped up from the front bench.

"This is an outrage!" he shouted. "This is a classified document deliberately taken out of context and distorted to mislead the House." His face red with fury. "I demand an immediate apology."

The Speaker shouted, "order! order! That is a scurrilous and inexcusable assertion by the Honourable Member for South Cambridgeshire. Who must retract it immediately or be disbarred from the House."

She raised her voice to reply, "I will not apologise for speaking the truth. And I cannot withdraw what I know to be true. If the truth cannot be spoken here, in the House. Then where can it be?"

The noise in the chamber was deafening.

"This government," replied the Prime Minister, almost shouting to be heard. "Is committed to achieving the best possible deal for this country. And that is exactly what we have done."

The Speaker banged his staff on the floor and shouted, "order! order!

For gross disregard of the authority of the chair The Honourable Member for South Cambridgeshire is hereby suspended from the service of the House, for a period of five sitting days. And must leave the Chamber immediately.

Her remarks are to be struck from the record. And the document she brought into the chamber to be surrendered and deemed property of the House."

On College Green, Louise waited to speak to the correspondent of the Politics Channel. The Home Secretary stood beside her.

"You spoke in the House today for the first time Ms Hemmings. And got yourself a week's suspension for your trouble. That must be some sort of record. Not even Henry managed that. Will you be apologising to the House?"

"I have nothing to apologise for," she said. "Everything I said was true."

"And the document you produced?"

"Is entirely genuine."

"How did you come by it?"

"I'm afraid I can't tell you that. But the Prime Minister and the government have not denied its authenticity. Because they can't."

The Home Secretary interrupted. "This young woman has shamelessly abused Parliamentary Privilege to introduce blatant falsehoods into the public domain. And to escape sanction for defamation and misleading the House."

Then with contempt in his voice he said, "but she's had her moment. And sadly she did not use it wisely. But that was her choice. Instead by her disgraceful performance today in the chamber she has shown herself unfit to serve in the House. And Parliament has duly dispensed with her. And I sincerely hope we will hear nothing more from her ever again. She has clearly demonstrated by her actions today, she has no intelligent or worthwhile contribution to make to serious political debate in this country."

"Harsh words, Home Secretary," said the interviewer.

"Not harsh. Just true," he said. "And I know I speak for all sensible and reasonable people in this country when I say that."

"So you can state categorically what Louise Hemmings said today in the House is untrue. And the document she produced is a fake?"

"I don't recognise that document at all. It would be quite impossible for her to have access to information like that. Even if it existed. Which of course it doesn't."

"So everything she said was false."

"Yes. I believe so."

"You believe so?"

"Yes, that's what I believe. And I think Ms Hemmings would do well to remember it's her late mentor Henry Douglas's mess we're clearing up here. But fortunately, unlike him this government will act responsibly and in the best interests of the British people."

In a ruling today, the European Court of Justice rejected all third party claims for loss or compensation relating to gold stocks formerly held in the Bank of England.

In a directive issued this morning, any organisation or national government seeking re-imbursement is instructed to secure redress directly from the UK Treasury.

This follows a European Court of Auditors' assessment, that due to non-compliance with EFR financial reporting protocols, Bank of England declarations of value and ownership of its former gold stocks cannot be authenticated.

Bank of England officials have played down the issue.

"This is just a minor misunderstanding," said a spokeswoman this afternoon. "And we anticipate an early and satisfactory resolution. It's nothing to worry about."

The Speaker called on the Prime Minister to address the House.

He got up from his place on the front bench and stood at the Despatch Box.

"Over the past six months," he said. "This government has successfully renegotiated the UK's relationship with the EFR. Allowing us at last to re-gain our rightful place at the heart of Europe."

Murmurs of "hear, hear" echoed around the chamber.

"And now that important work is done, the time is right to pass the leadership of this great and historic government to someone else. Someone who can bring a fresh energy and focus. And make the most of the huge opportunities that now exist for us within the EFR.

And so I wish to inform the House I tendered my resignation to His Majesty the King this morning, with immediate effect. It is the greatest honour any politician can have to lead their country. And it has been my privilege to serve as your Prime Minister.

And while I leave the country in a far better place than when I took office twelve months ago. There is still much work to be done.

We have been through difficult times. And past decisions regarding our relationship with the EFR have damaged us politically and economically. But that is behind us now. The foundations of our future prosperity and stability are now in place. And our prospects could not be brighter.

But I am mindful at this crucial time of Federal re-engagement, the process of selecting a new Prime Minister and leader of the Party could be an unwelcome distraction. So I have sought council from the President of the EFR.

And I am pleased to tell you, under the provisions of the recently signed Treaty of Augsburg, he has agreed to nominate an independent non-executive Chief Minister. Who will serve until the next General Election.

As laid down in the Treaty, this interim Chief Minister will be completely impartial and operate strictly in the role of facilitator. He will not lead the cabinet. Nor will he favour any particular course of action, or advocate any particular cause. He will merely create the environment in which every member of the cabinet will be able to contribute to the very best of their ability. And to arrive at a consensus view acceptable to all.

And I am delighted to say senior EFR Commissioner, Sir Stephen Fowkes has agreed to return to Westminster to fulfil this role. He will take a seat in the upper chamber as Lord Fowkes of Haslemere. And I know you will give him your full support."

Shortly after the EFR issued a statement.

"It was with regret we learnt from the British Prime Minister earlier today of his intention to resign. He is a loyal citizen and friend of the EFR. And we join the people of Britain in thanking him for the enormous contribution he has made to securing the future prosperity, not only of the UK, but also the EFR and its member states.

His wise and skilful re-negotiation of Britain's relationship with the EFR has cemented his place as one of the foremost European statesmen of his generation. And one of Britain's greatest Prime Ministers.

He leaves office at the height of his power, and with the unqualified support of his country and his Party.

And we are delighted to say his talents will not be

lost to the people of Europe, as he has agreed to accept a senior position within the Federation.

And we also welcome the new Chief Minister, who we are confident will maintain the excellent relations between the UK government and the EFR."

Sir Stephen Fowkes addressed the assembled media outside Number 10 Downing Street.

"It is an honour to return to London," he said. "To the land of my birth. And the country that made me. And it is with great humility I stand here before you. And pledge myself to the service of my fellow countrymen and women.

I will draw on my many years' experience working for the Federation, to further develop our great nation's new and harmonious relationship with the EFR.

I am well aware however, that without your support I can achieve nothing. But if we work together we can do great things."

And with that he turned away. And went back inside Number 10.

Next door his arrival was awaited in the Cabinet Office.

An attendant entered the room a moment or two ahead of him.

"Everyone is to stand when the Chief Minister enters the room," he said.

Sir Stephen walked briskly in.

Most stood immediately, some awkwardly. Others hesitated a moment, then got to their feet.

"Good morning ladies and gentlemen," he said. "I will be announcing a new executive process this afternoon in my opening speech to the House.

But I will run through the key points with you now. I will not be taking any questions. These measures are not for debate. They have already been agreed and ratified with the European Court of Justice.

And as you will hear over the next twenty minutes or so, there is little point in anyone resigning. As most of you will not be part of this new process anyway."

Three hours later on the floor of the Commons, the Speaker's voice rang out in a packed House. "I call on the Chief Minister."

Sir Stephen, sitting in the Prime Minister's place got up and stood at the despatch box.

"I would like to thank you for the welcome you have extended to me," he said coldly.

Then he continued. "According to the prerogative vested in me as Chief Minister under the Treaty of Augsburg, a Special Powers Bill will be expedited through the Commons and the Lords within the next forty-eight hours. This will permit the temporary delegation of all Parliamentary authority and executive functions to a Special Council of Deputies. Which I shall chair.

The members of this council will be drawn from across the full spectrum of British political parties and public life. It will be a collection of the most brilliant minds in Britain. Brought together solely on the basis of ability, irrespective of political allegiance. This will truly be a coalition of all the talents. And as Chief Minister my role is solely to marshal those brilliant minds, to achieve the greatest benefit for the country.

This Special Council of Deputies will be in place until the next General Election is called.

And during this time the doors of the two chambers will be locked. And MP's will return to their constituencies.

This will allow time for a deputation from the European Court of Justice to formally codify the UK's shambolic constitution. Thus ensuring harmonisation with all EFR requirements, as laid down in the recent Treaty of Augsburg."

The following morning, on the steps of a deserted House of Commons Louise spoke in front of the TV cameras.

"Today, for the first time since the Rule of the Major Generals, almost four hundred years ago, Britain has no functioning constitutional government. And how long until we see another?

And this Special Council of Deputies is not a cabinet of all the talents. And these are certainly not the most brilliant minds in Britain today.

But they are without doubt," she said. "The largest group of pro-EFR MP's and public figures ever assembled in one place."

The EFR President stood before the vast European parliament assembly chamber in Lausanne. As he spoke hundreds of interpreters translated his words into the twenty-four languages of the Federation.

"NATO no longer represents the EFR's world view," he said. "It is a relic of the cold war. And should be consigned to history along with it.

Old alliances with states outside Europe must be secondary to those within. And neighbouring Federations must exchange conflict for collaboration. And work together to eliminate the shared threat of nationalism.

Accordingly, I hereby announce our financial, military and political contribution to NATO will cease with immediate effect.

Henceforth all member states will wholly and exclusively commit their military resources to the new European Armed Defence Force.

The new command headquarters will be situated in Lausanne. Construction will commence later this year. For completion within three years at a cost of 3.5 billion Euros. To be borne equally by all member states.

And to ensure the EFR maintains a world-leading military capability, a new European weapons system called Epee will be manufactured in partnership between MBDA Missile Systems and Almaz-Antey in Moscow. This system will be operational within the next five years.

Responsibility for control and deployment of the UK nuclear deterrent will pass to the Federal Defence Commission in Lausanne. In accordance with the protocols annexed to the Treaty of Augsburg.

The UK's commitment to buy and maintain the Trident system and its successor will be cancelled with immediate effect. The UK government will unilaterally settle any compensation or other claims arising from this cancellation.

And I am pleased to announce an intelligence and technology exchange and collaboration programme with The Russian Federation. Russian defence experts will be granted full access to all military establishments throughout Europe this summer.

EFR military personnel plan to arrange a reciprocal visit to Moscow, at a date to be agreed later in the year."

"As I set out in my blog this morning," said Louise, speaking on the Politics Channel's *This Week in Westminster*. "The recent fall of President Maboteau, and the installation of a more open government in Kalatou has brought to light a number of key documents."

"Including, you claim," said the host. "Evidence of misappropriation of Federation Aid money. Perpetrated, amongst others, by the EFR President's son David Arnoud."

"That is correct."

"And despite being dismissed as crude forgeries and fake news, you believe these documents are genuine?"

"I am sure of it. And I have handed them over to the Metropolitan Police."

"But as a Swiss national, running a company registered in Zurich, shouldn't you pass this information to the relevant domestic authorities?"

"I could have. But under the Treaty of Augsburg the UK is a signatory to the Strategic Cross-Border Policing Protocol. Which gives all national police forces, including our own, equal jurisdiction over every citizen of the EFR."

"And the EFR President? Do you believe he is implicated in this?

"That would be for the courts to decide."

"Would it? Given he enjoys immunity from prosecution."

"He does. Although the full extent of European parliamentary privileges and immunity protocols is largely untested. As yet.

But leaving that aside for a moment, surely no father would pass up the opportunity to defend his son in a court of law?"

An uncharacteristically large and noisy British media contingent gathered at the weekly EFR Commission press briefing.

"What's your reaction to claims in the British press," called one of them. "That the son of the EFR President is stealing from the overseas aid budget?"

The spokesman ignored the question. And looked around the room for another to answer.

"… And the EFR is a haven for cheats and swindlers?"

"Of course it is not!" The EFR spokesman reacted angrily. "Look around Europe, what do you see? A highly successful economic super-power, yes?

And that is all thanks to the EFR. Any country in the world would be honoured to join our glorious Federation.

Certain nations and their media would do well to remember what the EFR has done for them. In just a few decades we have transformed Europe from a collection of tired, bankrupt old countries divided by language, trade barriers and social division, into the greatest brotherhood of nations the world has ever seen.

And let me tell you, Britain has done very well out of the EFR over the years. But don't ever expect to hear them admit it. They are never satisfied. Whatever deal they have ever got was never good enough. So we take no notice when they complain."

Outside her office window the watery light of a late winter's day was fading.

Her old college lecturer sat opposite. She held up a memory stick.

"People have risked their lives to get this information Bruce," she said. Before correcting herself. "People have lost their lives to get it. And I owe it to them.

And now the CPS has refused to proceed with the case." She looked intently at her old lecturer. "I'll have to do it."

She put the stick back in her drawer.

"If I learnt anything from you Bruce, it is the power of the law. I'd rather have a copy of Archbold in my hand than a gun any day."

She read the words on the screen. Again.

Please be advised I am initiating a private prosecution against your son, David Francois Arnoud, in the High Court in London.

This relates to alleged misappropriation of EFR aid and development funds from inter alia, the Mabatoville International Airport and New City Development project.

You are not a party to these proceedings. And are being asked to provide testimony voluntarily, about activities unre-

lated to your official capacity as President of the EFR. And in due cognisance of Articles 12 & 18 of Protocol No 36, on the privileges and immunities of the European Communities.

However, refusal to comply with this request would give cause to a formal application for a Witness Summons to be sought upon you, under Part 34 of the Civil Procedure Rules 1998.

And failure to observe will leave you liable to arrest for contempt of court, under the Criminal Procedure (Attendance of Witnesses) Act 1965.

She re-read the email on the screen. One last time.

Pressed *send.* And sat back in her chair. Her heart pounding.

"Good morning Ms Hemmings," said the visitor to her constituency office.

They sat at a table by the window, overlooking busy Sydney Street.

"As I explained in my letter, I am the legal representative of Mr David Arnoud in London. And I am instructed to inform you that should you proceed with your action, my client will issue a counter claim against you. For *Defamation* and *Malicious Prosecution without Reasonable and Probable Cause.*

And as part of this counter claim my client will seek punitive damages, for the egregious and wholly unjustified injury you seek to inflict upon his reputation. Particularly, but not solely with regard to his extensive charitable and humanitarian works."

He sat back in his chair. "However," he said. "At this stage my client has incurred relatively little expense in this matter. And is prepared to write off those costs if you sign this undertaking to desist from your action with immediate effect."

He opened his briefcase and took out a single typed sheet of paper. He placed it on the table in front of her.

"This offer is open for 24 hours. After which time it will be withdrawn.

And if I may say, as one lawyer to another, surely you cannot be unaware of the inevitable consequences of this ill-judged action you are contemplating. Which is certain to fail. And undoubtedly result not just in your financial ruin. But also the loss of your personal and professional reputation. Such as it is.

An outcome my client is generously allowing you the opportunity to avoid. You have until midday tomorrow to accept this offer. Which I must inform you, my client is making against my professional advice. The choice is yours Ms Hemmings."

He looked at his watch.

"As we speak, the High Court in London is hearing an ex parte application from the EFR Legal Commission for a Public Interest Immunity Order. On the grounds that your case is wholly without merit or substance. And motivated solely by malice.

And under instruction from my Client, a separate and further ex parte application has been submitted for a *contra mundum hyper-injunction*. Upon you and persons unknown relating to these allegations.

The effect of these applications, as you will of course be aware, would not only prevent disclosure of any documents. But also give rise to a complete reporting ban. And place a restraint upon you, or anyone else from speaking about or otherwise disclosing any information relating to these matters. Including even divulging the existence of the injunction itself.

And I am extremely confident the judge will find in favour of the applicant on both counts.

Ms Hemmings, surely it is obvious to you now, if it wasn't before, that this is a completely pointless action. With no possible prospect of success."

Then he said, "maybe you will get your day in court. Although I seriously doubt it. But with the injunction no one will ever know. And you will never get the President into the witness box. Instead, yours will be a silent action. One that will serve no purpose. And achieve nothing. Except your own downfall."

He got up to leave. "I have to say, I am very surprised someone of your legal background would even consider such a reckless and foolhardy action."

After he had gone she walked over to the window.

She stood there for several minutes. Looking out.

"A person has been arrested this morning in London for a public order offence involving the President of the EFR.

Details are still emerging. But it is understood the President was unharmed in the incident. Police officers detained a suspect at the scene. Who is currently being questioned at a central London Police station.

A further statement is expected within the hour. When we should learn more about the identity of the person in police custody.

Downing Street has expressed deep regret for the incident. And offered its profound apologies for the distress caused to the President and his family. And assured them the perpetrator will face the full force of the law."

A couple of hours later the Home Secretary spoke to reporters outside his home.

"It's outrageous a Member of Parliament behaving like that on the streets of London. She has caused enormous damage to the standing of Britain, within the EFR and the world. This is a civilised country. And that sort of behaviour cannot be tolerated. Even Henry Douglas never sank to this. Her career is finished. And she must surely be facing a lengthy custodial sentence. I cannot imagine what she was thinking."

Crowds had been gathering for several hours outside Barrington village hall, in her former constituency of South Cambridgeshire. Blocking the road and filling the wide green beyond.

Police officers in yellow jackets moved conspicuously amongst the crowd. And still more observed from a distance on horseback.

TV, cable and internet news trucks and wagons lined the length of the village.

Inside, the hall echoed to the sound of hundreds of conversations, in dozens of different languages. Journalists and cameramen vied with each other for a view of a small bare stage, with just a table and two empty chairs.

Her assistant walked to the front of the hall. The crowd fell quiet.

"Louise will be here in a moment," she said.

Word she was in the building charged the atmosphere. And the noise level rose sharply. News quickly spread to the crowd outside.

"She will be making a short statement," she said, raising her voice to be heard. "And will take some questions afterwards." But only a few at the very front could hear her.

"And she hopes you'll understand if she keeps it brief. As she is in some pain and discomfort."

A door at the back of the hall opened. Everyone turned to look. The room fell silent.

Louise walked slowly towards the stage. The crowd parted to let her through.

She climbed the short flight of steps. And lowered herself gently into the chair next to her assistant. The air filled with the sound of hundreds of camera shutters. Capturing images of her face, bruised and swollen. Images that would be seen across Europe and beyond. She looked out over the crowded hall.

"Thank you for coming," she said. Her voice slightly distorted by two stitches at the corner of her mouth.

"As you are all no doubt aware, I was arrested this morning."

She placed a piece of paper on the table in front of her.

"According to the charge sheet, I was detained under *Section 4 of the Public Order Act 1986*."

She read out loud from the document.

"For unlawfully and intentionally causing harassment, alarm and distress in a public place by the use of threatening, abusive and insulting behaviour."

Still so silent the hall, even those at the very back could hear her every word.

"That," she said. "Is a complete fabrication."

The eyes of all were fixed upon her. And the reflection of her face in every camera lens.

"However, thanks to the efficient reporting of the BBC and other media outlets, the incident is in the public domain. So I am able to show you a recording of it. Made with a hidden camera. And suitably redacted to comply with all legal restrictions. Including concealing the identity of the other party involved. Although of course, that too is now also a matter of public knowledge."

She asked for the lights to be dimmed.

"I'll be happy to take questions afterwards."

On the bare white wall behind her, images appeared of an expensive residential street. From the style and size of the architecture, probably Mayfair or Belgravia. And by the angle of the light, sometime in the early morning.

A large grey Mercedes with darkened windows drew up at the side of the road.

The front passenger door opened. Eyes obscured behind mirrored sunglasses, a tall powerfully built man got out. He opened the rear door. A second man, his face pixelated to mask his appearance stepped out onto the pavement.

A woman's voice is heard.

"My name is Louise Hemmings. I am an elected Member of the British Parliament. And I am here to…" The sound cut out for a second. *"… In accordance with section…"*. The sound cut out again. *"… for the offence of…"*. And again, for a third time. *"… And I must ask you to accompany me to the nearest police station."*

The two men turned to look towards the camera.

At this point Louise stopped the video.

"As you can see," she said. "These gentlemen were met by a calm and reasonable individual. Who clearly identified themselves. And made their intentions clear. As a former lawyer I know exactly what the law requires. And I made sure I complied with it, to the letter. Which is why I was released so soon this morning without bail.

She re-started the video.

The man in sunglasses runs towards the camera. The image spins wildly. Glimpses of the sky, the pavement and the sound of shouting.

Then silence. The image disappeared. Leaving a blank white wall.

The lights in the hall came on. And Louise spoke again.

"The camera was broken at that point," she said. "And the next thing I remember was being handcuffed in the back of a police car."

Then she said, "now, if there are any questions I will do my best to answer them".

Before she finished speaking, someone called out, "what were you trying to do?"

"For legal reasons," she replied. "I'm afraid I can't tell you."

"Were you making a citizen's arrest?" shouted another

"I'm sorry, I can't say."

"Why were you trying to arrest the President of the EFR?"

"I'm afraid I can't answer that. Unfortunately."

"Is there some sort of injunction?"

"I can't comment on that."

"Why is there an injunction?"

"What's the President got to hide?"

"Is this about the President's son?".

"Is the President involved?"

She raised her hands to try to restore some sort of order.

"I wish I could answer all these questions," she said, above the noise. "And in a free and democratic society I would be able to. But unfortunately, that is not the case in Britain today. Or in the EFR.

So I ask you this, in the name of free speech. And the long and noble tradition of independent journalism speaking truth to power, not to let this matter rest.

These are all extremely important questions. And they need to be answered. Each and every one of them. For all our sakes."

She bowed her head for a moment. Then she said, "I'm very sorry, but I will have to draw this press conference to a close. The effect of the painkillers is starting to wear off. And I'm feeling quite a lot of discomfort. But I want to thank you all very much for coming."

For a moment there was silence. Then, from all corners of the room the sound of applause began to fill the air.

Louise slowly got out of the chair. A grimace of pain on her face. Her assistant helped her down the small steps from the stage. And through the crowd, as the applause grew louder. Echoed by a similar sound from the crowd outside.

Chapter Seven

Not In Our Name

The EFR President stepped onto the raised platform.

"Good morning ladies and gentlemen, thank you for attending this special media briefing.

I regret the need to call you here. And I regret the need to be here myself."

The irritation was clear in his voice.

"The role of President is a lonely and selfless one," he said. "And requires many personal sacrifices." He looked around the room for a moment. His eyes briefly scanning the faces of the assembled press corps before him.

"And any public servant expects to be judged by the very highest standards of honesty and integrity. And I welcome that.

But regrettably, in any political career there will always be unscrupulous people, who seek to falsely tarnish the reputation of others.

So I would like to make it clear there is no legal action of any sort against myself. Either as President. Or in a private capacity. Nor against any official in the Commission or the wider EFR administration.

My legal counsel's advice is never to draw attention to any individual, by responding or commenting on anything they may have said about me. Or the Commission."

He paused a moment.

"But in this instance, I have chosen to disregard that advice. Sound as I know it to be."

He looked around the room again. His eyes lingering a little longer this time on the faces before him.

"Because I want to address you today, not as President of the EFR. But as a father."

His voice faltered. He stopped a moment to compose himself.

"My son has always had a passion to help those less fortunate than himself. It is in his nature. It always has been."

He paused again, and lowered his head for a moment. When he looked up there were tears in his eyes. "And yet, in trying to help others, he has become an innocent target for a malicious and cowardly attack on his character. And for no other reason than to have me as his father."

His voice was charged with emotion now.

"And just as I know all of you would protect your own child, I will protect mine.

And *that*," he said. Anger rising within him. "Is the reason for the injunction. And *that* is why I want to keep the details private. Because this is not political. It's personal."

Then he fell silent. And when a moment later he spoke again, his voice had returned to its earlier measured tone.

"But despite that, I have today authorised the opening of the Commission's files to an independent auditor. Who will have unrestricted access to every aspect of the Overseas Development Agency's activities.

Internationally respected lawyer Lord Smythson has been appointed to carry out a forensic audit. And to publicly report his findings within twenty-one days.

I do this not because it is necessary. But to show how deeply the values of transparency and accountability are embedded in this organisation. And the importance it attaches to due process in all its activities.

And let me give you my personal assurance. Here and now. In this room. That the Commission will be bound by the findings of this report. And will implement without exception any and all recommendations His Lordship may make as a result of his investigation. No matter the cost. Either to the EFR as a whole, or individuals within it. Including myself."

The Isle of Man TT, the Manx Grand Prix and Southern Hundred will no longer take place, due to their failure to meet the Common Health and Safety Directives applied throughout the EFR.

However, in recognition of the island's long and historic association with the motorcycle, we are pleased to announce a special licence has been granted for a new and exciting event. The Manx Motorcycle Festival will preserve much of the spirit and excitement of previous events. Enthusiasts will continue to have the opportunity to visit the island every June, to display their motorbikes in various static non-competitive events.

And following the Manx government's compliance earlier this year with the EFR regulatory tax and investment directives, the island is now fully harmonised with all EFR regulations. Allowing the lifting of sanctions and the resumption of economic, travel, trade and cultural links previously suspended. The EFR welcomes the return of the island as a valued partner. And looks forward to working with them to rebuild their economy.

Father and son sat either side of Lord Smythson, at the front of the Alcide de Gasperi Room in Brussels. Beneath giant live images of themselves, displayed on a huge LED screen on the wall behind.

They faced an audience of several hundred journalists and delegates. Seated in long semi-circular rows, stretching almost out of sight to the back of the chamber.

His Lordship spoke first.

"Good morning, ladies and gentlemen. Thank you for attending this press briefing, prior to the publication of my report into the EFR Overseas Development Agency's activities. The full report will be available at midday today, via download from the EFR website. But I will briefly summarise my findings for you now.

I would like to start by thanking the Federation for the openness and co-operation it extended to me during my investigations.

And after detailed and careful examination, I am completely satisfied there is no evidence whatsoever, of malpractice or impropriety in the way EFR aid money has been distributed over the past five years. Indeed, it is clear exceptional efforts are made to ensure this process of distribution is conducted as fairly, impartially and transparently as possible.

And as a result of this, I can say with absolute certainty that any accusations against the President's son are completely unfounded. And he has no case to answer.

Nor does any member of the Overseas Aid Commission. Or any other person within the wider EFR organisation.

And I would go so far as to say, any claims made to the contrary are not only false. But require such gross distortion of the facts, they could only be motivated by malicious intent.

Which is why one of my key recommendations is that the EFR should, as a matter of principle seek legal redress against any individual or organisation making such accusations. Either now or in the future."

Then he said, "thank you ladies and gentlemen that concludes my briefing this morning."

Then Jean Arnoud spoke.

There was a controlled anger in his voice.

"This report clearly demonstrates my son is an innocent and honourable man. And has completely exonerated him of any wrong-doing.

And to repeat His Lordship's words. He has…," he spoke slowly and precisely. Emphasising each word, individually. And with barely suppressed fury. "No-Case-To-Answer."

He paused a moment. And when he spoke again, his manner was calm and composed.

"And I commend the dedication of Lord Smythson

for producing such a thorough report. One that shows I have done my job with dedication and integrity. Which is why I have found the recent baseless and egregious attacks on myself and my family so distressing. Attacks from someone for whom such qualities mean nothing."

He paused again, to let his audience reflect upon his words. Before continuing, "but these allegations are not merely about attacking me or my family. It is much more serious than that.

It is about trying to destabilise the EFR. And that is something that cannot be allowed to happen. Which is why I will accept the Report's recommendation to take legal action against any person who seeks to discredit the EFR.

And why I will instruct the legal commission to commence a civil action in this instance for defamation and conspiracy.

But I stress I do this not for myself. But to protect the good name and reputation of the Federation. And let this wretched person's fate be a lesson to others, who seek to damage the Federation through unfounded and slanderous allegations.

Two hundred miles away, a hastily assembled press corps gathered on the grass of College Green. A spokesman for a cross party group of MP's read out a statement.

As today's Smythson Report clearly shows, the member for South Cambridgeshire has spoken repeated untruths in the House, and elsewhere. With the intent to falsely discredit an innocent and honourable public servant. And in so doing has seriously damaged the international reputation of Parliament for fair and honest behaviour.

And we hereby call for the impeachment of the Honourable member. On the grounds that by her actions she has proved herself wholly unfit to be a member of the House. And further should be barred from seeking election to public office in the future.

And it is our intention to table a motion to that effect on the first day of the new parliamentary session.

Shortly after, Sir Stephen Fowkes spoke at a special press briefing.

"I can understand my colleagues' concern about the presence of Louise Hemmings in the House. And the message this sends to the world, that our once-great parliament is now little more than a refuge for liars and scoundrels.

And so taking into account my Honourable and Right Honourable friends' views. And to demonstrate our commitment to a fair, free and open democratic process of government, I have ruled that the MP for South Cambridgeshire is to be expelled from the House. With immediate effect.

And upon the resumption of the next parliamentary session her seat will be declared vacant. And a writ for a by-election in the constituency of South Cambridgeshire will be issued.

Should she attempt to enter the Palace of Westminster to take her former seat in the House, she will be removed from the chamber. By whatever means necessary."

The recent Smythson Report has conclusively demonstrated there is no substance to the plaintiff's case against our client, Mr David Francois Arnoud. And that it has no prospect of success should it go to full trial.

So, we hereby request the court to exercise its powers under Civil Procedure Rules Part 24.2, to give a pre-trial summary judgement against the plaintiff. And dismiss the case.

Further, and in connection with the forgoing, it is our contention that without her salary as an MP, following her expulsion from the House. And with the prospect of further legal action against her from the EFR, the plaintiff may not have the means to meet our client's costs arising from her failed action.

Accordingly, we hereby make a separate application to the court for the plaintiff to submit a bond to the value of five hundred thousand euros. To demonstrate her financial capacity to cover my client's costs. And upon failure to do so, within a period of fourteen days, for a petition of bankruptcy to be issued against her. And the freezing of all her assets. Both joint and several, until such time as my Client's costs have been submitted to the court. And due payment discharged.

The President entered the room, followed by the Vice President and several senior Commissioners. He stepped up to the podium while they took their seats behind him.

The President looked around the room at the assembled press and media seated before him.

"Good morning fellow citizens," he said.

"To hold the office of President of the European Federal Republic is the highest honour any man or woman from our great continent can have bestowed upon them.

But I will not pretend I have been unaffected by recent unfounded and scurrilous allegations against me.

Anyone who has held high office knows this is something one has to accept. And I do. As I have always done.

But it is the distressing effect of these allegations on my family I have found much harder to bear. Even though they have always insisted I should not consider their feelings in the discharge of my duties. And be guided solely by what is right for the people of Europe.

But President of the EFR as I may be, I am also a father. And a husband. And the events of the past few weeks have led me to believe that perhaps." He paused a moment. "That perhaps I have given insufficient time to those other important roles in my life."

A sense of unease began to build in the room.

"And that after many years of loyal service to the Federation, my first responsibility should now be to my family.

And so it is with regret, I have decided to announce my resignation as President with immediate effect."

His words were met with a stunned silence. Then gasps of shock and anguish filled the air.

He continued. "And the time is right. Because the integrity of the Federation has been completely vindicated, following the unqualified endorsement of the recent Smythson Report.

And I can pass on the position of President to my successor, in the certain knowledge that I have left the EFR in the strongest and most respected position it has ever been."

Then he said, "I would like to thank you all for your support over the past four years.

And to wish you and your families all the best for the future."

He stepped away from the podium. And walked briskly to the exit behind him.

His Press Secretary took his place at the microphone.

"The President has no further comment to make," she said. "And will not be answering any questions. Now Vice President Alain Delois wishes to say a few words."

One of the delegates seated behind, got to his feet. He walked to the podium.

And when he spoke, his tone was sombre.

"This is a tragic day for the EFR," he said. "And for the people of Europe. We have lost a great President. And we have lost a great man.

And such is his integrity, to be completely exonerated was not enough. Just to have it questioned at all was a profound affront to him. And something he found completely unacceptable.

And maybe one day, the individual who has brought about this terrible situation will come to regret what they have done. And the price the people of Europe have had to pay because of her lies and deceit. But whatever fate the courts duly decide for her, no matter how harsh. Her atonement can surely never be complete."

He fell silent for a moment.

Then he said, "but perhaps we too share some of the blame."

He scrutinised the faces before him.

"Did we ever express our gratitude to the President for all he did for us?"

He slowly shook his head.

"No, my friends. We did not. And maybe, if we had let him know the loyalty, admiration and indeed love, that every man, woman and child of this great continent feels for the Federation and its glorious leader. Then perhaps…"

He hesitated. As if barely able to say the words.

"Perhaps he could have been persuaded to stay."

He lowered his head in contemplation.

A moment passed before he looked up and spoke again.

"And we must ask ourselves this."

His voice was grave.

"Have we been too accommodating to those who have no respect for our values of openness, tolerance, equality and fairness?"

He waited a moment for the audience to reflect on his words.

"Have we made it too easy for anarchists and agent provocateurs to take advantage of the freedoms the EFR has worked so hard for?"

He looked slowly around the room.

"Yes, my friends," he said. "I fear we have. As the events of the past few weeks have only too clearly shown.

And I know I speak for all, when I say this must never be allowed to happen again.

And that we must have the courage to stand up and defend those values we hold most dear. Values the Federation has fought tirelessly for on behalf of all its citizens. And if further regulation and control is required to safeguard and preserve these precious freedoms. Then surely we would all welcome that.

So as my first act as Interim President, I will be announcing a raft of measures later today to protect the authority of the Federation. And to enhance the powers of the President. For we must be strong. We must be bold. And we must be decisive. The well-being, success and prosperity of every citizen in this great Federation depends upon it.

And so my friends, never let it be said of us by future generations we did not learn from our mistakes. For despite our despair on this darkest of days, some good can still come of this."

It was Paul Reynolds from The Times on the phone. "Hi Louise," he said.

"Maboteau's been arrested in New York."

"What was he doing there?"

"We're not entirely sure yet. But the rumour is it involved $20m in cash and a private airstrip up in the lakes. It happened a couple of months ago. But the State Department kept it quiet, while they negotiated a plea bargain with him. And the word is he's been singing like a bird."

"Does the EFR know this?"

"Well," he said. "What do you think? Given recent events in Lausanne."

He continued, "and under US Freedom of Information protocols, transcripts and documents relating to the case will be available on line from midnight tonight. Then it'll become a legitimate news story under Article 10. And we've got a team ready and waiting to go through it all. Page by page, line by bloody line.

We'll be leading with it tomorrow morning in our print and on-line editions. All hell's going to break loose.

We've also applied to the Royal Court to have the injunction against you set aside. On the grounds it's meaningless now. And it's my job to make sure we talk to you before all the other buggers do. It will be the news story of the year. Maybe of the decade. And we're going to break it."

The following morning the Justice Commissioner spoke to the assembled press corps in Lausanne. Jean Arnoud stood impassively behind him.

"The Smythson Report has already cleared our former President of any wrong doing. And in a fair and reasonable society, built on the sacred principle of due process, that should be the end of it.

So I have today informed our former President he must forgo the opportunity to clear his name in a court of law. Understandably, and as you would expect this came as a great blow to him. But the principles of *ne bis in idem* apply to all. From the youngest to the oldest, the richest to the poorest. Irrespective of rank or status. And there can be no exceptions. Not even for distinguished former Presidents of this great Federation."

He stepped back, and the former President took his place at the microphone.

And when he spoke, it was in a slow and measured tone.

"I wish to make it clear I was very happy to forfeit the immunity from prosecution formerly granted to me as President when I resigned.

Indeed, I welcomed the opportunity to stand trial before my peers. And to speak my truth. As I have nothing to fear."

The muscles tightened in his jaw.

"So to be told." There was an edge to his voice now.

"I would be denied the right to publicly defend myself against false charges in a court of law. A fundamental right enjoyed by every other citizen of the EFR."

He studied the faces of the audience seated before him.

"Was a very bitter pill to swallow. And worse still," he said. Anger rising in his voice. "The person who has perpetrated this malicious and dishonest attack on me." He shook his head. "Will now never have to face the consequences of their wicked conspiracy against me."

He gripped the sides of the lectern. "Because they are the one who would have found themselves on trial." Fury blazed in his eyes. "Not me. And I would have been exonerated. And they would have been found guilty."

Then he fell silent. He bowed his head for a moment. And when he looked up his movements seemed calmer and less animated. His voice quieter, and more composed.

"But despite that," he said. "I have been persuaded by my colleagues, against my wishes and those of my family, not to appeal against this pardon. One I did not seek. And do not want.

But if this is the price I have to pay. And let me tell you it is a very high one. I do it solely for the people of this great Federation. Not for myself."

In the first session of the Federal Parliament after the resignation of the former President, the German delegate spoke.

"Recent events have given this chamber cause for deep reflection," he said. "And to consider its future direction, as we begin the process of appointing a new President.

We must win back the trust of the people. And prove we are worthy of the power and responsibility they have bestowed upon us. And to be seen to act not only lawfully, but also in a fair and reasonable manner. Something I believe we have not achieved in recent times.

For there is a belief in some quarters, that the conditions of the UK's recent re-negotiation of its relationship with the EFR were very harsh. Certainly I for one, am of that opinion.

And perhaps we should have given public voice to our private concerns earlier.

But what is it our place to comment on the internal affairs of another European state?

And was it not reasonable to presume the British government knew better than us what it could or could not accept. But perhaps that was not the case. And perhaps we should have spoken up earlier.

And I say this not for sentimental reasons, but purely out of common sense and pragmatism.

A politically and financially bankrupt Britain in the midst of Europe will poison us all.

You cannot undermine one of Europe's largest economies without undermining them all.

No, my friends, the Federation has gone too far. And we have been quiet too long.

This agreement offends the innate German sense of decency and fairness. And we are no longer prepared to stand by and allow these things to be done in our name. It is my government's official position that the conditions laid down in the Treaty of Augsburg are unacceptable. And we will not ratify it.

And we call on the incoming President, whoever they may be, to address this issue as their first priority.

The EFR is in danger of becoming a principality presiding over the rest of Europe. And no longer being seen to operate within a democratic process. And my country more than most knows the perils of that.

And there should be no conflict here. The EFR's interests should be our interests. And I have to say speaking to you today, that appears to be in doubt.

I think that perhaps in recent years, the European Parliament has not listened to its citizens as well as it should. And is in danger of acting in its own interests. At the expense of its member states.

And if the ordinary citizen comes to believe that is true. Whether they are right or not. Then we sow the seeds of very serious future unrest within the Federation. And possibly its ultimate failure."

Then the Belgian delegate spoke.

"I am a little older than some of my colleagues here today. And I can remember my grandmother speaking of their generation's gratitude to the British for the liberation of our country in 1944. She said from that day on there was always a special place in their hearts for Britain.

And before that, we should recall the millions of British lives sacrificed in the First World War, honouring their promise to protect our neutrality. It is to them we owe our liberty. Not once but twice.

And yet less than a hundred years later this is how we re-pay them.

The EFR was formed to ensure no European citizen should ever be subjected to such tyranny again. But what have we learnt from the lessons of history? What we are doing here is not right and my government will not support it."

The Swedish delegate addressed the chamber. "I think too many of us for too long have enjoyed the benefits of EFR membership, and closed our eyes to what has been done in our name. We are in grave danger of losing all the good things that have been achieved. I speak for my fellow countrymen when I say we are not prepared to support the present EFR policy towards the UK.

And the good name of the Federation and the office of President has been seriously damaged by recent events. We need a reconciliation candidate for President now. One who by their actions demonstrates great personal integrity, bravery and a commitment to the pursuit of truth and fairness.

And I believe there is only one person for that role now. Perhaps for the first time in the history of Europe there is overwhelming support for one candidate. The appointment of the President is not a democratic process. But if there was ever a time to listen to the popular will this is it. This is our chance to show the people we have heard. And we have understood.

For there is a now a very powerful sense of a need for reform at the heart of the EFR. It is time for a new European spring.

And it has to be her. She has demonstrated her courage and commitment to democracy. And at considerable risk to her own personal liberty and safety. She is universally seen as the right person for the job. There is no doubt in my mind that should she permit her name to be put forward she would be appointed.

And the sooner the better. Because the longer we delay the greater the vacuum of power at the top of the EFR. And the moment could be lost."

At the small village hall in Barrington in her former constituency of South Cambridgeshire, Louise Hemmings addressed a crowd of hundreds of media reporters from around the world.

"There is an important place for the EFR. But it must serve the nations of Europe. Not divide and control them. Measures must be put in place to curb the influence of the President. And to apply appropriate checks on the power of the Federation.

The new President and the Executive should pare back much of the bureaucracy and reduce the powers of the Commission. It should relinquish its tax raising powers, curb the influence of its central banking and financial institutions, disband its centralised defence and economic policies. All of these things and more should revert back to national level. And return the EFR closer to its origins as a trade based brotherhood of nations, working together for the greater good, tolerance, peace and understanding.

One that operates in an open and democratic way. Not conceals its workings behind increasing layers of impenetrable bureaucracy.

And sometimes, through a fortuitous combination of circumstance, the opportunity and the collective will comes together in a moment in history.

And I believe we are living in just such a moment now.

We stand on the edge of a great European political divide. One way lies reform and the other an ever deeper descent into the political dark ages.

Which way do we go? That is the great decision that confronts us now. And we must decide. And we must decide now. For we have it within our grasp to shape the future of Europe for generations to come.

Either we seize the moment or we let it pass. Maybe never to see the like of it again. Certainly not in our lifetime. And perhaps not in many lifetimes.

And I for one could not bear to look back in later years and think we let it slip.

So I have tonight accepted the position of President of the European Federal Republic."

Part Two: From the Heart

Hidden Agenda

Prologue

January 1990

If only he could have seen it.

Surely, it would have been proof enough.

Even for him. That his friends had not deserted him.

And his work did matter.

A large crowd looked on from behind the metal railings that separated the church yard from the road.

Many of them curious no doubt, to know who we were. Allowed to stand so close to the graveside.

His sister, to my right they could surely guess. His face so recognisable in hers.

And of course, they could not mistake Rachel. Standing to my left. Although they had never seen her look so pale and drawn.

At least the photographers kept their distance from her. Staying back on the path a few yards away.

"He was a very special person," she said quietly, without looking up.

"Yes," I said. "He was."

"I will always love him."

"So will I," I replied.

Chapter One

February 1989, A Chance Encounter

I hadn't seen him in years when we met by chance in the street. For a moment I barely recognised him.

I knew his face of course. But unlike his pictures, he looked tired and thin. And as we walked his movements seemed stiff and uneasy. To my surprise he knew me immediately. And even seemed pleased to see me.

We had never been close. Indeed, there had been times when I believed I hated him. But for those few brief moments at least, we spoke as old friends might on re-acquaintance.

He asked how I was. And what I was doing now. I told him I was late. And couldn't stop. He said he'd like to keep in touch.

I could have given him one of the business cards Sarah had printed for me. But I hoped instead he might lose the scrap of paper I scribbled my address on.

I didn't want to hear from him again.

I learnt later he had slipped back into the country a few weeks earlier. Unannounced and alone. At Heathrow a couple of press photographers saw him. But unexpected and so long out of sight, by the time they recalled his face it was too late.

There was no one to meet him. Even his publishers were unaware of his return. Outside he hailed a taxi and was gone.

"How awful for you," smiled Sarah the next day, when I told her of our chance encounter.

"I thought he was living abroad somewhere," she said.

So did I. And I envied her indifference. Happily married and content with her life, she could afford to be amused. But for me, meeting him stirred much darker emotions. The ease and good fortune of his life only deepened the shadows of my own. And I resented him for it.

And his apparent pleasure at meeting me was a surprise. I had barely known him at school. And that had been almost twenty years ago. I didn't dislike him then. He had yet to give me reason to.

I never followed his career. Quite the opposite. But every mention of his name fuelled still further my own sense of failure. I had never read any of his books. And had no intention to. I didn't know how many he had written. But I knew it was a lot.

It was some small consolation then, that he had already abandoned his own career when I lost my job. Better still, he had left the country. And for good he said. At least I would no longer hear his name.

Without a job I was totally adrift. So, it was a lifeline when Sarah offered to pay me to re-decorate some rooms in the village hall.

She worked in the parish office for her father. And knew all the local charities and old folks' homes. That winter, thanks to her I turned my hand to re-painting railings, sweeping leaves and clearing gutters. A little more work came from a small advert she put in the local paper for me.

A few days later a letter arrived, with an SW7 postmark.

It was from him. Had I known, I would have thrown it away unopened.

He wanted a price for some decorating work at a house he owned in the country. Now my humiliation was complete.

Not because of the work he wanted me to do. But because I could not refuse. He wouldn't even allow me that little pride. I needed the work. And I couldn't afford to turn anything away. Even from him.

Had I left five minutes earlier that fateful morning we would never have met. I didn't even remember telling him what I did. But obviously I had. And I regretted it now. He had come back to haunt me. And I was powerless to resist.

I called the number in the letter. Again, he seemed pleased to hear from me. We arranged a time and place to meet to view the work.

A couple of days later I waited outside Acton Town underground station. It was late afternoon. And already getting dark.

I saw an expensive German sports car approach. I guessed it to be him.

The journey passed in silence. I had nothing to say. I was too consumed with bitterness towards him. And life in general. And he, so recently returned from years in the wilderness, was out of practice with small talk.

We left the lights of the city streets behind. And headed into the darkness of a winter's night.

After about an hour he slowed the car and turned off the road.

We stopped in front of a pair of tall ornate iron gates. He got out of the car to open them. Even in the darkness, I could see they were several feet taller than him.

The house was reached down a long unlit track. A moment later part of it appeared in the headlights ahead of us.

When he switched off the engine, the silence briefly disturbed by our arrival, settled all around us. Even the slightest sound seemed magnified. Out there beyond the glare of streetlights it was completely black. Overhead the stars shone icy cold. Far more and far brighter than I had ever seen in the city. Yet cast no light upon the ground.

Inside the house I followed him across great expanses of uncarpeted floorboards, and past large shuttered windows.

The rooms were mostly empty. The few pieces of furniture unrecognisable under white dustsheets. That hung motionless, like brooding phantoms. Occasionally a chair or the corner of a table was uncovered. The sheet lay where it had been dropped at the time. Revealing his movements like a trail through the house in the weeks since his return.

The work he wanted was simple. Hardly worth doing

I thought. Painting a few rooms that looked fine already. And some re-papering where the damp had got in.

It would take a fortnight. Maybe ten days if I worked hard.

Could I have turned it down, I would have. But after I was finished at Sarah's I had no other work.

I took a few measurements. Sat at a table and worked out some prices.

Then doubled them. I needed the money. And he could afford it. Then I added some more.

If I had to work for him, at least it would pay very well. My humiliation would not come cheap. I gave him a price. To my surprise he accepted immediately.

I told him I couldn't start for a few weeks. He said that was fine. Just start when you can.

The next day I told Sarah about his letter and my visit to his house.

"It's a creepy old place out in the country near Oxford. It looks like he's hardly lived there."

"Yes?" she said disinterestedly.

I asked her when she last saw him.

"I don't know," she replied. "A long time ago."

Then she said, "maybe you ought to stop what you're doing here and work on his house instead. It sounds much more interesting."

"I don't want to work for him. But I don't have a choice. I haven't got anything after this."

"Maybe I could find you something," she said. "Perhaps at the church hall. I'll talk to dad."

So, in search of alternative work to his, I waited outside the parish office a few days later. I had never met her father before. Although I had seen him many times. He used to take school prayers every year, at the end of the Christmas and Easter terms.

"Hello Robert," he said warmly, shaking my hand. "Sarah tells me you may be able to help us." He invited me into his office.

"I'm retiring next year, after thirty years in the parish. And there's going to be a celebration to mark it. With the Mayor and the local paper, that sort of thing. So, we'd like to smarten up the church hall. Get it looking its best. Is that something you might be able to do for us?"

I told him I'd be pleased to.

"Splendid," he said. "Splendid."

I had never met a priest before. But he seemed quite like an ordinary person. Very relaxed and informal in fact. I followed him across the courtyard to the church hall. A bare high-ceilinged assembly room. With a couple of smaller rooms at each end.

But there wasn't a lot to do. And plenty of time to do it in. At the price I had agreed with James, I could hardly afford to put off his work for this. So, I resigned myself to starting at his house the following week.

I arrived early that first morning.

Unsure of the route, I left home before 6am and drove for a couple of hours. Until eventually, miles from the nearest town, deep in ancient woodland, I recognised the tall iron gates close to the road. The name *Studlands* carved high up on one of the large stone gate pillars.

In daylight the house looked as bleak and bare outside as I knew it to be inside. But even larger than I remembered.

I parked in the drive and unloaded what I needed. He had told me a side door would be open. It was very quiet inside, and quite cold.

There was no sign of him. And I didn't look. I got straight to work. The sooner I started, the sooner I could get paid. And be away. Never to see him again.

Around mid-morning I heard someone coming. I expected to see him. But instead, a middle-aged woman came into the room.

It was of no interest to me who she was. Or why she was there. I continued with my work in silence.

She introduced herself as Mrs Davies, the housekeeper. "I've worked here twenty-two years," she said. "Newton's the third owner I've known. And the worst. He bought it three years ago. Stayed a few weeks with a lady friend, then left. I didn't know where to contact him. He's let it go to rack and ruin."

I didn't respond.

"Then a couple of months ago he turns up. I don't know how long he'll stay this time. Just make sure you get your money."

I carried on with my work. I didn't want to talk to anybody. Even someone with a similar opinion of him as me.

I ignored her. And presently she left. I hoped not to see her again.

Later that afternoon he did come to visit me. As I knew he must. It would have been impossible to avoid him for the whole two weeks.

This time I was prepared. I had a blow lamp primed and close to hand. When I heard him coming, I started to burn paint off a door frame. I continued for as long as it took to discourage him from speaking to me.

After that I barely saw him. The house was easily big enough not to see him at all. For days I saw no one. And spoke to no one.

I started at 8am and left for home at 4pm. The travelling was hard. But it was the best paid work I'd ever had.

Occasionally working by a window, I might see him from afar walking in the garden. Or perhaps after dark as I was leaving, a distant light in another part of the house. But that was all. And it suited me fine.

But by the middle of the second week, I became concerned about finishing for the weekend. The work was easy. But my progress was slow.

Under different circumstances I might have quite enjoyed working in a house like that. The scale of the rooms and the quality of the workmanship was far in excess of anything I had ever seen before. But instead, my only thought was to be away as soon as possible. I re-doubled my efforts to make sure I finished by the end of the week.

So I was angry when he came to see me on Thursday afternoon, to ask if I might look at some other things for him. I told him I couldn't.

I told him I had other work. It wasn't true. But I couldn't face the thought of staying even another day. He said he understood.

Then he offered to pay extra for the inconvenience. "If that would make any difference," he said.

But the truth was it made no difference. No difference at all. For despite what I said, I had to stay. I couldn't afford to turn any work away. Not even his. Especially when it paid so well.

But I wanted to make him work for it. I felt it gave me some small sense of power over him. And I had to make the most of it while I could. Little as it was.

When I said the travelling was too much, he immediately offered to pay for local lodgings.

We agreed a price. I should have been embarrassed. At the money I asked for. And for my behaviour towards him. But I was still too bitter then to be ashamed.

With a heavy heart I returned the following week. I found a cheap boarding house a few miles away. And booked a room for a fortnight.

I had worked undisturbed for several days when he came to see me one afternoon.

"I don't know where you're lodging," he said. "But you could stay here during the week if you like. I'm sure it would be a lot more convenient for you. There are plenty of rooms."

I thanked him. But told him I was fine where I was. It was a lie. My room was cold and smelt of damp. But it was bad enough working for him. Without staying in his house.

After that we both worked silently in our different parts of the building. From time to time, he would come to see how I was getting on. When I was nearly finished in one room, there always seemed to be another to do. But at the price he was paying I couldn't refuse.

But at least Studlands was a decent place to work. It was inside and out of the rain. But more than that, it was a fine old building. And I began to find a pleasure in what I was doing. Something I had never known before. Or, as it turned out ever would again.

On another brief visit he told me Mrs Davies cooked dinner in the evening. "And you're very welcome to join me," he said. "It would be nice to have some company. I eat at seven. But it could be earlier if you'd prefer."

I thanked him. And said I would. If I was ever working late. But with the firm intention never to be. Yet only a couple of days later, I was.

Restoring the fine detail of a fibrous plaster ceiling rose, the afternoon slipped past unnoticed. It had been crudely and thickly brushed over with emulsion. And lost much of its definition.

It was the most intricate work I had ever attempted. And not something that could be rushed. My concentration was only disturbed by the sound of his voice behind me.

"I thought I saw a light on," I heard him say.

I looked at my watch. I would never make supper at the boarding house now.

"I've taken the liberty of asking Mrs Davies to lay an extra place for you," he said.

I was hungry. I had nowhere else to go. And I was angry. Once again, he was making me do something I didn't want to.

I followed him into unfamiliar territory, away from the part of the house I knew.

We walked down a long corridor with a polished tiled floor. Lined with painted rectangular wood panelling.

"The house had gas lighting originally," he said. "You can still see the old lamps in this part of the building."

I said nothing. He had outmanoeuvred me again. Not that it was deliberate. It was worse than that. He did it without even trying.

In a large dining room, two sets of cutlery were laid on the table. And an opened bottle of red wine. He took one place. And I took the other.

He poured a glass of wine for me. And another for himself. "The house came with a fully stocked library and wine cellar," he said.

I had no interest in his library or his wine. But I was quite prepared to drink it. In the same way I was quite prepared to take his money. He had plenty. And he was just paying his dues. At that time, I had yet to feel grateful to him.

He looked at the label on the bottle. "This is rather good," he said.

"Do you eat like this every night?" I asked.

"Not every night. Mrs Davies cooks three times a week. But I could ask her to if you'd like. With just me here it's not worth her coming in more often. It would be different if there were two of us."

He talked on a little more. But I was in no mood to listen. Although my irritation with him did not prevent me from enjoying the meal. It had been a long time since I had eaten so well.

So I gave myself to the food and the wine. We completed the meal in silence, save for the noise of the cutlery. Shortly after nine I thanked him for the food and left the table.

That night in my little room, I thought of him. Alone in that big old house. And the strange life he led.

I had never known him well at school. So I couldn't tell how much the last few years had made him the man he was now.

But certainly, they had me. I knew I had become something of an uncouth fellow. The lack of light and laughter in my life had dulled my spirit. Happiness and enthusiasm were emotions that had little place in my world.

Outwardly too, those years had taken their toll. Thinners and white spirit had reduced the skin on my hands to a rough and flaky texture. And my fingernails were cracked and encrusted with dried paint.

And until then my work had been of a similarly coarse and functional nature. But at Studlands I saw there could be more to it. Whatever imagination I could bring could be comfortably contained there. And I would never run up against the limits of what was possible.

And so, from that night on I resolved to go for a bolder approach. The following day I used one of the rooms he had asked me to redecorate to experiment in.

Where before I was content just to match the original colour, now I chose brighter and more vibrant hues. And a small sample patch was no longer enough. I wanted to see how the light fell on it across a large area. Covering and re-covering the same wall or ceiling, a whole day could pass until I was satisfied. The quantity of paint wasted must have been enormous. And the historical accuracy increasingly tenuous. But I was newly freed from the constraints of the past in those days. And experience had yet to stay my hand from excess.

Another week passed. And Friday came around again. Rain had been falling steadily for hours. By three o'clock it was getting dark, and the wind was rising. By four o'clock it was hurling the rain against the windows.

I was packing up to leave when he came into the room.

"Are you going back to London in this?" he asked. "It's pretty wild out there. If I were you, I'd only go back tonight if I really had to."

And I didn't really have to. It had been a long time since I'd had anything to go back for.

"I don't think we'll see Mrs Davies tonight," he said. "But there's plenty of food in the kitchen."

So, I didn't go home that night. Instead, I stayed all summer.

And it could have been a lifetime.

He cooked a meal of pasta and red pepper. And we reduced the stock in the wine cellar a little more. Like two waifs sheltering from the storm, we ate the food and drank the wine. While outside the wind and rain whistled around the balconies and the tall chimneys on the roof.

The wine warmed me and raised my spirits. And we talked into the night. I told him I had just finished some work for Sarah.

"Do you remember her?" I guessed they might have known each other at school. But that had been years ago.

"Yes," he said. "How is she?"

"She's fine. She's the one who got me started in this. I've just done some decorating work at her house. And she helps out with my accounts and to find me work."

Then, unsure of when they had lost touch I asked, "have you ever met her husband Ian?"

"No," he said, "but I know of him."

He re-filled my glass and then his own. I asked about his writing. "You've obviously done very well."

"Have I? I've always considered myself a failed writer."

"What do you mean?"

"I'm not proud of what I've written. I'm ashamed of it. I never wanted to be a popular writer. I wanted to be more than that. And the fact I've sold so many books, proves I've been doing something wrong.

And that's why I've come back. To finish the novel I've tried to write my whole career."

He was speaking with more emotion than I had seen before. In fact, for the first time.

"I tried three years ago. When I first moved here. It didn't work out then. But this time it will. This time it has to."

Outside the noise of the storm had subsided a little. It was after two by the old clock on the wall. He said he ought to find me a room. I followed him up the wide staircase to the first floor. This part of the house was in far better order than any of the rooms I had been working in.

He opened a door to a large airy room with a high ceiling, and a pair of tall French Windows. Apart from the elegantly crafted bed, there was a writing bureau, a pair of antique chairs and a wardrobe. All of the highest quality. And of the same period as the rest of the house. It was the finest room I had ever seen.

"There's a bathroom through there," he said. Pointing to a door by the bed. "I hope it will be OK for you."

Then he said he'd see me at dinner the next evening. And bid me goodnight.

We both knew I was never going back to the boarding house.

I lay on the bed and looked up at the magnificent vaulted ceiling high above me. Outside I could still hear the wind and the rain. It had been an extraordinary two months.

By morning the storm had passed. And the air was cool and clear.

As usual there was no sign of him. It was the first time I had been at Studlands on a weekend. And although every day there was the same, I felt more relaxed than I ever had before.

I walked the gardens for an hour or so. Then found a newspaper to read in the lounge before making some lunch. In the afternoon I did a little work. I went up to my room at six. When I came down an hour later, I found him sitting patiently in the dining room waiting for me.

"How was your day?" he enquired.

"Fine," I said. "And yours?"

"Very good, thank you. Very good." Then he said, "if there's anything particular you'd like, I'll ask Mrs Davies to get it in".

Then he leaned back in his chair. "Would you consider staying on and sorting the place out properly," he said. "Not just the house, but the gardens too? It's been neglected so long. I realise that's a big job. But there's no rush. You can stay as long as you like. I appreciate you have other work. And I wouldn't want you to give that up. In fact, I'd insist you didn't. But perhaps you could fit this in around it."

I had to admit I'd become quite fond of the old house. But more importantly I had a beautiful room of my own. With a splendid marble bathroom. And no bills to pay. It was an extraordinarily good arrangement. And as far as I was concerned, the longer it lasted the better. So I agreed.

"That's excellent," he said. "And when you're up in town working at Sarah's or anywhere else, you can stay at my apartment in Cornwall Gardens. There are several spare rooms. Just take one of them."

He picked up the bottle of wine and filled my glass. Then his own. "Here's to the summer," he said, raising his glass. "Wherever it is."

I raised mine. He was becoming a most affable host. And besides, it felt good to have someone seek my company. Even him. In fact, especially him.

For I began to sense a shift in the balance of power between us. That he had no idea such a thing existed, did little to diminish my satisfaction. I began to feel he wanted my friendship. And I didn't have so many to enjoy the luxury of turning any away. Indeed, except for Sarah I didn't have any at all.

But he didn't know that. And I would make him work for it. That would be his penance for the years of unhappiness he had caused me.

Then he said, "meeting you again is like coming home for me. Like returning to the good old days."

"What good old days?" I asked. "Were there any?"

"Maybe not. But I feel I'm returning to them all the same. Three years ago, I just wanted to leave it all behind. But now I've come home."

I couldn't see I had much of a part in his past. But I suppose I had been around for some of it.

Then he said, "you know when I was away, I forgot how cold this country can be in the winter. But I remembered the moment I stepped off the plane at Heathrow. The first thing I did was go to Simpson's and buy the warmest coat I could find."

It was the coat he wore the first day I met him in the street. It hung on a stand in the hall by the front door. He put it on every time he went out.

He got up and walked over to the radiator. He tried to turn it up. But I could see it was already at its highest setting.

"I never used to have a problem with the heating in this house" he said. "I think something must have happened to it while I was away. Or maybe I'm just out of practice with the English winter."

I wished I was out of practice with it. It seemed years since I had known anything else.

Then he asked if I had seen the Temple. I had no idea what he was talking about.

"Oh, you must," he said. "It's too late now. But we'll go and look at it tomorrow."

It was about 10pm when I went up to my room. He said he wanted to do another hour's work. It had been an enjoyable evening.

When I first met him a few weeks earlier, although only in his mid-thirties he seemed quite like an old man. His eyes were dull, and his manner distracted. Yet now returned to the discipline of writing, he seemed to grow more enthusiastic and vigorous each day.

We met every evening at dinner. But filled the days in our separate ways. I still saw him occasionally walking in the garden. He always looked pre-occupied. And I never approached him. I guess like me, he too was at work. But whereas mine lay in the physical world all around me. He had to withdraw into himself for his. And close his mind to all distractions.

Despite what he said though, the weather was changing. And had been for some time. But so used to the cold wet days by then, we failed to notice at first. Overhead the heavy grey cloud was beginning to thin. And the sun rose a little earlier, and a little higher each day. Inch by inch the winter was giving ground.

Until one morning a couple of weeks later, I stepped outside and the chill edge to the air had gone.

At last, we sensed winter had ended. And the siege had been lifted for another year. And now the change was swift and remarkable. Vast stretches of slender green daffodil storks appeared. And blankets of Bluebells and yellow Crocuses sprung up under the trees.

This change found an echo in us too, as nature in all its forms took heart. I felt my spirits rise. I'm sure he felt it too, as the nights receded. And the days grew warmer. Fine clear days gave way to fine clear nights.

Seen from across the valley, Studlands ceased to be a lonely outpost in a bare and barren landscape. Instead, it was fast becoming concealed in a rich green countryside of rolling fields, copses and hedgerows, white with hawthorn and elderflower.

In those early spring evenings, a simple pleasure of mine was to sit on the balcony of my room. Watching for the first lights of the distant villages.

My work was going well. Looking at the ornate plaster ceilings and intricate hardwood mouldings all around me, I realised this was what I wanted to do. Now, and in the future. What Sarah had started, James had given me the opportunity to take to a level I could never have imagined. What I lacked in skill and experience I made up for with interest and enthusiasm.

And now the weather was warming up, I didn't work every day.

One sunny spring afternoon, I drove to the nearby town of Woodstock.

Along a tree-lined pavement I walked, past old terraced cottages and small shops. I had emerged from a long dark winter of my own. To feel the warmth of the sun on my back. And a soft summer breeze on my face.

On an old wooden table outside an antique shop, I noticed a cardboard box of second-hand books. Looking through the authors' names, remarkably I saw a single slim paperback of his. The pages were yellowed and brittle. A pencilled price of just a few pence written inside the cover.

I put the money in the jar. And walked on in the sunshine. Perhaps I might read it one day I thought.

A week or so later he came to see me. It was still rare then for him to leave his study during the day. He seemed particularly jovial.

"I've been meaning to show you the Temple for ages," he said.

If it was a convenient time for him, it was not for me. But it was good to see him in such high spirits. And I knew he would be disappointed if I didn't go with him. Besides, I was unused to anyone seeking my company. And I liked it.

He opened the French windows and stepped out onto the lawn. I followed a few paces behind.

Even at this hour the sun was already high in the sky. It would surely be the hottest day of the year so far.

We left the formal gardens. And passed into a larger more expansive area of the grounds. Dominated by dense overgrown bushes and tall trees. I had never been this far from the house before.

We seemed to be tracing the route of an ancient path. Once perhaps quite wide. But now almost completely reclaimed by nature on all sides.

We walked for several minutes. But our progress was slow. The grass was thick and uneven underfoot. And the hot sun nearly overhead. Several trees lay across our path. Felled perhaps in the great storm a couple of years before.

Then he stopped. "There," he said. I followed his gaze into the distance.

"Can you see it?"

There was something ahead, through the trees. But no more than just a sense of sunlight on smooth stone.

We walked on. The ground rising steadily now. Then at last a grand and imposing structure came into view. A large dome of honey coloured Cotswold stone, soaring fully thirty or forty feet above us. Overgrown and discoloured by green moss. Supported on a dozen slender columns. I could just make out a Latin inscription carved around its circumference. Three broad steps surrounding its circular base led up to a flat stone floor, open on all sides. On a pedestal in the centre, stood a classical statue in female form.

We stood a few minutes in the cool shade of the great dome.

Then looking around he asked, "have you ever been to Oxford?".

I told him I hadn't. And it felt impolite to add I had no particular wish to.

"It's only twenty miles from here," he smiled. "Let's go at the weekend."

Then he said he ought to return to work. We re-traced our steps back to the house. And went our separate ways.

He used to return to London from time to time. Sometimes just for the day, sometimes longer. The house was easily big enough for both of us to come and go without the other noticing. Only when no place was laid for him at dinner, could I be sure he was away.

Yet that night his place was set, but I ate alone. I had never known him to be late. He was either on time, or not at all.

I was even more surprised a few minutes later when Mrs Davies placed his dinner on the table. In front of his empty chair.

"Is he in the house?" I asked.

"As far as I know," she replied.

But his seat remained empty. And his meal untouched.

"It's not the first time," said Mrs Davies as she cleared our plates. But it was the first time I had ever known it.

The next night I ate alone again. This time Mrs Davies left his place empty.

But twenty minutes later, he came into the room. He greeted me quietly and took his place opposite.

"How was your day?" I asked.

"Difficult," he said. Without looking up.

Mrs Davies brought a bowl of soup re-heated from earlier.

"No, no," he said, waving her away. "Just get me a sandwich or something."

It was not like him to be so abrupt. After that we ate in silence.

Until he said, "at least I haven't lied or cheated."

I looked at him. "I don't understand," I said. "Have I done something?"

"No, not you," he said. "You're the only friend I've got. If you don't mind me calling you that."

"No, of course not," I said. And I didn't mind. I didn't mind at all.

He was silent after that. And clearly in no mood for conversation. I finished my meal and said goodnight. I thought him best left alone. Later I came to see that was the worst thing I could do. But this was the first time. And I didn't know any better.

I crossed the hall and went into the lounge.

Usually, I watched television for an hour or so after dinner. Before going up to my room. And usually, he returned to his study for a couple more hours.

But not that night.

Instead, he came into the lounge and silently took a seat.

I had almost forgotten he was there when he said, "surely no one believes all this?".

I looked across at him.

"These adverts," he said. Gesturing at the screen. "All these happy families. No one really lives like that do they?"

"I know lots of happy couples," I said.

"Do you?" he replied. "I doubt it."

I didn't answer. It was clearly not a night for discussion. But I did believe it. I knew Sarah and Ian. And that was enough.

Shortly after he got up and left the room.

Looking back, the signs were there from the beginning. But I had yet to make any sense of them.

I worked quietly for the rest of the week without seeing him. I wasn't sure if he was in the house or not.

Until early Sunday morning. And a knock on my bedroom door.

"It's a beautiful day," I heard him call out. "Perfect for Oxford."

It was just after six by the clock on the bedside table.

"Don't be long," he said. "We want to be there before it's busy."

"Go away!" I shouted and rolled over.

But awakened so abruptly, I couldn't get back to sleep. I came down for breakfast shortly after.

"I knew you'd want to come," he said.

"Go on your own," I said irritably. "I've got things to do."

"It wouldn't be the same without you. And you'll regret it if you don't."

It was still early when we arrived. In those days Oxford was only a half hour drive from Studlands. And it was possible then to park on the street in the heart of the old city. He stopped the car by the Emperors' Heads outside the Sheldonian.

At that time on a Sunday morning, it had the feel of a private viewing. Just the two of us and eight hundred years of history.

The sun was not yet overhead. But high enough to clear all but the tallest spires and steeples. Through quiet courtyards and narrow alleyways, we took a meandering route towards the Botanic Gardens. Few colleges closed their doors to visitors then.

In the walled garden we admired the giant Victorian glass houses. And the colourful late spring beds beyond. Then stood a while on Magdalen Bridge in the sun. Watching the river pass slowly beneath our feet.

He had been right. It was a perfect day for it. And I was pleased I had come. We retraced our steps back into town. Past the magnificent dome of Queens College and under the Bridge of Sighs

The shops were starting to open. In Blackwell's I saw a large and beautifully bound photographic book of the city. I was earning good money. But I wasn't ready to spend that much. Later in the summer I would have bought it without a second thought.

"What a wonderful book," I said. James came over to look. "I wish I could take photographs like that."

"Are you going to buy it?" he asked.

"It's too expensive." I put it back on the shelf.

"Let me get it for you," he said.

"No, no it's too much."

It was late morning now, and our thoughts turned to finding somewhere to eat. Passing the chapel of Exeter College, I looked inside. It was very quiet. In the past I would never have gone into such a building. But working at Studlands sparked interests where none had been before.

Evensong was still hours away. But it was not completely deserted. The vicar, in his robes was preparing communion. I watched him quietly filling the sacrament cup with water. He reminded me of Sarah's father.

I thought James had seen him too. But before I could remark on it, he had turned away and walked out. I caught up with him on the pavement outside.

"I'm sorry," he said. His mood seemed to have changed. "I've got to get back to work."

"But it's Sunday," I said.

"I don't get weekends off. I'm sorry. We have to go."

We walked back to the car. The sun was now high in the sky. It was going to be a very hot day. I was disappointed to leave so soon.

When we returned to Studlands he went to his study. And didn't appear again until dinner. As usual he was already at his place when I arrived.

"I'm sorry we didn't stay longer today," he said.

He reached for the bottle of wine.

"But I must finish this book by the autumn."

He filled my glass.

Then he said, "maybe it's time you did some more work for Sarah".

He poured a glass for himself.

"I ought not to be selfish. And keep you entirely to myself. Much as I'd like to."

I was surprised he remembered my work at the church hall. Surprised and disappointed. I didn't want to work there. I wanted to work here, at Studlands. And to forget about everything else.

"I hadn't really thought about it," I said.

"Well, perhaps you should. I think you owe it to her. After all she has done for you."

"I suppose so," I said.

"You'll have to go back some time. It might as well be now."

I knew he was right. "I'll call her and get it over and done with as soon as I can," I said. "Do you mind if I ring her from here?"

"No, not at all."

After dinner I called her from the phone in the corridor outside his study. While he worked a few yards away.

The next day I worked harder than I had in weeks.

The prospect of leaving Studlands, and the uncertainty of how long I would be away, instilled a renewed sense of urgency.

After my brushes were cleaned and dustsheets folded, there was barely time enough for a shower before dinner.

Approaching my room, I saw a large hardback book against the wall by the door. It was the photographic book of Oxford from the day before.

Inside the front cover was a handwritten note. *To Robert, many thanks for your help and friendship, long may it continue. With my kindest regards, James. April 1989.*

Downstairs at dinner I thanked him for the book.

Then I said, "It's inspired me to look for a camera when I'm in town."

"Yes?" he said with mild interest.

"I'd like to photograph the temple."

"That would make an excellent subject," he said enthusiastically.

He filled my glass with wine. "And you will stay at Cornwall Gardens when you're down there, won't you. I gave you a key, didn't I?"

"You don't mind?"

"No, I insist. It's the least I can do to help."

After dinner I went to my room. I planned an early start. And of course, the offer of his place in town was far too good to pass up.

And despite my reluctance to return to the church hall, I was looking forward to telling Sarah all about him. It had been a long time since I'd had anything interesting to say. And I was sure she would be fascinated.

And there was so much to tell. In truth, it was the only reason I was going back. I didn't need her work anymore. Indeed, it had become a considerable inconvenience to me.

Chapter Two

May 1989, An Unwitting Accomplice

Early next morning I loaded my dust sheets and brushes into the van. It was very quiet. I didn't see him. I doubted he was even awake yet.

I arrived at the church hall just before nine. After unpacking I walked across the courtyard to the parish office.

But I was disappointed. Sarah wasn't there.

I finished at lunchtime that first day. I could have worked for another few hours. If I'd felt like it. But I didn't. I didn't want to be there. And but for James, I would never have come back. Perhaps I might have felt differently had I seen her.

I drove to Cornwall Gardens. To a split-level ground and first floor apartment. In a grand five storey stucco fronted Victorian terrace, just off the Cromwell Road.

But unlike Studlands, despite its period double height ceilings and arched windows, it was very modern inside. With recessed lighting, polished granite, and stainless steel.

He didn't own it. He said he had taken a twelve-month lease on it. Obviously, it wasn't cheap. And I couldn't see why he bothered.

But it was very fortunate for me that he did.

I hadn't paid rent on my room in Kilburn for months. The last time I left, I thought I'd be back in a week.

It would surely have been long since re-let. And my things thrown away. I didn't care. I had nothing worth keeping. It just saved me the trouble.

Cornwall Gardens was also very convenient for Sarah's house. Barely ten minutes' drive away.

It was a warm late spring evening, so I took a walk in my new neighbourhood. I dropped my old Kilburn door key into a skip by the side of the road. That was my old life. The one I had left behind. And I was never going back.

I took a room on the first floor at the front of the house. Overlooking the quiet and secluded gardens. A pink magnolia was in bloom across the road. And the tall plane trees were beginning to leaf.

I returned to the church hall every day. But progress was slow. What little enthusiasm I had brought with me quickly faded. I didn't see Sarah all week. She never said she'd be away.

At the rate I was working it could take weeks to finish. And I had no intention of being away that long. I resolved to work much harder the following day.

When I returned to Cornwall Gardens that night, I saw James' car parked outside.

I wasn't expecting him. He greeted me warmly. And asked how I was settling in. He said he had a meeting with his publisher. "I've been putting it off for weeks," he told me.

He hadn't returned by the time I went to bed. Several hours later my sleep was disturbed by the sound of slamming doors. I got up to investigate. By the light of the streetlamps outside, I saw him hanging up his coat in the hall downstairs.

The next morning, I asked if he'd had a good night.

"No," he said. "And I knew I wouldn't."

"Then why did you go?"

"To be polite. And so I don't have to go again."

"Well, you won't get any sympathy from me. I was in bed by eleven."

"Your evening sounds better than mine," he said.

I noticed a piece of paper on the floor. I picked it up.

It was a page carefully torn from a menu. Neatly folded in half.

There was a hand-written message on it.

"Who's Rachel?" I asked.

"Who?"

I passed it to him.

"Hope to see you on the ninth." He read the words out loud. And as if for the first time.

"Must have fallen out of my pocket," he said.

"Well? Will she?" I asked.

"No," he said.

"Didn't you like her?"

"I don't remember her. There were a lot of people."

He screwed it up. And threw it into the bin.

He left shortly after. I looked forward to following him down in a few days.

Work at the church hall offered little to occupy my mind. And my thoughts turned to Studlands. Inspired by books in his library, I decided to create an ornamental Italian garden. Of course, I knew nothing of such things. But everything seemed possible then. The summer was coming. And I had the enthusiasm. And but for the church hall I had the time.

In the evenings I made some simple sketches of a layout. The spot I had in mind was just a rough area of undergrowth. But emboldened by research in his library, I planned clipped hedges of juniper and cypress around a small fountain. A pergola climbing with wisteria. Surrounded by beds of white geranium, poppies, and cornflowers.

At last Friday came. I tidied up my work after lunch. And made good my escape for the weekend.

Studlands was very quiet and peaceful after London. I had only been away a week. But it felt much longer. It was a great relief to be back.

But the prospect of working at the church hall for weeks weighed heavily upon me. I wished I'd never gone back. But it was his suggestion. And as his guest I felt I could not refuse.

As usual, there was no sign of him. I guessed he was at work in his study.

It was a warm and sunny afternoon. I paced out the area for the Italian garden. And refined the sketches made earlier in the week.

After that, I sat out on the terrace and read the newspaper that came every day. I looked at them occasionally. James never did. Each day Mrs Davies put them on the table in the hall. Where they collected untouched all week. Until she took them away.

We met at dinner. It was good to be back. And to see him again. He opened the French windows. We ate our meal overlooking the gardens, and the late spring countryside beyond. Outside the clear blue sky was darkening. But the warmth of the day was still in the air. And the night drew in softly around us.

Unlike a few weeks before. When it closed like an iron grip. That drove us deep into the house for shelter. Now the whole summer lay ahead. And the prospect of many nights like this.

He asked how I was getting on at the Vicarage.

"It's the church hall," I corrected him.

"Now you're working there I hope you won't forget about Studlands."

I presumed he was joking. Although the way he said it, I couldn't be sure. I told him how much I enjoyed working here.

Then I asked if he knew any history of the house.

"There's a book in the library," he said. "It shows the house as it used to be."

"It's not always been like this?"

"It was much more ornate. But a lot of it was covered up or removed."

"Why would anyone do that?"

He shrugged his shoulders. "Tastes change I suppose. And circumstances too." Then he said, "Studlands was never an important country house. It was built a hundred years too late.

He looked up at the magnificent pale blue and white plaster ceiling above, with its inset painted panels. "That's not Adam or Zucchi," he said. "It just looks like it.

And those." He pointed at one of the finely carved and polished Mahogany doors. "They're not Chippendale. But at least the house survived. Hundreds like it didn't."

Then he said, "I've often thought it would be interesting to restore it back to the way it was. Is that something you might consider doing? As a longer-term project of course. In between other work I mean. Like the church hall."

I told him I'd like to very much. Then I asked if I could see the book. He said he'd find it for me.

"But first there's something else I want to show you." We had finished our meal and I followed him into the lounge. On a circular table in one corner of the room were several large cardboard boxes.

"You said you were interested in photography. And this is the place to do it. There's plenty of spare rooms for a darkroom."

There was a camera body, several lenses, and a tripod. An enlarger, various metal trays and bottles of chemicals. Even to my untutored eye it was equipment of the highest quality.

It was very generous of him. Although I was unclear why he thought I had an interest in photography. But it was a time of exploration and discovery. And surrounded by so many beautiful and fascinating things at Studlands, there did seem a certain logic to it. A logic that could only have existed there. And nowhere else.

It was well after midnight by the time I had examined all the equipment. The lenses felt heavy in my hand. And the camera body was machined from aluminium and magnesium alloy. The movement of the controls was smooth and silent. With a mechanical precision. It was surely the finest thing I had ever owned. And certainly the most expensive. It would take months to work out how to use it. And probably a lifetime to master it.

In the morning I saw he had left the book out for me. A slim hardback. With the title *Six Victorian Country Houses, A Photographic Record by Charles Latham*, deeply embossed in gilt lettering on the cover and spine.

Inside, a decorative frontispiece dated 1904 described the subject in characteristic period style, as *some of the most notable houses of England.*

Illustrated with beautiful glass plate black and white photographs. The text detailed the architectural features of each house and its gardens.

I read every word of the chapter on Studlands. And studied every photograph.

Just as he said, it looked quite different then. And much grander.

Where now the front of the house presented an unremarkable, flat and featureless aspect. With just a row of plain stone steps, leading up to a pair of double entrance doors. Back then, a tall and magnificent portico projected out over them. Supported on six circular columns, topped by a deep triangular pediment. Completely transforming the look and character of the building. Similarly lost now, a row of classical Greek or Roman statues lined the roof on all sides.

Later that day, looking up from the ground little evidence remained. Some small rather crude patchwork repairs. And a slight discolouration of the stonework. But that was all.

Several pages of text were devoted to the grounds. And there too, much had been lost. Nothing remained of the Dahlia Garden. Described as one of the finest in the land. Nor of the Statue Walk. An avenue of box hedge and Irish yew. Lined with over fifty antique Venetian figures in hollowed out recesses.

There was still some hedging in the gardens. And I wondered if any of the statues might still be there. Concealed by decades of growth. Later that summer I cut them back. And found nothing.

But at least the dome had survived. Referred to as The Temple of Indulgence. Described in the text as *a striking tholos. Much admired for its elegant form and magnificent setting at the end of a sylvan vista. Almost a quarter of a mile long.*

There was reference to the ironic humour of its Latin inscription: *in incerta temporum vivere bene.* Translated as *in uncertain times, live well.* Interpreted as an exhortation to the pursuit of pleasure. No matter the circumstances.

And mention too, of a mysterious faux gothic ruin somewhere in the grounds.

Photographs of the interior told a similar tale of loss and neglect. Although at least the double height entrance hall, lit by the light of a glazed rotunda above was still recognisable. And the grand galleried staircase with its ornate and slender curving bronze balustrade remained unchanged.

But in those days the walls were hung with huge and magnificent paintings. And instead of the old brown carpet, the floor was a beautiful polished patterned Sicilian marble.

Elsewhere, rows of long-lost classical busts, on raised pedestals seemed to line every corridor. And illuminated glass spheres hung on delicate brass chains. Where now bare light bulbs dangled on lengths of cable.

But most conspicuous of all, was the Grand Ballroom. I knew most of the rooms in the house. Certainly those of any significance. But I had never seen this one. Fully sixty feet long, with a heavily coffered Rococo ceiling. Four enormous chandeliers hung suspended high above a black and white porcelain tiled floor.

And at one end a huge and extravagant sculptured marble fireplace. Decorated with garlands of fruit and cherubs with trumpets. A vast gilt mirror on the wall reflected the depth and splendour of the room. And everything within it.

For page after page the architectural features of the house were described in great detail. But references to cipollino marble, yellow scagliola and green jasper meant nothing to me then. It was a language from another world. But one I believed I stood on the threshold of. About to enter.

Despite its bleakness as it first appeared to me, I had acquired a real affection for the house in the months since my arrival. But to see it like this. As it had been. And how it was meant to be, was a revelation. And to play a part in restoring it back to its former glory, would surely be the greatest achievement of my life.

That afternoon, book in hand I set out to solve the mystery of the grand room.

But tracking the direction of the shadows and the angle of the light, led only to a series of empty and unremarkable rooms at the back of the house.

There was no grand fireplace. No intricate plasterwork. Just plain walls and ceilings. And bare boards on the floor.

But a tap on one of those walls gave a hollow sound. I drilled a tiny spy hole.

And like an archaeologist opening up a new chamber, shone my torch into the darkness beyond. And there in the black of night, pierced by a single narrow beam of light I saw it. The magnificent fireplace, with its carved birds and fruit. Covered in thick grey dust. But there was no mistaking it. And the floor too, was still the black and white chequerboard tiles.

Other walls made a similar hollow sound. And surely the ceiling would have done the same. But it was early evening now. And too late to investigate further that day.

I told him of my discoveries at dinner. And asked if he knew any later history of the house, after the book had been written.

"It was requisitioned by the army during the war," he said. "Then a private school through the 1960s and 70s.

They only occupied part of the house and boarded up the rest."

Then he said, "if you're interested there are some old statues and other relics down by the folly."

I was very interested. And not just in the statues. But the folly too. Presumably, the gothic ruin mentioned in the Latham book. The house and its gardens were an endless source of fascination and discovery.

"Unfortunately, I can't carry on tomorrow," I said. "I have to go back to the church hall. I wish I didn't."

All he had to do was suggest I put off my return. And I would have. Probably forever.

But he didn't. Instead, he said, "it's important not to neglect Sarah's work. She's been a good friend to you. And there's plenty of time to work here. Just do it when you can."

So, with a heavy heart I returned to the church hall the following morning.

This time I saw Sarah's car. I thought about going over to see her at lunchtime.

But decided to finish early. And go to the west end instead. To look for a book on architectural photography.

When I returned to Cornwall Gardens that evening, a light was flashing on the answerphone. I guessed it to be a message from him. But it wasn't.

I knew I would disturb him at his work if I called. But so intrigued by what I heard, I called him anyway.

The phone rang for a long time. Eventually James answered. It may have been the first call he had ever received at Studlands.

And although it was only Monday, it was good to hear his voice again. I wished I was there.

"Rachel Adam left a message on your answerphone," I said.

"I didn't know we had one."

"It must have come with the apartment," I replied. "Anyway, she rang to remind you about some nightclub on Thursday."

"Rachel who?" he said irritably.

"Rachel Adam. That's not Rachel Adam from *Richmond Road* is it?"

"I've no idea where she lives."

"It's not an address. It's a TV show."

"I don't watch television," he said disinterestedly.

"What did she look like?"

"I don't remember."

"I wonder if it could be her."

"I doubt it," he said.

"Are you going?"

"No."

At the church hall next morning, my enthusiasm was at its lowest ebb. The work seemed to stretch out endlessly before me. And my mind was still on the weekend's discoveries at Studlands.

To revive my spirits, I walked over to the parish office to see Sarah.

She was working quietly in her cramped little office.

"I missed you last week," I said.

"I had a few days off," she replied.

I asked her how she was. For a second, I thought she hadn't heard me. I was about to ask again, when she told me she was fine.

"It was the church fete committee meeting last night," she said. "And it went on quite late."

Maybe she was tired. But it struck me how much of the happiness had gone out of her in the last few years. As if life had become a very serious business for her. It seemed especially apparent that day for some reason.

"It's the time of year," she said. "Spring is always the busiest for committee meetings."

The summer before she had asked me to help her on a stall at the church fete. I hoped she might ask again this year. But as it happened, she never did.

And although she was clearly not in the mood for conversation, I was keen to speak of James.

"I thought he was a bit odd at first," I said. "But actually, he's alright."

"Does he know you're working for me?" she asked.

I told her he did.

"And he doesn't mind?"

"No, of course not. But there's a lot to do at his house. I could be there for months. It's quite a place."

"Yes," she said. "I can imagine."

There was something in the way she spoke. Something that made me feel she didn't approve of my association with him. But if she knew him better, I was sure she'd change her mind. Just as I had.

I told her I would never neglect her work for his. But thought better of telling her what a fascinating house it was. I didn't want her to see how quickly I had lost interest in her work. Now something better had come along.

Later that afternoon, working quietly and alone in the church hall, I thought maybe I could re-introduce them. Each was missing out not knowing the other.

After all they had done for me, this was something I could do for them. And I was sure they'd thank me for it.

Perhaps I could invite her to Studlands. To show her my work. I didn't think James would mind. Maybe tomorrow I'd suggest it to her.

That night at Cornwall Gardens he rang. He had never called before. And it was good to hear from him.

After enquiring politely about progress at the church hall, he said, "I suppose it must be very dull for you up there in the evenings."

I told him it was fine.

Then he said, "well although I think it will be dreadful. If you really want to, we could go to that nightclub tomorrow evening. You might enjoy it."

It seemed a shame for him come all the way into town. Especially for something he didn't want to do. But the prospect of an evening out. And for the first time since I could remember, was too good to pass up.

And I was still intrigued by the answerphone message earlier in the week. So I told him I would love to go.

"Especially if Rachel Adam will be there."

"Who?" he said.

I didn't visit Sarah the next day. On reflection, I hadn't enjoyed our last conversation. If she didn't approve of James that was her business. He was my friend. And I didn't have to justify him to her. It was her loss. I packed up early in anticipation of my big night out.

It was a brief taxi ride from Cornwall Gardens to Berkeley Square. A short journey for him perhaps. But not for me. I had come a long way since we'd met. After so many empty years, a simple taxi ride across town on a spring evening felt exhilarating.

And when we arrived, maybe it was just the heat of the moment. In that crowded space, beneath a Georgian town house in Mayfair. But I sensed the lost spirit of Studlands' glorious past in its wood panelling, paintings and porcelain. Red velvet sofas and silk wall coverings. And it captivated me.

"Isn't this awful," he said.

A few minutes later, presumably on a signal we never saw, everyone made their way to a dining area. Under a low vaulted ceiling, supported on shiny brass clad columns.

As we took our seats, I heard someone say his name. I didn't need to look to know who it was. But I instinctively did.

At the time Rachel Adam was just 24. And the new darling of British television. At 8pm every Tuesday evening, millions tuned in to follow the fictitious lives of three girls sharing a south London flat.

But naturally, and surely uniquely in the room, James knew nothing of this. And even if he had, would have been completely indifferent to it.

But everyone else in the room, myself included certainly were not. And by extraordinary good fortune she sat next to James on his left. While I sat opposite.

She introduced herself to me and shook my hand.

Thrilled as I was to meet her, I felt sorry she had us for company. When there were so many interesting people in the room.

And like me, he was long out of practice meeting people. Although at least in his case it was by choice. But to her great credit she didn't seem to mind. And spoke to us for most of the meal.

But I doubted he made a good impression. He listened politely to her. While I strained to catch her every word. He sat with his head bowed slightly to hear what she was saying. And with his hands clasped together in front of him, I thought he looked like a priest taking Confession. And he seemed to be enjoying it about as much.

Seeing James in public was not the same as seeing him at Studlands. He was much less at ease in a crowd. He was polite as always. But quiet and reserved. Just as he had been when we first met. I knew he would have much preferred to stay at home. And I was grateful he was doing this for me.

Once the meal was over most people left the tables. Rachel stood a few yards away, talking in a small group.

"What a lovely girl," I said.

"Yes, I suppose," he shrugged. Then he said, "if we leave now no one will notice".

It seemed a shame to go so soon. "Shouldn't we say goodbye to Rachel?"

"Why bother?" he said. And made his way across the

room towards the stairs. I caught up with him outside, in the cool night air. Looking up the road for a taxi.

"It was a great evening," I said. "I really enjoyed it."

"Did you?"

"Yes. And wasn't it incredible to meet Rachel Adam."

"Was it?"

I was delighted to return to Studlands a couple of days later. And on a sunny Saturday morning I went in search of the folly, and the lost statues he had mentioned. They had been on my mind all week in town.

His directions took me far beyond the edge of the formal gardens. Towards the furthest reaches of the grounds. It was hard to imagine anyone ever venturing this distance from the house. Finally, out in open countryside where the long grass stretched away waist high in all directions. A bare stone wall rose tall and jagged against the sky. Shattered blocks of stone lay all around. And pigeons nested in the huge arched and empty window opening.

Then, in the shadow of that great wall I saw them. Deep in the undergrowth. Amongst heaps of cracked marble paving slabs and broken Grecian urns. A dozen or more small stone statues. A mix of classical and medieval figures. Some holding swords and shields. A young woman holding a bouquet of flowers, another carrying a basket of fruit. And an old man with a cloak wrapped around him. Even weathered and caked in dirt the quality of the carving was plain to see.

Returning to the house to investigate how the statues had been fixed, I went in search of access to the roof.

Hopefully from within. For no ladder could ever reach that far from the ground.

The third floor was a part of the old house I rarely ventured. There was none of the ornate detailing up there found elsewhere. The ceilings were lower. And the corridors narrower.

The rooms too, were smaller and mostly empty. Save a few forgotten relics from the past. Some antique framed maps stacked against a wall in one. Battered Louis Vuitton trunks with faded travel labels in another. Whatever events had taken place on the floors below, up here at least the years passed slowly. Tranquil and undisturbed.

I tried every door. Until one, unlike all the others opened not into another room. But onto a narrow flight of wooden steps instead. Leading up to another door at the top.

I climbed the stairs. And turned the handle. It opened into brilliant sunlight and onto the roof. A vast flat open space. Dominated by a dozen tall brick chimneys, like the funnels of a great ocean liner. And beyond, lay a fabulous view of the countryside for miles around.

I told him of my day's work that evening at dinner. He expressed his usual level of mild interest. I described the view from the roof. He said he would like to see it one day. But he didn't give the impression that it would be anytime soon.

We shared a bottle of wine from the cellar, as we did most nights at Studlands. A few months before I asked if there were many down there.

"Enough to last us years," he had replied.

I liked the sound of that. As if it would always be like this.

And yet very little from those days remains with me now. So many were the things I left behind when I went. But a love of wine and architecture have stayed with me. And often been a source of comfort since in darker days.

But back then my education in such things was just beginning. And where better to learn than in the rooms and grounds of that great house. Just to live within its walls and to tread the soft grass of its gardens, was to open a gateway to worlds of which until then I knew nothing.

And the wine cellar was an important part of that. A low red brick passageway under the old kitchen. Quite wide, and with a fine barrel-vaulted ceiling. Lined with shallow bays to the left and right. Racked with wooden shelves. The bottles neatly stacked on their side, thick with the dust of ages. From the dates on the labels some were twenty or thirty years old.

Often on warm clear evenings, with a notebook and a selection of bottles drawn from different bins, I compared regions and vintages. I knew there was a science to it. But like everything else that summer, I learnt instead by trial and error.

Some nights James would join me, before returning to his work. And together we gave thanks to those whose unseen hands had laid those bottles down, years before.

But my pursuit of knowledge led me to one room more than any other. There were many smaller bookcases around the house. But it was the library that was its heart and soul.

A magnificent double height room and gallery. Lined with books on every subject. Between its marbled floor and heavily coffered plaster ceiling, it offered a complete classical education. And one I indulged myself in that summer.

From Vasari to Temanza, I read them all. Something I would never have done anywhere else. But the heroic landscape at Studlands gave their words a special resonance.

And the more I read of those ancient texts, the better I came to understand many of the references in the house and the grounds beyond.

For I was in search of history in those days. And at Studlands it seemed to lay all around. Sometimes right in front of me, in the clear light of day. Sometimes in the shadows, waiting to be discovered.

And it wasn't just the history of the house that came to fascinate me. But also of James himself. I knew so little about him. And his work. And I wanted to know more.

One night I asked if there were any of his books in the house.

"No," he said. "That would be far too depressing."

I didn't tell him I had brought one in a few weeks before.

"Good writing," he said. "Is a wonderful thing. I wish I could do it."

And I knew he wasn't joking.

He got up from the table. And walked over to a small bookcase in the corner of the room. He pulled out a small paperback. "If I could write half as well as this," he said. "I'd call myself a writer"

He handed me a copy of *Nostromo*.

"Have you read it?" he asked.

I said I hadn't.

"You should."

I took it. And I thanked him. But I knew I never would. I wasn't interested in other writers. It was his work and his life I wanted to know about. Not anyone else's.

But his past was not a subject that came up naturally. So much so, I felt uncomfortable raising it. He was too polite to say. But I got the impression he considered enquiries about it to be in poor taste.

So, if he wouldn't talk about it. I'd have to find another way. After all, he had been if not exactly famous, certainly quite well known. Information on him must exist. It was just a case of finding it. But in those pre-internet days that was not so easy.

Maybe it was the wine that emboldened me to ask if he had ever spoken to the press. "I was just wondering," I said.

"No, I don't think so," he replied. And carried on with his meal. Then he stopped a moment. "I did do an interview once."

"When was that?"

"Oh, years ago," he said. And returned to his food.

"Was it for a newspaper or a magazine?" I asked cautiously.

"I don't remember. I had lunch with a journalist. He'd obviously never read any of my books. Not that I held that against him. Far from it. I respected his good taste. And I was sure he had better things to do than listen to me talk about myself. I know I did. After that, I vowed never to do it again."

Then he asked me if I was going back to the church hall on Monday. "It's important not to neglect your other work," he said. "There's nothing at Studlands that can't wait. And it would be a shame for you to lose contact with Sarah."

I wondered why he thought that. He had. And it didn't bother him.

Before I went to bed that night, I took his book from the shelf. And opened it for the first time. It was just as well he never came into my room.

I read a couple of pages. I planned to take it with me to Cornwall Gardens in the morning. And read it there. I was only going back to the church hall to humour him.

Although as it happened, I didn't return until later in the week.

Instead, I went to the Westminster Reference Library. A fine old Portland stone clad building. A short walk from Leicester Square tube station. Renowned, I heard for the depth of its literary archive.

I was in search not of what he had written. But what others had written about him. It was a little after nine when I arrived. And I had the Square almost to myself in the warm morning sunshine.

But the visit was not a success. Looking through endless books and bound volumes of magazines yielded barely the briefest of references to him.

Returning to Cornwall Gardens that afternoon, I found a handwritten envelope on the mat. Addressed jointly to James & I.

That evening I called him. "Rachel's invited us to a party."

"How awful," he said. "I'm not going."

"Too late. I've already RSVP'd it."

There was silence on the other end of the line. It wasn't true. But I would. First thing in the morning.

Then I said, "you may get invites like this all the time. But I don't. Can't you just go for me?"

The next day I continued my research elsewhere. In those days, the National Newspaper Library lay almost beyond the most northerly outpost of the underground system. Far enough out of town to re-emerge onto the surface. And into the light of day.

Behind its austere 1930's red brick façade and art deco entrance, it was a library unlike any I had seen before. Instead of shelves of books and reading tables, there were forms to fill in. And rolls of microfilm to view. This was not a place for casual browsing. But of serious research. If there was any information on him, it would surely be here. Precisely catalogued and filed.

But I felt uneasy. Save for Sarah, he was my only friend. And I knew he wouldn't approve of what I was doing. But he would never find out. He had no idea where the church hall was. He couldn't possibly know if I was there or not. And he hadn't seen Sarah in years. He probably wouldn't recognise her if he passed her on the street. So I tried to put such thoughts out of my mind.

Ignorant of any significant events in his career, I made a random selection of newspaper titles and dates to view. I feared it could take days to find anything. Fortunately, I had the time. I didn't care if I ever went back to the church hall.

By the faint glow of microfilm readers, I took my place in the darkened reading room. A hand-wheel on the side of the machine wound images of newsprint across the screen. Sweeping through days and weeks in seconds. The days and weeks of his life. And mine.

How different things would have been if we had met years before. But it was an extraordinary coincidence we had met at all. And if I believed in such things, I might have thought fate had been on my side for once.

By lunchtime I had found nothing. And briefly exchanged the airless reading room for the daylight outside.

But later that afternoon, in the first week of September 1986, something caught my eye. A headline half-way down an inside page. *Popular Author Calls Time on Career.*

I read on. *In a brief press release from his publishers yesterday, best-selling author James Newton, 33, unexpectedly announced his retirement from writing.*

Reading those words brought it all back again. The satisfaction and the relief I had felt at the time. But now I was ashamed. What I had rejoiced in then, upset me now.

According to the article he was leaving the country. And with no plans to return. There was a quote from him thanking his publishers for releasing him from his contractual obligations. No reason was given for his decision.

A second paragraph offered a brief resume of his career. *"Widely hailed eight years ago,"* it concluded. *"As one of the country's most promising new young writers. Yet despite his prolific output and huge sales, many critics believe that early promise remains largely unfulfilled. And following yesterday's announcement, now seems destined never to be.*

I had read enough. I was beginning to find what I was looking for. And I didn't like it. It troubled me to think of him unhappy.

And I knew something of that unhappiness remained with him still. He needed a friend. And remarkably, chance had made me that friend. And I was determined not to fail him. I returned the rolls of microfilm and left.

I arrived back at Cornwall Gardens shortly after five. To my surprise James's car was parked outside.

Even more unusually, he was not in his study. But in the lounge instead. He looked up as I passed the open doorway.

"How's it going at the church hall?" he asked. "You must be nearly finished there."

"Yes, nearly," I lied.

"Has she got any work for you after that?"

"I don't think so," I said. And thank God for that I thought.

"I was wondering," he said. "If you might help me out up here. Just for a day or two a week. Replying to letters and taking a few telephone calls. I find those things such a distraction."

Staying up in town was the last thing on my mind. Studlands was where I wanted to be. And as far as I could see he hardly received any letters or calls. But if that was what he wanted, I felt obliged to do it.

I moved a table and chair into a spare room on the ground floor. Later he came to see me, with half a dozen envelopes. A couple of unpaid bills, the rest junk mail. It was going to be a very quiet office.

And that suited me fine. I had no intention of staying there long. But at least it would be easier to keep in touch with Sarah. Not that that seemed so important now.

It was Rachel's party that weekend. So I stayed in town. But I didn't return to the church hall. I went to the west end instead. Walking for hours in the sunshine around Piccadilly and St James's. I counted his books on the shelves in Hatchards and Foyles. I wasn't buying. Just curious.

I did buy a shirt for the party. And not a cheap one. But I could afford it. With the money James paid me and no cause to spend it, I had more than I'd ever known before.

On Saturday evening we took a taxi ride across town. Rachel lived in Cloudesley Road then. A few hundred yards from the Angel. I travelled in high expectation. And James under sufferance.

Unlike now, many of the town houses in that part of the city had acquired a fashionably shabby quality. Some divided into two or three flats. And it was one of these Rachel shared with two other girls.

And once inside, the crush of people, the heat and the noise gave me a tremendous rush of exhilaration. I had never felt so alive.

James leant across to me. "Isn't this awful."

"I can't see Rachel," I said.

"We won't stay long, will we?" he asked.

"Just long enough to say hello," I lied.

I wanted to look for her. But James refused to move from the spot we found ourselves in. He guarded a can of beer close to his chest, against the endless press of people pushing past. But in time, the constant movement around us as we remained a fixed point brought her to us.

"I'm so glad you could come." She seemed genuinely pleased to see us. "I didn't think you would, after you left so early last time. I hope you'll stay a lot longer tonight. I'll be very disappointed if you don't."

I could see others looking at us. Wondering who we were. I struggled to think of anything to say. And James had fallen quite silent in her presence. But unlike me, he had no excuse. He was used to this sort of thing.

Yet remarkably, despite that she talked to us for several minutes. And I could sense it in the room, who *are* those two?

Eventually, she moved on of course. But promised to return. Sadly I watched her go. And as she did, the eyes of everyone in the room followed her. But I knew we had had far more of her time than we could have hoped for.

James said, "we've seen her now. Can we go?"

"Not yet, you heard what she said."

"She was just being polite." But he could see my disappointment. "OK, OK," he said. "We'll stay a bit longer."

Until the very end if I had my way. But I knew he was struggling. Another hour would be about as much as he could take. It seemed such a shame to go so early.

Not that I felt I belonged any more than he did. Far from it. But unlike him I enjoyed being there. To me it was very exotic. I was a traveller in a foreign land. Admiring the views. And enjoying the atmosphere. Whereas he had seen it all before.

Shortly after eleven he went to get our coats. I offered to wait behind, in the hope of seeing her one more time. When he didn't return, I went to look for him.

I saw him in the hallway. Talking to her. Or at least, listening politely. Had I gone for the coats, that would have been me. But as I approached, I could see he was saying goodbye. And I only got to thank her for the evening before we left.

A few minutes' walk in the still night air brought us to the busy junction at Highbury Corner. Where he hailed a cab.

He was very quiet on the journey home. Staring out of the window at the passing streets.

"I wonder if we'll ever see her again?" I said.

He seemed so pre-occupied I tried to lighten the mood. "Or were you arranging a secret meeting you didn't want me to know about?"

"Not exactly," he said. Still looking out the window. "She asked if I'd go with her to the premiere of some dreadful film."

"That's astonishing," I said. "I'm stunned. And very jealous."

"Then why don't you go instead."

"I'd love to," I said. "But she asked you. So you'll have to go."

I was jealous. But more than that I was pleased for him. Very pleased. But amazed. Then I said laughing, "although I can't imagine what she sees in you."

"No," he said, his mood unchanged. "Neither can I."

Next morning, we returned to Studlands. And went our separate ways, to meet up again at dinner.

During my week in town, I had had a lot of time to think. The Latham book in his library had inspired me. And I planned to produce a modern version of my own. To record the restoration of the house. That afternoon in preparation, I laid out all the photographic equipment for the first time.

At dinner I told him of my plans to photograph the house and gardens.

He said he thought it was an excellent idea.

Then I returned to our conversation of the night before.

"So, are you going with Rachel to that film premiere?"

"No," he said.

"Why not?"

"What's the point?"

"You have to go."

"I don't have to do anything," he said, slightly irritated.

"You'll regret it if you don't."

Then in a sudden flash of anger he said, "no I won't. And I don't see what it's got to do with you."

I'd never seen him angry before. And it was a shock to see in one normally so placid. I was taken aback.

"I just think she'd make you happy" I said. "I only want what's best for you. That's all."

"OK, OK," he said. "I'll go."

But he made it sound like he was doing me a favour. Now it was my turn to be irritated.

"Don't do it for me," I said. "I don't care if you go or not."

"Look, I've said I'll go." From the tone of his voice, it was clear that was his last word on the subject. Shortly after he pushed his plate away. He wished me goodnight and returned to his study. Leaving me to finish my meal alone.

But later, in my room that night I thought about it. I did care.

His quiet and introspective personality may have been well suited to writing. But it made him a solitary character.

He almost never went out. And on the rare occasions he did, it was with very little enthusiasm. In fact, none at all. And yet remarkably, despite that he had met someone. But left to himself the opportunity would just slip away. Quite possibly he had lost others like that in the past.

But this time I could help him. And I was determined to do whatever I could to make it happen for him. It was the least I could do. After all he had done for me.

While in town thoughts of restoring the roof statues had been much on my mind.

But of all the work benches to be found amongst the many outbuildings, none were big enough. I had plenty of suitable materials, however. So I resolved to build one myself.

And there was space enough for it in the old stable block. Just inside the wide double doors where the light was good. I tried to make it in the spirit of the fine old building it was in. Using similar rectangular section wood, I copied the type of joints and bracing in the beautiful vaulted timber roof above.

It took several days. And although I had never done anything like it before, when it was finished, I was pleased with my handiwork.

It shared the space with his cars. But to me then, they were nothing more than a row of shapeless dustsheets. A useful surface sometimes to lay out my tools. But mostly just an inconvenience to work around.

I brought a single statue in at a time to work on. I decided to add some colour to the figures. The better I thought to highlight the fine detailing. And enhance their character. Mixing paint from my stock, I worked on the basis the bolder the better. Later with more experience, I would have respected convention and left them unpainted. But in those days, I was untroubled by historical accuracy. Although I have since learned, in my ignorance I may have been honouring ancient tradition more than I realised.

Chapter Three

June 1989, An Unexpected Complication

As usual, there was nothing to do in his office at Cornwall Gardens.

I read a newspaper.

The doorbell rang. A sound I had never heard before.

No one ever called. And James would have let himself in.

I opened the door. To see Rachel, standing on the step.

She must have sensed my surprise.

"I was just passing."

"It's lovely to see you," I said.

"Please come in. I'm afraid James isn't here."

I feared she would leave at that point. But fortunately, she didn't.

I showed her into the lounge. I wished James was there.

And no doubt she felt the same I thought.

We exchanged small talk for a few moments. But it wasn't as easy as before.

Then she said, "actually I'm quite relieved he isn't here".

I didn't understand.

She looked at me. "You know James better than anyone."

"Do I?" I said. "He's not an easy person to know."

She smiled, slightly. And I realised for the first time since she arrived.

"At least I'm not the only one who thinks that."

Then she said, "I've already made a fool of myself coming here like this. So I might as well ask." She hesitated a moment. "The two of you living together."

I could see she was uncomfortable.

"What I'm trying to ask…"

I wanted to laugh. But I knew that would add to her discomfort.

"It's not like that," I said. "He doesn't have any friends. And I've got nowhere else to go. So we're stuck with each other."

"I'm very sorry to ask," she said. "It's none of my business."

I didn't want her to leave. So I tried to lighten the mood. "I understand James is going to a film premiere with you next week."

"Is he?" she said. "It's hard to tell."

"Yes, he told me."

She smiled, a rather sad smile. Then she said, "I don't think it's a good idea. It's not his sort of thing, is it?"

I tried to think of something positive to say.

"I get invites to these things all the time," she said. "And I never normally go. But when I saw him with the coats the other night, about to leave. I knew I'd never see him again. So I had to say something. And it was all I could think of. I'd meant to get back to you both all evening. But I was nervous. And kept putting it off."

Then she said, "he must meet so many interesting people. What chance could I possibly have. Hopefully neither of you have ever seen that silly programme."

I said I had.

She looked at the floor. "Then you'll know what I mean."

"I like it."

"Thank you," she said. "But you don't have to be polite."

"No, really I do." Although like everyone else, I only watched it because of her.

"Well, I'm surprised," she said. "But please tell me James has never seen it."

"He doesn't watch television."

"Thank goodness. I doubt he'd be as understanding as you." Then she shook her head. "Next week will be a disaster. I know it will."

"No," I said. "It will be a lovely evening. He's looking forward to it."

"Really?"

"Yes, he said so," I lied.

"You're so positive and encouraging," she said. "I was so nervous about coming here. Even on the way over, I didn't think I'd really do it. Now I'm very pleased I did. But I'm worried about being on my own with him. I don't think I'll be able to keep him interested."

I thought what a ridiculous idea.

"If I got you an invite would you come too? If you were there, he might not get so bored."

"I'd love to come."

"That's settled then," she said. "I'm beginning to think it might be alright after all." Then she said, "he is a very special person. I knew it the first time I saw him. He was very quiet. And looked out of place. Just like I always feel. I could see he didn't want to be there, any more than I did. And I thought if we could only meet somewhere else, in better circumstances. And I've been trying to find those circumstances ever since."

Then she said, "there's something sad about him. And I just want him to be happy".

"Meeting you is the best thing that could ever have happened to him," I said. "It's just what he needs."

"I'm so pleased you think that," she smiled.

"I only hope he realises how lucky he is," I said.

"I'm the lucky one. Meeting him. I guess it's the job." She shook her head. "The phone company have to change my telephone number every few weeks. It can be a lonely life. But I don't plan to do this much longer."

"No?" I said.

"I'd love to give it all up and do something else."

"Such as?"

"Live in the country, have a dog, start a family." She smiled. "That sort of thing."

I could have listened to her all day. James truly was the luckiest man. But he deserved it. He was a gentleman. And I was delighted for him. And for her.

"Please don't leave on my account," I said. "I don't have anything to do for the rest of the day."

"We could go for lunch," she said. "I know a nice little place not far from here."

We walked in the sunshine to a small and discrete Italian restaurant in Old Brompton Road.

She was totally relaxed now. And talked enthusiastically, just as she had before.

I asked her if she had read any of his books.

"No," she said hesitantly. "I've been carrying one around in my bag for a couple of weeks. But I don't think that counts. Presumably you've read them."

"No, not one," I said.

"Isn't that funny. We're the two people who care most about him. And we've never read any of his books". Then she said, "that's because we love him for who he is. Not just because he's a brilliant writer."

"Is he?" I asked.

"I've no idea," she laughed.

Of all the happy times I spent with her that summer, few remain more vivid in my mind than that. It was late afternoon by the time we left the restaurant. We shared a taxi back to Islington. Then I went on alone to South Kensington.

I returned to Studlands the following day. I had more or less abandoned work at the church hall. Only to waste my time in his ridiculous office at Cornwall Gardens. But hopefully he'd come to see how pointless it was.

And the sooner the better. For many were the rooms in that fine old house I was anxious to work in. And at that time, one in particular weighed heavily on my mind. Accessed through a pair of tall double doors, lit from dawn to dusk by a full height window. Overlooking a small secluded terrace with an empty pedestal.

The walls were lined from floor to ceiling with shelves of old classical records.

Several hundred at least. He said they were there when he moved in.

But the damp had got in. And I feared for the damage it would do. To them. And the grand old Bluthner piano that stood in the middle of the room. Fully six foot long, at least. With elegant square tapered legs and faded mahogany case.

Looking back, I suspect it was a collection of a quality to match even that of the books in his library. But with no means in the house to play them, they remained ever a mystery. And perhaps because of that, like the books and the statues in the garden they came to intrigue me. Unable to hear them, instead I examined the covers. And studied the sleeve notes.

Even now, years later some I can still recall. Walter's 1958 New York recording of Mahler's second Symphony. Fritz Reiner's Bartok at the Chicago Orchestra Hall. And Callas and Di Stefano's Tosca at La Scala in '53. And others too. Whose names occasionally overheard by chance come back to me.

At dinner he asked after my time in London.

Naturally Rachel's visit went unmentioned. But I did ask if he had called her.

"Not yet," he replied. Then he said, "It must be very boring for you out here in the country. It's my birthday next month. We could have a party if you like. Of course, it won't be as exciting for you as Rachel's."

But he was wrong. On both counts. Living at Studlands was the most fascinating and extraordinary experience I could imagine. And a party there would be just as exciting as Rachel's. Especially if she was there. Rachel at Studlands was a perfect combination.

"And you could invite some of your friends," he said.

"I'd love to ask Sarah."

"Whoever you want."

I would definitely invite Sarah. I wanted her to see Studlands. And I wanted her to see my work. She would be my only guest. I had no one else.

I had been putting off a return to the church hall. But I knew I couldn't do that forever. Now I had a reason to go back.

I could have just sent her an invite. Or called her. But it was too important for that. I had to ask her in person. To make sure she came.

I returned to the church hall on Monday morning.

At lunchtime I went to tell her about his birthday party.

"It's at his house near Oxford," I said. "It's a beautiful old place. I'd love you to see it. I think you'd like it very much. You could stay over if it's too far. There are plenty of spare rooms."

"No, I'm afraid I won't be able to go," she said. She didn't even look in her diary to check the date.

"Are you sure?"

She shook her head. "But thank you for asking."

I was very disappointed. Not just because she couldn't come. But the way she said it. She didn't even seem to consider it. I felt foolish.

It was clear she had no time for him. But that was only because she didn't know him. Which was precisely why she should come.

And besides, he deserved better than that. Not that he would have cared what she thought of him. But that wasn't the point. It was exactly the mistake I had made about him. And I didn't want her to make it too.

"It would be such a shame to miss it," I said. "It may be the only opportunity you'll get to see the place."

She was quite indifferent to it all.

Then I said, "he asked after you." I don't know why I said it. It wasn't true.

Maybe to make her feel a little better disposed towards him.

"I'm surprised he remembered me," she said.

I wasn't at all sure he did. I was the one who first mentioned her name. It was clear she was very busy. And I had obviously picked a bad time. In fact, it was the least friendly I could remember her. She was so business-like and pre-occupied there seemed nothing more to say.

I had arrived full of enthusiasm that morning. Now I just wanted to go back to Studlands. And forget all about the church hall. And about her.

I decided that was exactly what I would do. I'd leave at the end of the day. And never come back.

But as I worked that afternoon, I realised I was wrong. I had dropped her work for his. The church hall should have been finished weeks ago. But despite what she thought. It wasn't his fault. It was mine. He had always reminded me not to neglect her work.

I saw a lot of my old self in her attitude. And I understood that. Of course he wasn't going to change her life. Not the way he had mine or Rachel's. But someone as special as him might only come once in a lifetime. And it had been my great good fortune to meet him again. And I just wanted to share some of that good fortune with her. But so far, I hadn't done a very good job.

And I thought it would be good for him too. I was sure if he got to know her, he would value her as a friend as much as I did. I had no idea the last time they had seen each other. And I doubted either of them could remember.

So I resolved that afternoon to arrange, or if necessary engineer, a meeting between them before the summer was out. And if not at his party, then somewhere else.

Back at Studlands for the weekend, I returned to my work on the roof statues.

The early summer sun, rising ever higher now. Penetrated a little deeper into the old stables each day. And that morning, a glint of sunlight reflected on chrome caught my eye.

A dust sheet had been disturbed, partially exposing what lay beneath. Bright red and freshly polished, I was drawn to it. I pulled back the cover a little more. To reveal a teardrop roof, with twin rear windows. Tapering elegantly into a flat rear deck. Flanked on either side by rear wings rising gracefully to a crease line as sharp and true as a mason's rule. I had never seen anything like it. And it astonished me.

I lifted the cover of the one next to it. Then the next. Revealing more magnificent shapes and colours, textures and surfaces. Crafted in steel, aluminium, fibreglass and leather. Cast, machined, welded, turned and stitched. At that moment, illuminated in the first shafts of the morning's early light, they seemed as special as any of the other treasures in the house or the grounds beyond.

And I wanted to know more. But these were not subjects to be found in any bookcase there. At least none that I was aware of.

But no matter. Back in London the great bookshops of Gower Street, Charing Cross Road and Piccadilly were my library.

Returning to town on Monday, I took the opportunity to read everything I could about them. I learnt of their history, and about the great workshops and factories of Sant'Agata, Modena, Stuttgart and St Louis that created them.

The night of the film premiere arrived. James and Rachel were going to the screening. My invite was for the party afterwards.

A car arrived to collect him at six. He looked very smart in a dark suit and white shirt.

"You are still coming tonight?" he asked. With the air of someone expecting to be abandoned for the evening.

I assured him I was.

A couple of hours later my cab pulled up outside a smoked glass doorway in Jermyn Street. The crowd of photographers waiting outside, as much as discrete twin brass plaques either side of the entrance, indicated this to be the place. A doorman checked my invite and let me in.

I made my way down a wide dimly lit wood panelled stairway. And through the crowd towards a distant bar. I was beginning to get a taste for this.

I saw Rachel, her arm held up to catch my attention. But it would have been impossible to miss her. Tall and elegant in a black dress. Her long strawberry blonde hair almost golden under the lights. James was with her. At least he was still there. When I reached them, Rachel said, "thank you so much for coming". And not without a hint of relief in her voice I thought. "Let me get you a drink." She turned away to look for a waiter.

I asked James how it was going.

"Awful," he said. "People have been bothering us all night."

Rachel returned with a glass of wine for me. She leaned in close. "Thank goodness you're here," she said. "I don't know how much more of this he can take."

Just as she said that a photographer motioned with his hand for them to stand closer together. James waved him away. "For Christ's sake. Haven't they got anything better to do?" he said to me.

"Rachel's a big news story."

"Is she?" he said irritably. He still didn't understand who she was.

"And so is anyone with her."

"Are they?" He looked unamused. From anyone else that would have sounded ridiculous. But not from him. He really didn't know.

"So, you'd better get used to it," I said.

Less than an hour later Rachel took me aside. "I think James and I ought to go," she said. "I don't think he can last much longer." I said I would go with them. I was sorry to leave. But if we pushed him too far, there might be no more nights like this.

The next morning James accompanying her was in all the papers. Pictures appeared of them together on several front pages. Fortunately, he never read them. So knew nothing of this. And I thought it best not to tell him.

But his association with her made us all see him differently. And I include myself in that. In the company of anyone else that summer, he would have passed unnoticed. But not with her.

It was a dramatic return to public life for him. Disappearing for three years, to re-appear on the arm of the most eligible woman in London. It seemed proof of a charisma unappreciated before. But now so self-evident and compelling no one ever doubted it after that.

If he wanted to quietly keep himself to himself, he couldn't have gone about it in a worse way. From then on, he became much more than just a writer. No longer familiar only to those who read his books. People who had never heard of him before knew him now.

And for her too, their association was a cause for re-evaluation. For he was not an obvious choice. And it hinted at a depth to her not previously imagined. Proof she was more than just a pretty face.

After that night the work in his office suddenly increased. Large quantities of mail arrived every day. And instead of junk mail and bills, there were requests for interviews, signed photographs and personal appearances. All of which of course he ignored.

Looking back now I can see after that his life, what little remained of it, was never the same again. And neither was hers. But typical of him, it was some time before he became aware of it. But eventually even he could not fail to notice.

One evening at dinner a few weeks later he said to me, "it's rather extraordinary. I seem to have become quite…" He searched for the right word, "… fashionable".

"Very fashionable," I said. "And all because of Rachel."

"All?" He said a little disappointed.

"Well mostly because of her."

"Yes, I suppose so," he said. "Sales are up for all my old books, even the last one."

"And your publisher keeps calling."

"I thought they would never speak to me again," he smiled. "Who would've thought it three years ago."

But I wasn't being fair to him. And I knew it. That summer he was the most talked about and written about man in the country. Whose modest and unassuming manner, despite the huge attention paid to him, never failed to charm all who met him.

His new book, still barely half-written was already a guaranteed success on a scale he had never known before. He truly was a man whose time had come.

And maybe I was worried the truth might spoil him. But that was never going to happen. He was never that interested. Briefly amused perhaps. But nothing more than that. He never sought the attention now focused upon him. All he wanted was to be left alone to write and to live his life quietly and contently at Studlands. Public enthusiasm or indifference, and he had known them both, were all the same to him.

But there was one event that promised to disturb the tranquillity at Studlands that summer. And in ways none of us could have imagined.

His birthday party was only three weeks away. He had left all the planning to me. And I intended it to be a very special night.

And I knew he was only doing it for me. It certainly wasn't for his benefit.

I had some stylish invites made. With gold embossed lettering printed on thick card.

Looking back now, I'm sure he hated them. But he never said. He asked for twenty for himself. "There's a few people I suppose I ought to invite," he told me.

The rest I gave to Rachel. Except one.

The one I sent to Sarah. I still hoped she might come.

When he had left three years before, the house was shut up. Outside the seasons changed. But inside it was always winter. Always night. The air was silent and tomb-like. Disturbed only occasionally by the footsteps of Mrs Davies. And she rarely ventured beyond the main entrance hall.

But now the shutters had been folded. And the light streamed in. Penetrating into the deepest recesses of the house.

Even in the short time since my first visit, I had seen the life return to it. His birthday party was to be at least as much a celebration of Studlands itself. And I wanted to create a night to match any in its history.

To me it was a special place. An historic building. And a glorious testament to outstanding architectural and artistic style. Created in an age of confidence and unshakeable optimism. But one that had fallen since on harder times.

Much of its extravagant detail and character had been stripped out. Or covered up. But at least the house had survived. Where so many had been lost.

And now after years of uncertainty, its future was as bright as James'. And soon to be restored to its former glory. For I had the time. And he had the money.

In the weeks that followed, I tidied the gardens close to the house. And installed several of the roof statues.

The Grand Ballroom of course, would not be ready. I had barely started in there. But maybe by Christmas. When hopefully he could be persuaded to do it all again.

Rachel was a frequent visitor to Studlands. Sometimes just for a day or two. Sometimes longer.

She often came to help me while James worked in his study. One afternoon painting a roof statue she said, "I'm hoping he might propose to me at the party".

She smiled shyly. "You probably think it's too soon. But it's not for me. I've always known. From the first moment we met." Then she said, "well I can dream, can't I?"

"It would be the best thing that could ever happen to him," I said. And I meant it.

She reached out and squeezed my hand. "And you'll meet someone. Then all four of us can live here together."

The first I knew of it was a headline on a news stand:

Best Selling Author Dies in Road Accident.

Photographs of the two of them appeared on the front page of every newspaper. Most describing them as soon to be married. Clearly unaware they had not seen or spoken to each other for months by then.

And it had been several months too since my last contact with him.

I saw a picture on the news that night. A black Porsche 930. The front half shattered beyond recognition. It must have been a massive impact. Local press reports attributed it to a tired driver. And a notorious stretch of road. Deep in the Aosta Valley.

I never read any details of the crash. I couldn't bring myself to.

But perhaps I should have.

Maybe it would have helped me come to terms with it better. And more particularly, to the part I played in it. Which haunts me still. To this day.

Yet despite all that had happened, I don't want to think it was in his mind to end it all. But dwelling on the hopeless future he saw ahead, I know he would have been at his lowest ebb.

When he quit the country three years earlier, he still had hope.

Hope that even in his absence, circumstances might yet bring her back to him.

But as the years passed, he came to believe that was not going to happen.

So he resolved to return. To write the book that had cast a shadow over his career. And to reclaim the woman who had cast a shadow over his life.

He spent the first few weeks in an apartment he had rented in South Kensington.

Drawn to his muse, it was not the first time he had driven the three or four miles across town to her house in Clapham. But never with the intention of trying to contact her. He always knew it would be much more difficult than that.

Then one day he saw someone. Someone he recognised from years before. Unloading dustsheets and tins of paint from an old van outside her house.

This was it. This was the opportunity he sought. And in a way he could never have anticipated. Now all he had to do was contrive a chance meeting in the street.

And then, as he might develop the plot of one of his novels. Set about creating the circumstances and manipulating the characters to achieve the denouement he sought.

But Rachel, and later Julie were complications he never allowed for. But all that lay in the future then.

And so it was, his influence rippled out across the water towards her. In the early days when it was just the two of us, it was easy to bend me to his will. But as the weeks passed, and spring turned to summer, he began to lose control of events. And by late summer he found himself instead, a hostage to fortune.

But despite all that, it could still have worked out for him. If perhaps not in the way he had planned. But by then he had come to trust someone else more than himself. Someone who never understood the powerful forces at work that summer. At least not until it was too late.

Something in the past his solitary nature would never have allowed. And so, when the moment finally came. As he always believed it would. His confidence was broken. And he had despaired of it.

I did return to Studlands one more time. I received word from Julie's solicitor I could go back to collect any property I had left behind. There was nothing. But I needed to see the house again. One more time.

It was a long and desolate drive. The sight of the distant spire at Church Hanborough, that always signified the last few miles to Studlands, held no comfort for me now.

Turning off the old familiar road onto the long drive, it was clear how much the winter had closed its grip on the place. The house was visible for some distance through the bare trees. Cold and lifeless now, against a low grey sky. I didn't know what Julie planned to do with it. I guessed it was hers now. I doubted she'd have any interest in it.

Inside everywhere was evidence of decay. Most of the furniture had gone. A few papers lay scattered across the floor. The house had become an empty shell.

I walked from room to room. My footsteps echoing on the bare floorboards. The slow decline I thought I detected when I had left three months before, was as nothing to the desolation I saw now.

To see it like this was the final proof he was gone. Until then his loss had had an abstract quality. As if it were some sort of misunderstanding. Or a mistake soon to be corrected. But now confronted with this. I could see it was all over. That there would be no thaw for him in the spring. No return to complete unfinished work. And I would never see him again.

Yet, as the days turned to weeks. I found myself retreating into a deeper and less rational part of my mind. A part where there lingered still a belief that perhaps he hadn't died that night.

Haunted in waking hours and fitful sleep by the thought he might still be out there somewhere. Laying in the snow, unconscious. And if I could only find him. I could bring him home to Studlands.

But as time passed. And his loss receded further into the distance, another thought took hold. Though badly injured, he had survived the crash. And made his way home. But only partially recovered, didn't remember me. And if we met, he wouldn't know who I was. For months after I might see a distant figure on the street. Or someone turning a corner out of sight. Of course I knew it couldn't be him.

But still I had to follow them. To be absolutely certain.

It was the night before James's party. And preparations were almost complete. A freshly erected marquee stood on the terrace. And only a few minor jobs remained.

Engineers had been working all day to set up the lighting and sound systems. The final checks were nearly complete. And a trial run was set for 10pm. Rachel and I went to watch. James returned to his study.

It was nearly dark, but still warm. A few minutes later to the quiet hum of a generator somewhere out of sight, the final connections were made. And Studlands was illuminated.

It was a breath-taking sight. The house a towering beacon of light in the darkness. Visible across the fields for miles around. Like a great ocean liner out at sea.

The effect was exactly as I had hoped. Spotlights positioned around the gardens highlighted the architectural features of the façade. Dramatically framing the mortar joints and window reveals in deep shadow, against the pure white Portland stone. The brilliant reds, blues and gold of the roof statues stood out bold and bright in the night sky.

And the sight of Rachel's face, lit by the floodlight's dazzling glow. And the reflection of the house in her eyes, recalled to mind an earlier conversation.

When she spoke of her hopes he might propose at the party, I couldn't see it. I felt it was too soon for him.

And maybe it was just the euphoria of the moment. But now I thought perhaps he might. There seemed a sense in the air that night, that something significant was about to happen. And I say that not just because of what I know now.

It was after midnight when I finally went to bed. It had been a beautiful warm and sunny day. And the forecast was for the same tomorrow. All week I meant to call Sarah one last time to ask her to come. I was sure it was going to be one of the greatest nights in the history of the house. And I wanted to share it with her.

But with all the preparations I never did. And now it was too late. Perhaps I might have made more of an effort, if I'd thought it would have made any difference.

The first guests began to arrive just after seven. Cars soon filled the wide space in front of the house. And the long gravel drive that led to the road outside. We had sent less than fifty invites. But it seemed much more.

By eight the terrace was full of people. With still more arriving. As the sun finally set, the spotlights came on. And the brilliance of the house filled the sky.

I took a few moments to sit quietly on my own. No matter how many glorious nights lay ahead. Few surely would ever surpass this. And I wanted to preserve the memory of it.

Looking out across the gardens, I saw Rachel in the half-light and shadow beyond the spotlights. She was walking barefoot and alone across the lawn. Holding her shoes in one hand and treading so lightly she barely seemed to bend a blade of grass. I wanted to call her name. But so serene did she seem. Newly in love and for the first time, I didn't for fear of breaking the spell. Instead, I stayed silent. And watched her until she skipped up the stone steps and re-joined the party.

Even James seemed drawn into the spirit of the evening. Playing the good host to a degree I didn't know he could. For tonight he seemed to make an effort to speak to every guest. And not to miss anyone. Constantly appearing and disappearing amongst groups of people. Sometimes for just a few moments. Sometimes longer.

It must have been a little after ten when I learnt Sarah had come after all. I saw her husband in the marquee.

When I asked, he told me she was somewhere nearby. The sudden realisation she was there, and the effect of the wine made me feel very light-headed.

I saw Rachel and told her there was someone I wanted her to meet. But I never did find her. I must have been more drunk than I thought. It had been quite late when I saw Ian. And now it was very late. The crush of people from earlier in the evening had thinned.

I returned to the marquee. It was quieter now where before it had been packed. I was re-filling my glass when I heard James say my name.

I turned to see him with a young woman.

"This is my sister Julie," he said. Until that moment I didn't even know he had a sister. It was yet another reminder of how little I really knew him. But I recognised her immediately. I could see the same pleasant features of his face in hers. Only softer and more rounded. And the colour of her hair was just the same. She smiled shyly and shook my hand. I guessed her to be a few years younger than him.

And there was in her manner too, a similar reserve. He had always seemed so alone and unlike anyone else, it felt extraordinary there could be another like him. Another who might think like him. And feel things the way he did.

But typical of him that night it was only a moment or two before he was gone. Taking her with him.

A couple of hours or so later I saw him again. Alone this time. He was sitting quietly in the now almost deserted marquee. He had a bottle of beer in his hand. And his energy from earlier in the evening was spent. I sat down next to him. It was very late. And we were both very tired.

"Sarah was here earlier," I said. "Did you see her?"

"Yes," he said.

"I guess she went home hours ago?"

"I guess so," he said.

I was delighted she had come. But disappointed not to have seen her myself. It seemed ironic. She was my guest. Yet he saw her. And I didn't. But at least they had met. Now she had come to Studlands once, she could come again. And as far as I was concerned the sooner the better. I was more determined than ever for them to get to know each other. Things were working out much better than I had hoped.

We walked back to the house in the faint glow of first

light. Through a thin film of mist that hung suspended an inch or two above the ground.

It had been quite a night.

And things would never be the same again.

I got up late on Sunday and did very little. On Monday the workmen took down the marquee. And dismantled the light and sound systems.

Seeing Ian reminded me how much I had neglected the church hall in recent weeks. But much more than that, I wanted to know what Sarah thought of Studlands. And Rachel. So I resolved to return to London the next day.

I saw her car when I arrived. But so long had I been away, I thought it best to put in a good morning's work first. My brushes, dustsheets and tins of paint were still where I had left them weeks before. At lunchtime I walked across to the parish office.

"I hear you were there on Saturday night," I said.

She said she was. But seemed as busy and pre-occupied as ever.

"I'm sorry I missed you," I said. "I looked for you". She nodded her head and carried on with her work. "What did you think of Rachel? Isn't she lovely?"

"I didn't see her."

"That's such a shame. I so wanted to introduce you. I wish I'd known you were going."

"Well, it was a last-minute thing. We didn't think we could, but…"

Her manner was typically brusque. Perhaps more even than usual. It made me feel awkward.

All I wanted to do was talk about James and the party. But I guess all she wanted was for the church hall to be finished. I was already weeks behind the date I had given her father. My long absences were coming between us. I went back to work determined to make good progress. I didn't leave until after seven. And my van was the only one in the car park when I left.

That night James called from Studlands. It was good to hear his voice. And I wished I was there. He asked if I was coming back on Friday.

I told him I was. "That's a great relief," he said. "Julie's coming up for the weekend."

I left for Studlands on Friday afternoon. I worked hard all week. And hadn't seen Sarah since Monday. I hoped my good progress had not gone unnoticed.

"Thank God you've arrived," he said when he saw me. "Rachel's not here yet. I hope she's not late."

It was not like him to be concerned about such things.

"I'm always nervous when I have to meet Julie," he said. "Fortunately, it doesn't happen very often. I wish she wasn't coming."

Then he said, "I would never have invited her to the party if I'd thought she'd actually come. She doesn't approve of me."

"I'm sure she does."

"No," he said. "Not at all. She thinks I should get a proper job. Although she may have a point there."

He opened a bottle of wine. "Maybe this will help. But I doubt it."

"So why is she coming?"

"I don't know," he said. Pouring himself a glass. "She's never bothered before."

"What does she do?" I asked. Feeling a lot less relaxed now about the evening ahead.

"She's an accountant." He poured another glass of wine.

"You'll probably need one of these too." He handed it to me. "I've hardly seen her in the last ten years. She's very serious."

Then he added, "she used to draw and paint in her room for hours when she was young. She was very good. But she gave all that up a long time ago. Probably enjoyed it too much."

He finished his wine and re-filled the glass. We heard a car arrive. He checked his watch. "It's too early for Julie. It must be Rachel."

I let her in while James went to check on Mrs Davies in the kitchen.

An hour or so later Julie arrived. James met her in the entrance hall. Rachel and I waited in the lounge.

Certainly, seeing the two of them together there seemed little warmth or connection for a brother and sister. And their similarity in looks and speech only emphasised still further the distance between them.

Rachel poured us all a drink.

James' comments earlier hardly made me feel comfortable in her presence. Only Rachel amongst us tried to make conversation. After about half an hour we went through to the dining room. In time, thanks to the wine the atmosphere became a little lighter and more relaxed.

I had selected a '63 Romanée-Saint-Vivant for its taste of summer fruits. Fortunately, deep red and smooth in texture, it had aged well. And my confidence in it was not misplaced. But it was not one of the more enjoyable evenings at Studlands. Although James said later he thought it went better than he expected.

After the meal we briefly walked out onto the terrace. It was a clear evening. And we admired the view over the gardens and the countryside beyond. Julie said she was tired. James walked her to her room. Leaving Rachel and I alone.

"She seems very nice," she said.

"I suppose so," I replied. I doubted she thought much of Rachel.

Then she said, "I think James could have made more of an effort though."

"Do you know how long she's here for?" I asked.

"For the weekend. James has asked me to stay while she's here."

The next evening there was only three of us at dinner. James sent word he would join us later. But never did. I had spent the day working in a distant corner of the grounds.

It was Mrs Davies' night off. Rachel cooked. Julie and I helped in the kitchen.

We worked with what we found in the cupboards, fresh leaves of rocket and basil. Green and black olives, mozzarella and tomato. And from the cellar a couple of bottles of '66 Mirafiore Barolo.

They told me they had played tennis on the old courts. And walked out to the temple. Despite what James said,

Julie seemed easy to get along with. I didn't think she was as difficult as he made out. Maybe she felt more relaxed without him.

The following morning, I saw Julie's bags in the hall. Packed and ready to go. I found James in the lounge reading a book. I guess now she was leaving, he felt it was safe to come out of his study.

"Has Rachel gone?" I asked.

"Yes," he said from behind his book. "She said to say goodbye."

Then he added, "Julie's taxi will be here in a few minutes." With I thought, a hint of relief in his voice.

We were alone for the first time since the weekend before.

There had been no word of any engagement. And it was not my business. But I was worried he might never seize the moment. There were plenty of others, only too willing to take his place. Then what would become of him? I feared that day. I couldn't bear him to lose her. More even than that, I couldn't bear to lose her myself.

"You and Rachel," I said.

"Yes?" he replied. Without looking up.

"Have you thought about the future?"

"How do you mean?"

"Together."

"No," he said. "There's no future for us."

"Why not?" I said suddenly shaken.

From outside, the noise of car doors slamming. And the sound of footsteps in the hall. Julie opened the door to say goodbye. I was too rooted in the moment to look up. James lowered his book to say goodbye. After she had gone, I said it again. "Why not?"

He put his book down. And got up from the chair. He walked to the window.

I asked a third time. "Why not?"

He stood with his back to me. Looking out over the garden.

Then he said, "it's Sarah. It's always been Sarah."

For a second, I was stunned into silence.

"I don't expect you to understand," he said. "But we will be together."

"She's married, for Christ's sake."

"It's not a marriage. It's a lie." There was a sudden edge to his voice.

"If it was a real marriage, you and I wouldn't be here now. Having this conversation."

"It will never happen," I said.

He turned to look at me. "How do you know? What has she said to you?"

"Nothing."

"What has she said?" he persisted.

"She's never mentioned you."

"I don't believe it," he said. Becoming agitated in a way I'd never seen before.

"She must have said something. You see her all the time. She knows you're working here. She must have."

He was staring at me. "Tell me what she said." He raised his voice and seemed barely able to control himself. "Tell me! Tell me!"

"So that's why I'm here. To be your spy. I thought I was your friend. But you've just used me."

"No, no that's not true," he said. Suddenly losing his anger. "You're the one good thing to have come out of this awful business. I would never do anything to risk our friendship."

"So that's why you got me to invite her to your party."

"I never asked you to."

"You put me up to it."

"No, no," he protested.

"What did you think would happen?"

"I don't know. I just wanted to see her again. To have a few minutes alone with her."

"And did you?"

He shook his head. "No, Ian was there."

He was silent for a moment.

Then he said, "she warned me. Three years ago. She told me they'll try to take me away from you. And you mustn't let them. She made me promise. But I didn't understand."

He took a small photograph from his wallet and handed it to me.

"That was on my birthday, three years ago."

It was taken in a restaurant. He was sitting at a table with a crowd of others. Sarah was behind him. Her arms around his shoulders, looking into the camera.

But it was hard to believe it was her. I had never seen her look so happy. I'd never seen such life in her eyes.

"That's a beautiful picture," I said quietly, handing it back to him.

"A fortnight later she was gone." He put the picture back in his wallet. "I went away for a few days. When I got back…" He slowly shook his head.

"It was as if she'd never been here. I tried to contact her."

He turned back to the window and looked out over the garden again.

"But she wouldn't speak to me."

He fell silent again for a moment. Then he said, "I tried to continue writing. But I couldn't. I put all my papers in a drawer. Shut the house up and left. I thought it was all over. My career. My life. Everything.

But now I've come back. To put things right while I still can. It's the only thing that's kept me going. It's brought me back from the brink."

That night I sat on the balcony of my room. It was another warm clear evening. But I felt nothing. I was in shock.

After several hours turning it over in my mind, I finally fell into a troubled and fitful sleep.

I awoke early next morning. And left for the church hall.

I had no plan. And no idea what to say to her. Or even why I was going.

All I knew was I cared too much to stand by and do nothing. I did very little work all morning. At lunchtime I went over to the parish office.

She must have sensed my unease.

Before I even spoke she said, "I'll come and see you".

A few minutes later she came and stood in the doorway where I was working.

"I take it you know," she said.

"Yes."

"I should have told you. I knew it was just a matter of time. But I couldn't face it. That's why I avoided you the first week you started."

"Did you?"

"Wasn't it obvious? But I knew I couldn't do that forever."

She was silent for a moment.

Then she said, "it's the thing I dreaded all these years. That one day he might try to come back for me. So, when you said you'd met him." She shook her head. "But I realise now that's silly. I wasn't thinking straight. Of course that's not why he's come back. I'm sure he hasn't thought of me in years. Thank God."

She brushed the hair from across her face.

"What I did to Ian was unforgivable. And I could never leave him. Fortunately, he doesn't know the details. We've never discussed it. And we never will."

She looked at the floor. "So, going to his party was the last thing I wanted to do. But I knew how important it was to you. And I didn't want to let you down."

"I had no idea," I said. "I'm so sorry. I'll never mention his name again."

Chapter Four

July 1989, Hostage to Fortune

It was clear. I had to return to Studlands that night. He had to understand the reality. And he had to understand it now. Once and for all.

But I was nervous. He had reacted very emotionally. Revealing a side to him I had never seen before. And I didn't want to see it again. I feared for his mental state.

We met at dinner that evening. He seemed relaxed and pleased to see me. Like nothing had happened. When Mrs Davies left the room I said, "I went to see Sarah today."

"Oh yes?" he replied. As if I had raised a subject of only mild and passing interest.

"You know I only want what's best for you."

"Yes, of course," he said, continuing with his meal.

I had to make it plain to him. This was too important for any misunderstanding. "There's no future for you and Sarah. She told me herself today. You have to put it behind you."

"And it's as simple as that?" he said calmly.

"I know this is very hard for you to accept. And I wish there was an easier way to say it. But you and Sarah will never be together. And there's nothing you or anyone else can do to change that."

Until then his attention had been politely shared between his meal and listening to me. Now he carefully put down his knife and fork and looked at me.

"So I should just forget all about it?" His manner remained personable. But measured. Quite unnervingly so, given how strongly I knew he felt.

"Yes," I said.

"I don't expect you to understand. It's taken me a long time to make sense of it myself. But as my friend, I hoped you might be a little more supportive."

"No, I do understand," I said. "It's very simple. It's over. It finished years ago. Rachel's the future. Not this ridiculous fantasy with Sarah."

"That's exactly what it's not," he said calmly. He picked up is knife and fork and returned to his meal. I had barely touched mine.

"There are things you don't know," he said. "Just because it's not on the page, doesn't mean it's not in the book."

He seemed alarmingly in control of himself. Unlike the day before.

"This is complete madness," I said. "You're not listening to me at all."

I slammed my hand down on the table.

"I can't take any more of this," I said. And got up from the table.

"Wait," I heard him call out as I left the room.

But I knew I had nowhere to go. And he knew it too. Returning to Cornwall Gardens was all I could do.

In the morning before I left, I found a hand-written note under my door.

My dear Robert, I'm very sorry about tonight. Your friendship means everything to me. And there will always be a place for you here. I hope to see you at dinner tomorrow night, James.

Fortunately, it was still early. And I knew he wouldn't be up. But rather than Cornwall Gardens, I went to the church hall instead.

In the past I had lost myself in my work. At least for a few hours. But not this time.

I hadn't been working long when Sarah came to see me. She must have seen my van outside.

"Hello," I said. "How are you?"

"OK," she replied.

She sat quietly on a chair while I worked. We remained like that for some time. Each alone with our thoughts. Until she spoke.

"You know I said I didn't want to go to his party."

"Yes."

"That wasn't true. When you told me you were working there, it brought back so much. Things I hadn't thought about in years. Like the gardens. And the places I used to walk. That's why I went. Just to see Studlands again. One last time."

She fell quiet for several minutes. Then she said, "it was years ago. We've both moved on. And put it behind us. But I wish I'd had the opportunity to explain. When it ended we never talked."

"I wouldn't worry about it," I said. "He's very happy with Rachel."

"I'm pleased to hear that," she said. "They say she's a lovely girl."

"She is."

"Well, if you think so, then it must be true. And I'm delighted for him. He deserves to be happy."

Then she said she ought to get back to work. I carried on. But achieved very little. I left in the middle of the afternoon.

When the phone rang at Cornwall Gardens that evening, I guessed it to be him.

But it wasn't. It was Julie.

She asked if I'd like to meet up. Caught unprepared, I couldn't think of an excuse quickly enough.

I returned at the church hall the next day. But I knew I couldn't stay away from Studlands much longer. For fear of what might become of him, left alone with his thoughts. And but for Julie, I would have returned that afternoon.

Instead, it would be my first evening alone in the company of anyone else for a very long time. And it was not by choice.

I don't know why she wanted to meet. For news of James presumably. He was the only common ground between us. And we didn't stray far from it all evening.

She knew nothing of recent events of course. And naturally I didn't speak of them.

But despite what he said, she was pleasant company. And easy to talk to. Away from James she did seem more relaxed. And surprisingly, perhaps because the reality was less daunting than the expectation, I quite enjoyed our evening. It made for a brief and welcome distraction. It helped too that their similarity in speech and looks, created a faint illusion in my mind we were distant acquaintances. Rather than the complete strangers we actually were.

I returned to Studlands the next morning. It was a beautiful sunny drive down. But I felt a deep sense of unease. Nothing had been resolved between us. Storm clouds were gathering darkly over a future that had seemed so bright just days before.

Yet those few hours with Julie had felt like a break in that cloud. And I thought about calling her after the weekend. I had asked James to go with me to a photographic exhibition at the Hayward Gallery. But he was sure to have forgotten. And at that moment anyone's company seemed preferable to his. Even Julie's. In fact, especially Julie's.

There was no sign of him when I arrived. And I was relieved. I wasn't looking forward to seeing him.

I was reading a newspaper by the pool when we met a couple of hours later.

But the encounter was not as I expected.

From the start he was at his most conciliatory.

"I'm very sorry about the other night," he said. "When you left I thought you'd gone for good. I was so worried. I never meant to upset you. I never want us to fall out."

He pulled up a chair and sat down beside me.

"I thought about what you said. You're right. It's like a sort of madness. I can see that now. I've got to look to the future. And it's here with you. And Rachel. Thanks to you I've laid a ghost to rest. One that's haunted me for years. You are the best friend anyone could ever have. You've saved me."

Then he said, "I thought it might be a good idea to get away for a few weeks. Would you come to Italy with me and Rachel?"

I told him I would like to. Very much.

"She's coming up this afternoon. We could all go out for a meal tonight."

I was delighted. But even then, as much as I hoped. I doubted it could be that simple. But with my spirits lifted, I resolved to invite Julie to the photographic exhibition.

I asked if he had her phone number.

"Yes, somewhere", he said. "Why do you ask?"

"I want to call her."

"Do you?"

"Do you mind?"

"No, not at all. I just can't imagine why you'd want to."

Having resumed work at the church hall, I felt I had to carry on. But working there was not good for him. Or for her. So I resolved to go back for a single week. Finish what I could. And never return.

Early on Monday I started. And inspired by the prospect of my last few days there, I worked with an enthusiasm I hadn't known in weeks.

But only for a couple of hours. Until Sarah came to see me.

She sat on a dust sheet a few yards away while I worked.

I had almost forgotten she was there when she spoke.

"Has he ever said anything about me?"

"No" I replied. "Nothing at all."

"I'm sorry to ask. But I've never talked about this to anyone before."

"Please don't apologise," I said. Without looking up. I had a lot to do.

It was a minute or two before she spoke again.

"When I was young, dad used to say how special it would be if I was married in his church. I know he was disappointed I never shared his faith. So I grew up believing that was the one thing I could do to make him proud of me."

I said nothing. I hadn't the time to stop and talk. What didn't get done this week wouldn't get done at all.

"Ian and I were far too young. And I hadn't really known him that long. But by the time I came to my senses, the announcement was in the parish magazine. I told Dad we had to stop it. He said it was just nerves. Lots of couples feel that way.

But the truth is I was the vicar's daughter. Getting married in his church. To call it off would have been unthinkable."

I was sorry for her. But I had to get on.

She continued. "James and I had always been close at school. I used to joke one day I'd marry him. And I think we both thought it would happen. When I married Ian, it broke his heart. And mine too."

She fell silent. Several minutes passed before she spoke again.

"I saw a poster on the underground. He was doing a book signing in town.

I said to myself I'd go and stand somewhere out of sight. Just to see him. That's all. He'd never know I'd been there. I didn't think I'd actually do it. It was just something to daydream about.

She was starting to irritate me now. I wished she would leave.

"But I did go. There was a large crowd at first. An hour later though, we were almost alone. He asked how I was. And I told him. I told him everything.

He had just bought Studlands. We moved in together. I thought I'd stay forever. They were the happiest days of my life.

But it had a devastating effect at home. Dad said marriage was a contract with God. Divorce Ian and you divorce God. Of course, what he meant was divorce Ian and you divorce me."

She fell quiet again. I hoped she had finished. I waited for the sound of her footsteps down the hall. But instead, the silence behind me betrayed her presence.

Finally, she spoke again. "Then Ian tried to kill himself."

I turned to see her looking out of the window. Her gaze lost in the distance.

"I sat all night by his hospital bed. He was unconscious. With a tube down his throat. Connected-up to all sorts of machines. It was a terrible sight. I'll never forget it."

I put down my paint brush. And sat on the dust sheet beside her. I put my arm around her. The sound of traffic outside carried through the open window. But she didn't hear it.

"Then as the hours passed," she said. "I began to feel this tremendous anger towards him. Not because he'd tried to kill himself. But because he'd failed. I couldn't stop thinking if he was lying in his grave, instead of that hospital bed. I'd be free. Free to be with James."

She shook her head. "And that really frightened me. What sort of person had I become? The next day dad drove me back to Studlands. James was away. He helped me pack. And leave behind the wonderful new life I had just begun. I didn't even write him a note. I couldn't. It was all too much.

Instead in the weeks and months that followed, I convinced myself James had died that night. It was the only way I could carry on. So when you said you'd met him." She looked at me. "It was like you'd seen a ghost."

She fell silent again.

Then she said, "none of this will ever get back to him, will it?"

"Not a word of it. I promise you."

"I hoped if I gave up James, maybe in return God might let me be happy with Ian. But I don't think He does deals like that. Dad was delighted though.

I went to his service the first Sunday after Ian came out of hospital. Just before we went in, he said he always knew I'd come back. As if everything was OK now."

A minute or two passed before she spoke again.

"You know you said none of this will get back to James."

"Nothing at all. I assure you."

"Well, maybe I wish it would. So he might understand. And perhaps forgive me."

"But what's the point?" I said. "It's all in the past."

"You're right. I'm sure he's forgotten all about it."

She wiped a tear from the corner of her eye.

Then she said, "I know I've been a very bad person. And I've done a terrible thing. But even bad people can do good things, can't they? And maybe one day make up for what they've done. That's why I spend so much time working in the charity shop and helping out at the old people's home."

It was a huge relief to get back to Cornwall Gardens that evening.

It had been an awful day.

And I knew I couldn't abandon her and the church hall now as I had planned. I'd have to finish it. And there was another couple of weeks' work at least. Probably more.

But I had to get away as soon as possible. My presence there wasn't just bad for them. It was bad for me too.

An hour or so later, James rang from Studlands. Something he very rarely did. It revived my spirits to hear his voice.

He asked how I was. And made uncharacteristic small talk about Rachel's birthday party in a few weeks. Then he said, "I understand you're going to an art gallery with Julie tomorrow night."

"It's a photographic exhibition," I corrected him. "Do I need your approval?"

He was silent for a moment. Then he said, "no, of course not. I hope you have a nice time." Then he enquired if I was coming up at the weekend.

After that I watched TV for another hour or so, then went to bed. Despite what he thought of her, I enjoyed Julie's company. And looked forward to seeing her again.

My route to the Hayward Gallery took me through the piazza at Covent Garden. On a warm summer's evening, I stood on Waterloo Bridge. Watching the sunlight reflecting on the surface of the water.

But I had felt a sense of unease all day. Out here, in the real world I barely knew her. Any familiarity I felt was just an illusion. Created by her similarity to him. And she had no such illusions of me. I wished I was going with James. But it was too late now.

Looking back on that evening, I recall feeling out of place. In the gallery. And with her. I hoped it didn't show.

This time the subject of James barely came up. But resting a moment on a bench beneath Man Ray's *Glass Tears*, she briefly spoke of him.

"Now he's back," she said. "I've promised myself we'll get on better. His party the other week was the first time I'd seen him in years.

But this summer it's my ambition to bring us closer together. Neither of us are the easiest of people. And until recently I wouldn't have bothered. But I don't want it to be like that anymore. It's something that's become very important to me."

A couple of hours later, under the art nouveau glazed brick arches of Covent Garden underground station, we parted. She seemed to have enjoyed the evening. And my confidence was beginning to return.

I'm not sure when the thought first occurred to me, that she could be more than just a friend. Maybe it was that night at the gallery. Possibly before. Perhaps the very first moment I saw her. Given the extraordinary way his life and mine had been drawn together that summer, it didn't seem so ridiculous.

I returned to the church hall on Monday. Spurred on by the thought that five more good days would set me free. I didn't see Sarah all week. I told myself I couldn't spare the time.

I finished late on Thursday. But my work was almost done. And I knew when I packed up the next day, it wouldn't be just for the weekend. But forever.

I had been thankful for the work when I started. And the opportunity it offered to get away from Studlands. But now it was a huge relief to be done with it, so I could return there. My time at the Church Hall had not been happy.

I did a couple of hours in the morning to finish up. Then made good my escape. In my haste I never said goodbye to Sarah. And I left a box of tools. But no matter. My days of doing that sort of work were over. And I was never coming back.

I took the Westway out of town. The city streets gave way to open fields. And the sun rose high overhead in a cloudless sky. It was a trip I had made many times. But one I never tired of. Indeed, it always revived me. No matter how I felt. And never more so than that day.

I had few regrets for not speaking to Sarah before I left. And by the time I saw the spire at Church Hanborough, I felt a huge sense of relief at the growing distance between us.

I was surprised to see Julie's car when I arrived. Parked next to Rachel's red Lancia. Surprised and pleased.

As usual there was no sign of James.

I went up to my room. Julie had taken one for herself in the same part of the house. Her door was open. I knocked. And heard her say come in.

She was working on a drawing of Studlands in a large art pad. Propped up on the dressing table. A couple of small black & white photographs of the house were pressed into the mirror frame.

She looked up. "Hello," she smiled. "James said you'd be back for the weekend."

She saw me looking at the art pad.

"I haven't drawn anything for years. I'm afraid it's not very good."

"I think it's excellent," I said. "When it's finished, we should put it up somewhere." And I meant it. He was right. She drew very well.

"I didn't know you were coming up," I said.

"I thought I'd get away for a couple of days."

I noticed another larger black & white photograph, on the dressing table.

It was an image of James at work in his study. Partially lit by sunlight through an open window. The room fading to black around him in the shadows.

I thought it captured the solitude and introspection of his life perfectly.

"I hope you don't mind," she said. "I used your camera and darkroom."

I didn't mind at all. She had made far better use of it than I ever had.

"That's as good as anything we saw the other night," I said.

"Do you think so? I'm pleased you like it."

She got up from the dressing table. "I've been sitting too long," she said. "Do you want to go for a walk?"

In the warmth of the late afternoon sun, we traced the route of the old Statue Walk. Then I showed her the space where I planned to create the Italian Garden.

When I asked how long she was staying. She told me she was leaving in the morning.

"Will you be back soon?"

"I hope so," she smiled. "Work permitting."

"I hope so too," I said.

Dinner that night was a much more relaxed affair than our first, a few weeks before. And we cleared a little more space for new stock in the wine cellar.

I was always happy to be at Studlands. But never more so than that night. I was home again. Amongst friends. And felt the need for no others.

But more, much more than that, my work at the church hall was done. And I had no reason ever to see or speak to

Sarah again. At last, the shadow of her presence had been lifted. And not just from James. But from me as well. And Rachel too, if she only knew it. Out here she couldn't reach us. And the future could not have been brighter.

Around midnight Julie said she had to make an early start in the morning. And went up to her room. I watched her go. And hoped one day we'd spend more than just a couple of hours together.

I said to James, "I didn't know Julie was coming up."

"Neither did I. She rang and asked if she could. It's not like her at all."

When I came down in the morning, I guessed she had left hours before.

I picked up a newspaper and went into the lounge.

Shortly after James came into the room. I carried on reading the paper.

A moment or two later he spoke.

"I'm concerned."

"Yes?" I said. Without looking up.

"About my sister."

I lowered the paper. And looked at him.

"What about her?"

"I'm not sure it's a good idea to get too friendly with her."

"What do you mean?"

"Maybe you understand her. But I doubt it. I never have. I don't want to lose you because of her."

"Is it really me you're worried about? Or her?"

"Not her. She can look after herself."

I returned to the newspaper. And he fell silent.

No, I thought. He didn't understand her. But I knew that said more about him, than about her.

In the days that followed I saw reminders of her around the house. I noticed she had sanded and re-painted an old chest of drawers. Of which there were many in the house. All of them dark, unattractive, and barely noticed. But now in a fresh coat of satin French Grey, it revealed beautiful fretwork and reliefs previously unnoticed.

She had drawn finely pencilled outlines of summer flowers and trailing leaves on the drawer fronts. And working in oil had begun to colour them in. In soft reds, pinks and greens. To my mind, even unfinished it looked as striking and attractive as any piece in the house.

Free at last of the church hall, the pace of life was slow. I had never felt so relaxed.

I had spent too long away from Studlands. And had no plans to leave.

Rachel was staying all week. Every evening the French windows were open to the warm evening air. Some nights after dinner we sat out on the terrace. Other nights we stayed at the table and talked for hours.

And it is these long summer days I try to recall now, when the shadows of later, darker times fall across me.

I finally began to lay out the Italian Garden. My thoughts had moved on since the spring. With his library a constant source of inspiration, the more I read, the bolder I became. To prolong the period in flower I planned to add walkways lined with Rhododendrons, Azaleas and other colourful early spring shrubs.

And there were several rolls of film to develop. A few of the house. But mainly of the temple and the folly. I had made little progress with my book. But there would be plenty of time for that next year.

After dinner, the three of us usually walked the gardens. Drawn by the scent of Evening Primrose and wild Jasmine.

One night we heard his voice behind us, as we walked on ahead.

"Look at those stars," he said. "You couldn't live out here and not be fascinated by them, could you?"

I did. And I wasn't. But now I looked. He was right. It was an extraordinary sight. A million stars spread across the unbroken arc of the night sky. It reminded me of my first visit. It seemed so long ago.

He pointed out the constellation of Cygnus and the Northern Cross. And several stars by name. But I was uncertain which ones he meant. And I suspect so was he.

Rachel's birthday party, an event that had always seemed so far off, was now almost upon us. And we prepared to return to London for the first time in weeks. A prospect that held little fascination for me now.

Waiting to leave on Friday morning, Rachel read a book on the terrace in the sun.

"One of his?" I asked.

She looked up. And smiled. I could see it was.

"Only when I know he's not around," she said. "I doubt we'll see him before lunch."

But to our surprise he appeared soon after. And asked if we were ready to go. Rachel closed her book. And slipped it discreetly under her chair.

At Cornwall Gardens the front door was hard to open for the weight of post behind it.

Rather than stay close to home that night, we headed north. To Hampstead. And a lively cocktail bar and grill. Behind an unassuming shopfront of maroon painted brick under a canvas awning.

The food and wine recalled his mind to thoughts of an Italian holiday again.

He spoke of a house in Pietrasanta, he had rented two summers before. In the foothills of the Apuan Alps. A place he had been happy he said. And where, inspired by several bottles of Chianti, we made plans to visit before the summer was out.

I knew nothing of Italy, save what I had read in his library. But to hear him speak of it brought it alive for me that night. Talk of classical marble and bronze sculptures. Ancient sunlit squares, and towering medieval campanili fired my imagination. Just as it had the craftsman who built Studlands a century and a half before.

And whose spirit, through my own work there. And the heady effects of the wine no doubt, I felt some small kinship with myself.

And it was not like him to talk about himself. Or his past. In fact, I believe that was the very first time. And it felt like being taken into his confidence. In a way I had never known before.

And eager for any opportunity to share their company, I asked if he had seen his invite for the Book Society Awards. At the Grosvenor House Hotel, in a couple of months. Naturally he hadn't.

"It might be a good evening," I said.

"I couldn't think of anything worse," he replied. And refilled my glass. "Writers aren't my type."

Then he said, "we must go and see Arthur Middleton in the morning".

"Who's Arthur Middleton?" asked Rachel.

"To buy a telescope."

We were none the wiser.

"To look at the stars."

It was still early when the taxi dropped us off outside The Wyndham's. Few were about at that hour. James led the way. Rachel and I followed close behind. But our progress was slow. Detained by the vintage maps and theatre ephemera in the shop windows of Cecil Court. But resisting the temptation to buy. And promising ourselves to return, we crossed over St Martin's Lane. And continued towards Covent Garden.

Where presently he stopped, in front of an old-fashioned brass shop front. Behind the glass, highly polished antique sextants, microscopes, and other Victorian scientific instruments glinted in the early morning sun.

Dimly lit inside, more like a museum than a shop. Filled with display cabinets of intricate weighing and measuring devices. And optical instruments of every size and shape. Vintage clocks and barometers lined the walls.

And on the floor, antique globes hung suspended on brass meridians in finely crafted wooden stands.

But it was a slender, tapered copper tube that captured his attention. Four-foot long and mounted on a sturdy mahogany tripod. The barrel engraved with the maker's name, *W. & S. Jones, Holborn.* And the lens as clear as the day it was ground and polished.

It was a beautiful piece. From a time when art and engineering were still as twin points of a compass, yet to be divided. And now I understood. It was far more *simpatico* with Studlands than a modern one could ever be.

It fitted inside a stained and lacquered rosewood box. There was no price on it. But I doubted it was cheap.

After that we went our separate ways. Rachel returned to Islington. And James and I to Cornwall Gardens. Before she went, she asked us not to be late. "I don't want to get stuck with a lot of people I don't know."

She was even starting to sound like him.

By the time we returned to the west end, the lights were coming on along Park Lane. It was another beautiful evening. The warmth of the day still in the air.

The taxi took us past Marble Arch. And into Oxford Street. Turning onto Welbeck Street, he leant forward and said something to the driver.

The cab slowed. And stopped at the side of the road, fifty yards short of the venue. We walked the rest of the way in the fading light.

As we did so the empty taxi passed us. And pulled up outside the double glass doors of *Ristorante Cinecitta Roma*. Drawing the interest of a couple of photographers waiting outside. Just long enough for James to slip past unnoticed behind them.

Safely inside, I could see he was amused by his little ploy. "You do get some unsavoury characters hanging around the streets," he smiled. It was good to see him so jovial. A few months ago, coming somewhere like this would have had quite the opposite effect.

Looking down from the top of the stairs, we saw Rachel and Julie. Talking on the floor of the crowded basement below. But it took several minutes to reach them. Delayed by the attentions of everyone he passed. Complete strangers all of them. Eager to shake his hand. Or worse, hug and kiss him. Just the things I knew that made him very uncomfortable. But for that night at least, he hid it well.

Rachel and James went to the bar. Julie and I sat at a table in the shadows.

"I've missed you," I said.

"Me too," she replied quietly. She reached out and took my hand. It was the first time I had felt the touch of her soft skin. "Me too," she repeated. More firmly this time, as if in affirmation to herself.

I asked when she was next visiting Studlands.

"I could come up at the weekend."

"Yes," I said. "I'd like that."

"But only for the day. Work's very busy at the moment. And I can't stay long tonight. I've an early call in the morning."

"This is hopeless," I said.

"No, it isn't. Please don't say that." Then she said, "I'll work something out. It won't always be like this."

Rachel and James returned with drinks for all of us. And the conversation moved on. The room was crowded. "Who are all these people?" I asked. "Colleagues mostly," she said. "A few friends." She was definitely starting to sound like him.

And it was a rare opportunity to speak to her on a night like this. Normally I knew better than to try. Although she always said she wished I would.

It might be nice she once told me, to talk to someone I actually want to.

But she was always far too polite to ignore the crowd that inevitably gathered round her. I didn't mind. I was just delighted to be there.

A few minutes later, to the sound of cheering and clapping someone stood on a chair to say a few words. A ragged chorus of *happy birthday* rang out. Then to more cheering, Rachel thanked everyone for coming.

I hadn't seen James for some time. Given how much he hated this sort of thing, and his habit of disappearing. It was quite possible he had slipped out for a walk. Or even gone home.

I checked upstairs. But the doorman said no one had left. Coming back down the stairs I saw him. Sitting alone at the bar. With his back to the room.

I went over and sat next to him. "It's a great evening, isn't it?" I said.

He didn't react.

For a moment I thought he hadn't heard me. Then he said, "I'm going to call her."

For a second, I didn't understand.

"And say what I should have said at the party."

"No, not this again!" I slammed my hand down onto the bar. I saw a couple of people look round.

He suddenly got up. "And I'm going to do it now."

I grasped his arm and roughly pulled him back. "For Christ's sake we're at Rachel's birthday party."

I was suddenly aware we were making a spectacle of ourselves. Not tonight I thought. Not in front of all these people. I could see others close by backing away. I saw a look of rage on his face. For a moment I thought he was going to hit me. If it was the drink talking anything was possible.

But instead, he slowly smoothed out the creases in the sleeve of his jacket.

"You're right," he said calmly. "I'm better off without her." Then he looked at me. "I don't know what I would do without you."

"Come on," I said. "We ought to go back and join the others."

We stood a few yards from the crowd around Rachel. He seemed to have returned to his old self again. He leaned over to me. "I don't know how she puts up with it," he said above the noise. Then he asked if I was coming up to Studlands for the weekend.

I told him I was.

"I wouldn't bother," he said. "There's a village fete or something in the garden. I meant to mention it earlier. The whole place will be overrun. We won't get any peace."

Then he added, "do you know if Julie's coming up?"

Now I felt a surge of anger. "Yes, just for the day," I said. "How long does this bloody thing last?"

"All day, I think. You don't mind, do you?"

Stung by the thought of rare and precious hours lost with Julie. "Yes," I said. "I bloody do mind."

I walked away. Better that than cause another scene on Rachel's special night.

"Come back, come back," I heard him call out.

I was still angry minutes later, when Rachel rushed up to me.

She threw her arms around me. "James has just asked me to marry him."

At last, I had heard the words. The glorious words I feared might remain ever left unsaid. And in that moment more even than joy, I felt an overwhelming sense of relief, that surely I would never lose her now.

Yet the opportunity to share this special moment with her was only fleeting. The news was out. And a crowd of well-wishers swept her away.

James too, found himself forced to endure the enthusiastic and unwelcome attention of strangers again, for a second time that night.

"I'm absolutely delighted," I told him. When I reached him through the crowd. "I couldn't be happier. For you. And for her."

I shook his hand. For the first time. And with an enthusiasm I had never felt before.

"It would never have happened without you," he said.

I could see he was quite emotional. "When we first met, I never imagined it could lead to anything like this. You've saved my life."

"I don't think it had much to do with me," I smiled.

Then he said, "this won't affect you at all. Studlands will always be your home.

There's plenty of room for all of us." Then he added, but the significance was lost on me at the time, "I need you now, more than ever."

He was becoming very emotional. It was hard to tell in the half-light, but I think there were tears in his eyes. I told him it was the best thing he could have done.

Now no longer just another birthday celebration. But one of the nights of our lives. One we would never forget. No matter how hard we tried later.

Early the next morning I brought his car round to the mews behind Cornwall Gardens. And the three of us slipped away unnoticed. An hour and a half later the sight of the distant spire at Church Hanborough welcomed us home.

Upstairs I lay on my bed. And reflected on the events of the last few days.

It was as if he had been ill. And this illness had cast a shadow across us both. But morning had broken. He had made it through the night. And the fever had passed. Now we could all look to the future again, with great hope and expectation.

My thoughts turned to Julie. It would be another week until I saw her again. But only briefly. If at all. Because of this damn fete.

A couple of days later they went to visit Rachel's family in the west country. But I had no plans to leave. I would have Studlands to myself.

Before they left, I told her if she picked a room she liked, I'd decorate it for her.

"It will be my wedding present to you," I said. "And when you're married it can be your special room."

"What a wonderful idea," she said. "I would love that."

There were a number of empty rooms on the ground floor at the front of the house. All quite large and in reasonably good order. I laid out some colour charts and she made her selection. I told her I would make a start while she was away.

Then she said, "I really liked it when you said *when you are married.* I am a very lucky person. But I know without you, I wouldn't be here now. When I first met James, I didn't think he liked me. And I was going to give up. But you convinced me not to. We're only together because of you. And I'll never forget that. Meeting you has changed my life."

Then she said, "you will stay, won't you? My being here won't make any difference to you will it? We must all stay together. It's very important to James and I that you do. You will, won't you?"

I assured her I would.

"This is just as much your home as mine. You must always stay. Always, always, always."

Then she said, "I know it's a lot to ask. But it would mean so much to James and I if you would be our Best Man."

"Of course, but I'm sure there's far better people than me."

"There's no one else we'd even think to ask. It will be a small private affair at Studlands. But I guess there's bound to be some press interest I'm afraid."

"You're not having a church service?"

"James has no time for that sort of thing. Although I'd have quite liked it. I think it would have been very romantic."

The next day I started work in her room. But the pace of life was slow. I removed the old skirting and replaced it. There was plenty left over from work elsewhere in the house. And the old carpet went into the skip by the stables.

For me, those truly were the halcyon days of that extraordinary summer. Indeed, of my whole life.

Chapter Five

August 1989, Indian Summer

His telescope had remained untouched in its lacquered rosewood case since he bought it. It took just a few moments to assemble. I placed it by the full height window in the hall. Next to the painting of Vertumnus and Pomona. It could stay there until I found somewhere better. So it was only by chance I was in that part of the house to hear a knock on the door.

I opened it to a smartly dressed middle-aged woman.

She said she was from the Parish Committee. And thanked me for the use of Studlands for the fete on Saturday.

She said the marquee would be delivered in the morning. I offered to walk the grounds with her to find a suitable location for it.

"This is our twenty-sixth year at Studlands," she said. "And it goes in the same place every year."

She handed me a copy of the programme for the day. A single piece of paper, neatly folded in half. That night I took a moment to read it.

The next day under a clear blue sky the marquee went up. It wasn't as big as the one for his birthday party. But it was in the same place. The gardens were busy with people setting up stalls for the fete. Vans and cars arrived all day. Delivering materials and equipment, canvas banners and wooden tables. Large tents were going up all across the lawn. It was obviously a significant local event. Preparations continued long into the evening.

James and Rachel returned late. I didn't see them until the morning. He greeted me warmly when we met on the terrace. He looked out over the sea of tents.

"Do you know what time this thing starts today?" he asked. "It looks like they've got a lovely day for it." Then he added, "it's a lot bigger than I expected".

"The fete starts at eleven o'clock," I said, recalling the programme. "Lunch for the Ladies of the Parish Committee is at midday. Followed by a musical soiree in the evening."

Then he said, "they're not expecting me to open the bloody thing are they?"

I shook my head.

"Thank Goodness for that," he said with relief.

"No, you're hosting Lunch for the Parish Ladies."

He looked at me. And saw I wasn't joking.

"What have I let us all in for?" he said.

"It's not really your fault," I replied. "They've been doing it here for the past twenty-six years."

"Have they?"

A few hours later, from the balcony of my room I saw him walk across the lawn in his suit, under the burning midday sun. And watched him awkwardly shaking hands with the ladies of the Parish Committee. Then standing stiffly with them to have a picture taken for the local newspaper.

I felt it was his atonement, for the loss of what little time I might have had with Julie. For as pleasant and well-meaning as the Ladies of the Parish Committee may have been, I knew he hated meeting strangers.

Mid-afternoon came, and with it no sign of Julie. But amongst the red and white striped and sun-bleached canvas of countless stalls and several hundred people on the lawn, it would have been easy to miss her.

It was still hours before we could reclaim Studlands for our own. But it was good to see the old house so busy again, just a few weeks after his birthday party. The sound of jazz carried on the air from a band playing beneath a cloudless sky. It had truly come back to life that summer.

I wandered among the stalls again, in the hope she might be there. If she had come at all. I was about to retreat back to my room, and out of the sun when I saw her.

Sitting on the stone steps of the terrace. With her art pad. Sketching the people and the stalls. I sat next to her.

"This is awful," I said. Now I was starting to sound like him. "I haven't seen you all day."

"It's alright," she said. "I'm not going back tonight. We'll have plenty of time later."

After the musical soiree, a car arrived to take Rachel back to London. James went to see her off. When he came back, he said he was tired and going to bed.

At last, Julie and I were alone. Just as she had promised.

"I thought you were only coming up for the day?" I said, as we settled down on the large sofa in the lounge.

"I told them if they wanted the work done by Monday, they'd have to ask someone else." She put her arms around me. I felt her soft cheek against mine. "I said I had more important things to do."

"How long are you staying?"

"A week, maybe longer if I can."

I closed my eyes and listened to her voice quietly in my ear.

Later we slept on the sofa in each other's arms. I awoke in the early hours to a light breeze through the open French windows. I got up to close them. She stirred, and I walked her up to her room. In the doorway she asked me to stay with her.

Many were the hours we spent that week, sitting by the folly or in the cool shade of the temple. I read a book from James' library. While she drew views of the house and gardens in her art pad. And in the evenings, we talked long into the night.

James had revived me and made me feel alive in a way I had never known before. But now with Julie, I found something beyond even that.

All the disappointments of the past fell away. All the regrets I had carried so long lost their power over me. They ceased to be regrets. They ceased to be anything at all.

Even the empty wasted years before we met, I now saw had a purpose. I had been on a journey. Out of the dark, and into the light. A journey that led me here. To this place. And to this person.

One afternoon she said, "I've come to feel much closer to James these past few weeks. More than I ever have before. I hope it will always be like this."

"I'm sure it will, why shouldn't it?"

Then she said, "he's asked me to stay." She saw I hadn't understood. "Always I mean. To make this my home."

"Would you?"

"I could."

"What about your job?"

I just wouldn't go back. If I stayed here, I wouldn't have to."

I was very surprised to hear her talk like that. It was not the way James had described her.

"Then we could always be together," she said. "I think we could be very happy here. Don't you?"

"Yes," I said. "I do."

Then she said, "it's something I've thought a lot about lately."

Julie's week at Studlands stretched to almost a fortnight, when she told me she had to return to London.

"Not for long. I promise. Just to sort a few things out. No more than a week at the most. I'll be back as soon as I can."

She took my hand.

"You will wait for me, won't you," she smiled.

The next morning, I walked with her to her car. She put her arms around me.

"When I come back," she said. "I won't be going away again. It will be for good."

She held me tightly. Then she said, "think about me when I'm away. I'll think about you all the time."

Rachel had returned to town a few days before. Leaving James and I in sole possession of the house. We dined alone for the first time in weeks. But it was always a pleasure to be in his company.

"I understand you've asked Julie to stay."

"Yes. It's something I never thought I'd do. But I have to admit things are very good between us," he said. "We're getting on like never before. She seems very happy these days. Quite like a different person. Somehow, you've brought us together. I don't know how you've done it. But thank you."

I told him I didn't think I had done anything.

"No," he shook his head. "You've changed my life. Meeting you is the best thing that has ever happened to me. You saved me."

As far as I could see I had very little to do with any of it. But I was pleased he thought that. Although I knew it could never compare to what he had done for me.

It had been a beautiful summer, but it was now late September.

By day at least, the countryside remained a rich and vivid green under a clear blue sky. But the nights were drawing in. There was an almost imperceptible change in the light. And a new and unwelcome chill in the morning air. Autumn was in sight.

But this year the prospect of winter held no fear for me. James noticed it too. But he seemed more unsettled by it.

"It's been such a long hot summer," he said at dinner a few days later. "But I can feel the winter's coming." And then with a haunted look on his face he said, "I've forgotten what the cold feels like".

Hearing him talk like that reminded me of the early days. When we first met. It was exactly the sort of thing he would have said then.

"But everything's different now," I said. "You're getting married to a wonderful person. You've got me. And you've got Julie. Your writing's going well. These are the best days of your life. And long may they continue."

He slowly nodded his head.

Then I asked if he had heard from Julie. It had been a couple of weeks since she returned to London.

"She rang the other day," he said. "You know, it's a funny thing. She told me she was going back to quit her job. But instead, she's become a Partner in the firm."

"Did she say when she's coming up next?" I asked.

He said she didn't.

"I think I ought to go down to Cornwall Gardens. To check the post."

"I wouldn't bother," he said. "I don't think I'm ever going back there."

But it was not about the post. It was to see Julie.

I called her office as soon as I arrived. She told me she was leaving for Frankfurt in the morning. "I'm not packed yet," she said. "And I need an early night." She sounded distracted.

"Why are you going there?" I asked.

"To carry out due diligence on a company."

Sounds awful I thought. "Sounds interesting," I said. "When are you coming back?"

"Depends. Could be a few days. Or a few weeks."

"So, if I'd have called you tomorrow, I'd have missed you?"

"Yes," she said.

I told her it was very quiet at Studlands without her. "Please hurry back as soon as you can."

There was silence for a moment. Then she said, "I don't think Studlands is a very healthy place. You get drawn into a way of life up there. It clouds your judgement. And you don't want to leave."

"Perhaps we could get somewhere together?" I said.

"I have to pack," she replied. "I'll call when I get back."

After our conversation I poured a glass of wine. I couldn't see what was wrong with living at Studlands. And I knew how much James valued my company. But if I had to give all that up to be with Julie, I would.

And with her away there was no reason to stay a second night in town. In the morning I checked the post. Then left for Studlands.

Barely half a mile into the journey I saw a car like his. Just a few yards ahead. There were others like it in town. But not many.

To this day I don't know why I followed him. Perhaps it was just curiosity. I was sure I'd catch him in traffic on the Cromwell Road. And if it was him, I might as well stay another day.

But instead of bearing right for Cornwall Gardens he continued south. Down Gloucester Road towards the river. And across Battersea Bridge. Where was he going? Ten minutes later he turned onto a street I knew well.

I drove on. And returned grimly to Cornwall Gardens.

I didn't hear him come in. And I didn't see him until dinner that evening.

I asked if he had a good journey.

He said he had.

"Did you come straight here?" I asked.

He said he did. And poured himself a glass of wine.

"No detours?"

"No," he said.

"That's not true."

He looked at me.

"I know where you went. What did you say to her?"

He put down his glass on the table in front of him.

"I didn't speak to her. I just drove past her house."

He was silent for a moment.

Then he said, "I have this awful dream. I get up in the night. And I see myself in the mirror." He shook his head. "I'm an old man. And I know I've lived my life without her."

He looked at me. "I can't go through with this marriage. If Sarah rang tomorrow, or next week. Or next year, I'd leave Rachel immediately."

"But that's not going to happen."

"I believe you're wrong." He raised his hand to silence me. "And even if you're not, the fact I feel this way surely is enough. For the sake of our friendship, I've lied to myself for months. But it can't go on. I have to end it."

"It will be the biggest mistake of your life," I said. "You're giving up everything for something that doesn't exist. I know. She told me."

"Then why did she come to the party? Tell me that?"

But before I could speak, he said, "because she feels the same way I do. Her coming to Studlands proved that."

"No. It doesn't. She went because she's moved on. Just as she thinks you have. If she knew how you felt, she would never have come."

He shook his head. "It meant something. You just can't see it."

"As your friend I cannot stand by and let you make this terrible mistake," I said.

He looked at me. "I have to do what I believe is right. And as my only true friend I need your support. And I need it now. More than ever. Even if you don't agree with me."

There wasn't any more to say. I knew the truth. And I spoke it plainly. But it was not enough. He wouldn't listen.

I was too angry to stay in. I must have walked for miles around the streets. I longed to return to Studlands. And to the way it had been. But now I feared for the future. And felt the chill of winter drawing in. I had forgotten what it was like. It seemed so long since I had known that feeling.

When I returned, he was sitting quietly in the lounge.

"I told her," he said.

Three words. That changed everything.

"But it's not just her I'm giving up," he said. "It's Sarah too."

"She's not yours to give up, for Christ's sake."

"It's all I can do, to show how important you are to me. I can't be with Rachel. Even though I know how much you want me to be. But if I give her up, I fear I'll lose you too."

"If you're giving up Sarah, why can't you be with Rachel?"

"Look, it's the best I can do. If I could offer you more I would. I asked Rachel to marry me because I knew that's what you wanted. And I tried to convince myself. But I can't go through with it. So, I'm giving them both up. You know how much Sarah means to me. Doesn't that make up for what I'm doing? I can't be with Rachel. But I can't lose you. So, I'll give up the only other thing I can for you."

"I don't want you to do anything for me. It's none of my bloody business. Any of it."

I went up to my room. I didn't want to see or speak to him. Ever again.

Hours later, I heard a knock on the front door. It was late by then.

It went unanswered. I heard it again. I went downstairs to see who it was.

Rachel was standing on the step outside. Very distressed.

I had never seen her like that. And it shook me.

"I just want to talk to him," she said. "Please let me in."

"Of course, of course," I said. "Come in. I think he's in his study."

So many were the things I wanted to say to her in that moment.

But I had no words. No words to say so much.

I went upstairs to my room. There was nothing I could do.

I feared deeply what would become of her now.

A fury welled up inside me. The like of which I had never felt before.

Rage at what he had done to her. But not only that. At Sarah's weakness. And at James for wrecking my hopes for the future. At my failing Rachel. Losing my job at the bank. His success and my failure.

I hurled the bedside lamp across the room. It smashed into a thousand pieces against the wall. I wanted to hit him. To shake him. So violently he might come to his senses. I gritted my teeth and clenched my fists, until I thought my teeth would break. And my fingernails split my palms.

Then it passed. And I sat down on the bed. My head sank onto my chest. I felt an emptiness. That slowly filled with a deep and desperate sadness. Left only with the knowledge things could never be the same again. And that I would stay because I had nowhere else to go. And I would carry on because I had nothing else to do.

I heard her leave shortly after.

I needed to speak to her. To hold on to her somehow.

In the cold light of morning, I called.

"I'm very sorry about last night," she said. "I should never have come round. I'm so ashamed."

"Please don't apologise. If there's anything I can do." And I meant it. More than she could ever know.

"Thank you," she said quietly. "And thank you for calling." There was silence for a moment.

Then she said, "I thought he was happy with me. Where did it go wrong?"

"I don't know," I lied.

"You know him better than anybody. Is there any hope for us?"

"I don't know." Again, I lied. "I think he's struggling with his writing."

It was all I could think of to say.

I felt her slipping away. I was desperate for the conversation not to end. I didn't know if I would ever speak to her again. And I couldn't bear the thought. But I was powerless to prevent it.

The following night James and I met at dinner. It was a subdued evening.

We were alone again. Just as it had been in the beginning, all those months ago.

"I haven't seen Julie for weeks," he said in passing.

"She's working in Frankfurt."

"Yes?" he said disinterestedly.

We ate on in silence. After dinner we parted. I went to the lounge. And he to his study. I sat alone with my thoughts. But they were no comfort to me. I felt very tired. The last two days had been the worst I had ever known.

But it was not over yet.

I must have fallen asleep. When I opened my eyes, the room was in darkness.

And I could hear Rachel's voice. Just outside in the hall.

"I don't understand what went wrong," I heard her say. "But whatever it was, we can fix it. I know we can."

Trapped in the dark, I dared not move, or make a sound. Forced instead to overhear this dreadful scene. With its inevitable and sickening outcome, of her hopes dashed to pieces.

Devastating to learn of it afterwards. But to hear it first-hand was unbearable. I could feel my heart pounding in my chest.

Finally, I heard his voice. "It's no use," he said quietly. "There's no future for us."

I put my head in my hands, at the sound of her heart silently breaking. Just a few feet away.

Perhaps it was only a moment or two. But listening for every noise in the darkness it seemed like an age. Then I heard the front door slowly shut. And with the click of the lock it was over. They would never see or speak to each other ever again.

I waited in the darkness, until I heard him go up to his room.

I didn't see him the next day. I wasn't sure if he was even in the house. I hoped he had gone. By dinner time

I knew he had. And I felt a sense of relief. I had nothing to say to him. And it was easier not to say it to his face.

I rang Rachel again that night. I hoped our friendship might somehow survive. She said she was pleased to hear from me. And agreed to meet for lunch. She said she'd call back. But never did. Then her number changed. And I couldn't reach her anymore.

James rang a couple of days later from Studlands. He sounded very low. And said he would like to come up to Cornwall Gardens.

I told him it was none of my business where he went.

"I'd like to see you again," he said.

"Please yourself."

So he returned to Cornwall Gardens. By then my anger had turned to a deep sense of sorrow and regret. That weighed heavily upon me. But if that was how he really felt. Crazy as it seemed. Then that was his business. No matter what I thought about it.

He said he was very pleased to see me when we met at dinner. "I don't know how I would get on without you," he said.

We returned to our routine. I spent an hour or two each day in the office. While he worked in his study. I usually went out in the afternoon. To the cinema or for long walks. Given the time he spent on his work I presumed it was going well. Every night we met at dinner. We ate simply in the expensive kitchen. Some nights we shared a bottle of wine.

In a way it reminded me of how it had been in the days before Rachel. Without her life and enthusiasm to lift us, we were a quiet and sombre pair.

A few days later he said he was meeting Julie for lunch.

"I thought she was in Frankfurt?"

"She got back a couple of weeks ago. Didn't she tell you?"

His words jarred me.

"No," I said. "She didn't."

That night I wrote her a letter. I thought it would be clearer if I put my thoughts down on paper. So there could be no misunderstanding how I felt about her. And my hopes for our future together.

I recalled things she had said. And things we'd done. We had talked about it. But not at length. It didn't seem necessary then. But that had been at Studlands. Here in London six weeks later, what had been left unspoken needed to be said.

I posted the letter that night. And resolved to call her the next evening. Although I was sure when she read it, she would ring me.

But she didn't.

When I called I asked if she'd received my letter. She said she had. But there was little warmth in her voice. I suggested we meet up.

But we never did. At least not on our own. I forget the rest of the conversation. Brief as it was. Brief and irrelevant.

The truth is I hardly knew her. But because I knew him, I felt I did. But as he said, they were not so alike as people thought. People who didn't know better. People like me.

Our meeting brought her closer to him. And created the circumstances which drew us together. But for her it wasn't enough. And she soon saw that. She had a life outside that summer. Whereas for me that summer was my life. It was all I had. It was all I wanted. And all I could offer her.

When she gave it up, she gave me up as well. She could have stayed with me there. She said as much. But in the end chose not to.

At least she was prepared to do what Sarah had been too weak to. But then she was always far too strong to ever allow anything like that to happen to her.

We did meet again. One more time. At the Book Club Awards at the Grosvenor House Hotel. James decided to go after all. And invited us both.

He never said, but I think he thought it might be like old times. And in some respects it was. But not in the way he had hoped.

Instead, the mood of our party was very subdued. In the twin shadows of Rachel's absence, and our telephone conversation a few days before. It reminded me of the first night she came to Studlands. I didn't know her then. And I didn't know her now.

Yet despite the sombre mood I thought she seemed untroubled. And it made me feel what had come to pass between us meant little to her.

And later in the evening I saw her talking to someone, and I sensed a lightness in her mood. And the thought stung me that perhaps it was borne out of a relief to be free of me. And I resented her happiness. Coming as it did, at the expense of my own.

And so it was that night, I knew I too would soon be leaving.

And it would be because of her. I would do it to spite her. Because I knew it would hurt him very much. And he would hate her for it. Then she too would lose what she wanted. Just as I had. And she would feel as I felt now. It would be my revenge on her.

I don't know if she ever said anything to James. But in the days that followed he tried very hard to take me out of myself.

Where before he wanted to stay in, now he suggested places we could go every evening. It was not his fault. And I knew he would have done anything to save the situation for me. But there was nothing he could do.

Chapter Six

November 1989, The Longest Winter

I retreated back to Studlands. And left him in town. I returned to my work there. Back to where it had begun, all those months before. I tried to lose myself in it as I had then. But I couldn't. I was sharing the house with too many ghosts. And haunted too, by something I had said.

In my anger I had told him the worst day of Rachel's life was when she met him.

But I knew that wasn't true. It was a fortnight later. When she met me.

But for my meddling their first meeting would have been their last. And her disappointment would have soon been forgotten. In a few days, or a couple of weeks at the most. Certainly nothing like this, that threatened to overwhelm her.

At least Julie had come to her senses about me. Before I ruined her life too.

When I wasn't working, I spent my time reading in the old library and walking in the grounds. The summer was gone. And every day the darkness drew in a little earlier across the valley. And into my heart.

Inside the house the temperature was beginning to drop, as the winter outside started to creep into it. Preparing to take it soon. Not by open assault. But by stealth, through a thousand tiny cracks and joints. Each day drawing a little deeper into it. And into me.

A week or so later James arrived. But didn't stay long. He asked when I was coming back to London.

"I could do with some help," he said. "And some company." Just before he left, he looked around him. "I hate this house," he said. "I can't bear to come here now. It's so full of unhappy memories. Whatever you're doing here just stop and come back to London. I don't want to come here ever again." And as far as I know he never did.

I said I'd be back in a day or two.

When I returned, he told me how pleased he was to see me. We had dinner together. It was a bit like it used to be.

In the morning I looked through the post. Then read a newspaper in the lounge.

By mid-afternoon it was already dark outside. The room was getting cold. I lit the fire and stood in front of it. I felt a warmth in its crackling glow I hadn't known in weeks.

Shortly after he came into the room.

"I've written her a letter," he said. Holding an envelope in his hand.

"To Rachel?" I asked.

"No, to Sarah"

"Give it to me."

"You want to read it?" he said surprised.

"No, I'm going to tear it up."

He looked at me. "At the very least she owes me an apology. That's all I'm asking."

"For Christ's sake leave her alone. This has got to stop. Now. Once and for all. Give me the letter."

He handed over the envelope. I threw it on the fire.

He watched it burn. "You're right," he said. "It's like a madness that comes over me. I don't know what would become of me without you."

By the end of November, the thoughts of many were turning to the new year. And the new decade just a few weeks away. It was a time to look to the future. And what it might bring. And I was determined to do just that.

I spent hours in the office. Partly dealing with his mail. But mostly calling all the painters and decorators I could find in the phonebook.

A few days later I went into the West End. To take some papers to his solicitor. He said he was in town. And offered to meet me afterwards.

I waited for him by the doorway of Fortnum & Mason, out of the cold wind that blew down Piccadilly.

Looking up the road towards Hyde Park, I saw him in the distance. Wearing the heavy Burberry coat I last saw the previous March. He looked very serious. With his collar turned up and his hands thrust deep into his pockets. Several people turned to look as he passed.

I stepped out onto the pavement and walked towards him. We met under the colonnade of the Ritz. He seemed preoccupied and very business-like.

He said he was parked in a side street. And turned to go back the way he had come.

I walked beside him. It was late afternoon. And the light was fading under a heavy grey sky.

"I've found a job," I said as we walked.

He looked startled.

"You've already got a job," he said. "With me."

"No, a proper job. Working for someone else. I'll have to find myself somewhere to live."

"Why can't you carry on working for me?"

"I've got to think of my future."

"You've got a future with me. I can give you money to start your own business if that's what you want to do."

I didn't answer.

"I don't understand," he said. "Why do you want to leave? You've got everything you need with me. I know the last few weeks have been very difficult. But things will get better."

He stopped walking. "I don't want you to go," he said. "I want you to stay and always be my friend. What do I have to do? Just tell me."

"It's not as simple as that," I said.

"Why isn't it?"

But he knew. I could see he was distressed. Even in my hurt and anger I didn't like to see that. I said I wouldn't rush into anything. But it was a lie. My plans were well advanced. And I was ready to leave.

I made the journey back to Studlands the next day. I packed what little I needed. I had brought nothing with me ten months earlier. And so many of the things I had acquired since would have been out of place anywhere else. And anyway, I didn't want to remember. I wanted to forget.

I left the expensive picture book he had bought me in Oxford. And all the photographic equipment. What use were they to me now? I took just enough clothes to fill a single suitcase.

I returned to Cornwall Gardens that afternoon. He was out.

So I went without seeing him. And I preferred it that way.

He didn't know I was leaving that day. He didn't know for sure I was leaving at all.

I left no note. Or forwarding address. I didn't want him to find me. He would only try to talk me out of it.

Once he found I had gone, I knew he would never forgive her. In my hurt I felt I had lost the future I wanted. Now she would too.

And as much as he disliked it, I hoped the winter might help him work. I believed the cold and dark would concentrate his mind after I was gone. For his work already months behind, now appeared to have ground to a virtual halt.

I turned my back on his world. And returned to reality. Which included a visit to the Church Hall. For the box of tools I thought I'd never need again.

Sarah would see my van. But I doubted I would see her.

But I did. And it should have changed both our lives. And his. Forever.

The door to the church hall was unlocked as usual. I let myself in. The box was still where I left it months before.

I heard the sound of footsteps.

"Hello," I said to whoever was coming.

"Hello," came Sarah's voice.

She stood in the doorway. "We wondered when you'd be back for that."

I asked her how she was.

For a moment she didn't answer.

Then she said, "Ian and I are no longer together."

I should have told her I was very sorry. I should have asked her how she was.

Instead, I said, "you told me you could never leave him."

She slowly shook her head. "It was always more complicated than that."

Then she said, "It was inevitable."

"Was it?" She heard the edge in my voice.

"We're both older and wiser now. And know it's for the best."

I felt a surge of anger well up inside. I raised my voice to her. "Then why now for Christ's sake? Not before?"

I saw my reaction startled her.

"I'm sorry," I said.

She brushed her hair from across her face. Her hand was trembling.

Then she said, "when Ian came out of hospital, I promised myself I would never leave him. Not so long as there was the slightest possibility for James and I. Even though that meant living a lie. So while it breaks my heart into a million pieces he's getting married."

I could see a tear in her eye. "I kept my promise."

Then with a sad smile she added, "by marrying someone else, he's finally made an honest woman of me."

"You must call him," I said quietly.

She shook her head. "What's the point. You said so yourself."

"I was wrong. You two are meant to be together."

"He's marrying Rachel Adam. I read it in the papers."

"He's not marrying her. Because he's still in love with you. I know. He told me."

For a moment there seemed no reaction to what I said.

Then her gaze fell away from mine. She sat down on the floor. Pulled her knees up under her chin. And bowed her head.

I sat next to her. And put my arm around her shoulder.

I could feel her shaking.

For I had spoken the unspeakable words. Words from another life. One long since lost. When love, hope and happiness still existed in her world.

For long minutes we stayed like that. Tears streamed down her face. And mine.

Finally, I broke the silence. "We have to return to Studlands."

She looked up. Her eyes red and her cheeks wet with tears.

"Yes," she said. "Please take me home."

I went into her office and dialled his number. I wanted to be the bearer of the great news. And I wanted to do it now.

I heard his voice.

But it was only a recording. I listened for a moment. Then hung up.

"He's away," I told her. "Until the end of the month."

Despite how badly we had treated him, I knew he would welcome us back. And there would be no recriminations. And no questions asked.

It had been a terrible autumn. But now the future was wonderfully bright. For him. And for those of us fortunate to be his friends.

I didn't return to work that afternoon. I had felt so cold and detached for the past few weeks. But now in the sudden rush of emotion, I felt quite euphoric.

I was coming home too. I thought I had strayed too far ever to return.

But I was wrong. Gloriously wrong.

That night I rang his number again. Just to hear his voice.

I had never known him to leave a message on his phone before. And I suspect it was in the hope someone might call. And someone did.

But I was happy he had finally gone to Italy. I knew how much he wanted me to go with him. And I wished I had. But it didn't matter now. There would be plenty of time for that later.

This time I did leave a message.

"Hurry home," I said. "I have fantastic news for you. Give me a call the minute you get back."

And I knew he would.

Epilogue

May 1992

I did see Rachel again, one more time. A couple of years later. But she didn't see me. It was at a film premiere in Leicester Square. She only had a small part. But everyone wanted to see her as much as the big stars.

And I wanted to see her again too. Maybe I thought I might even speak to her somehow. I stood in the crowd and waited.

When we saw her approach, you could feel the love and affection surge towards her like a giant wave. And I saw that beautiful smile again. One I used to know so well.

I wasn't at the front. But close to it. I hoped she might see me. At one point she looked in my direction. And just for a second, I thought I saw a flicker of recognition in her eyes. But no, she walked on. Smiling and waving.

Shortly after I left the lights of the West End and made my way home. I was pleased to have seen her again. But so sad there was no connection between us anymore.

She had clearly coped with losing him better than I had. And I tried to draw some strength from that. She had moved on. Maybe one day I could too.

Although I was sorry to hear the next day, she had been taken unwell shortly after. And left early. I saw an upsetting photograph in one of the papers, of her being escorted from the building. Looking very distressed. She had been fine when I saw her.

Printed in Great Britain
by Amazon

20417414R00192